SURVIVORS AND OTHERS

ALSO BY ROBERT DRAKE

Fiction

Amazing Grace
The Single Heart
The Burning Bush

Criticism

Flannery O'Connor
(Contemporary Writers in Christian Perspective)

Memoir

The Home Place:
A Memory and a Celebration

―――――――――――

When the Abbé Sieyès (1748–1836)
was asked what he had done
during the Terror,
he replied,
"I survived."

SURVIVORS
AND
OTHERS

ROBERT DRAKE

MERCER

ISBN 0-86554-253-8 (cloth)
ISBN 0-86554-254-6 (paper)

The paper used in this publication meets
the minimum requirements of American National Standard
for Information Sciences—Permanence of Paper
for Printed Library Materials, ANSI Z39.48-1984.

Library of Congress Cataloging-in-Publication Data
Drake, Robert, 1930–
     Survivors and others.
     I. Title.
PS3554.R237S8   1987   813'.54   87-5644
ISBN 0-86554-253-8 (alk. paper)
ISBN 0-86554-254-6 (pbk. : alk. paper)

Contents

I
WANDERERS, WARRIORS, ORACLES
1

II
ANN LOUISE: THE MAKING OF A SURVIVOR
131

———————————

FOR

Betty and Ray Ashley
Mary Marley and Bob Reed Pipkin
Mary Kate and Jimmy Wyatt
and
Catherine Fields Atkins

Acknowledgments

————————— • ● • —————————

I am grateful to the Yaddo Corporation for the hospitality extended me during several visits at Yaddo, Saratoga Springs, New York, during which times I completed a substantial number of these stories. I should like to express my thanks also to Dr. Walter Herndon and the graduate school of the University of Tennessee, Knoxville, for making my task much easier during one term of the academic year 1982-1983.

The publication of this volume has been assisted by a subvention from the John C. Hodges Better English Fund.

"Survivors," "Mrs. English," and "On the Side Porch" appeared originally in *Modern Age*. "The Birthday Picture" appeared originally in *Motif*. "Remember the Errol-mo!" appeared originally in *Southern Partisan*. "Mrs. Picture Show Green" appeared originally in the *Arizona Quarterly*. "Now, Baby, Do You Know One Thing?" appeared originally in *The Reformed Journal*. "Miss Effie, the Peabody, and Father Time" and "The First Year" appeared originally in *The Southern Review*. "I Am Counting with You All the Way" and "Were You There?" appeared originally in *The Christian Century*.

Survivors

·●·

All my life, I realize now, I have been surrounded by survivors. First, I was the only child of middle-aged parents, the fat little boy who always had to sit in the corner at family gatherings and listen to the old folks talk, with a Confederate veteran for a grandfather and no contemporaries among his cousins. (No one ever said to me, "Go out and play." Whom was there to play with?) It's one reason, I'm sure, that I write: always I was listening to people talk about themselves and their concerns, but usually they were older and wiser and any kind of equal intercourse in conversation was out of the question. So early on I became a good listener, especially for the stories that seemed to emerge between the lines and the resulting counterpoint thus set up with the acknowledged, intended stories. Indeed, so good a listener did I become that often the talking elders seemed to forget that I was there; rarely did they remember to say, "Children should be seen and not heard," or "Little pitchers have big ears." So there I sat, soaking it all up, like a big blotter—and with a memory as long as death!

I quickly became used to older people, and to this day I'm often more at ease with people twenty and thirty years my senior than I am with those nearer my own age. And there have been times, too, when I have viewed this situation as difficult, even burdensome: it often seemed as if I were being immured in the past, shut off from any "normal" relationships with my own time and my own place—perhaps even left to float between two worlds and at home, really, in neither. Thus I was always somewhat outside the group, whether young or old, in it perhaps from time to time but almost never of it—the listener, the observer, but rarely the actor, the participant. And, as I said, there were times when this all seemed a mixed blessing, to say the least. I often found the past and the old voices wearisome, perhaps even destructive—like the "ravenous grave" of Allen Tate's "Ode to the Confederate Dead." But I never quarreled with the past and my relationship to it. I suppose I was more like Quentin Compson in *Absalom, Absalom!*, oppressed by the past, fascinated by it, even tormented by it, but of course never renouncing it. Thus I avoided what Yeats called the quarrel with others, out of which, he said, we make rhetoric (I would call it *argument*); and instead I came nearer to finding my real battle in what Yeats called the quarrel with the self, out of which, he said, we make poetry.

To have tried to renounce the past would, for me, have been tantamount to trying to renounce my very self. The past was simply part of the world that, for better or worse, defined me—like my skin—and I could never slough if off and would try to do so only at my peril. So I had to live with it, try to come to terms with it. And it wasn't ever easy. Often, indeed, I found myself drawing near people my own age whom I didn't even particularly like—with whom I felt I had very little in common except chronology—purely for the reason that they were young and I could somehow warm my hands at the fires of their burgeoning youth. I often wanted to get to know them better, perhaps even become intimate with them. Yet all my knowledge of the world seemed conditioned by things that had happened—and people who had lived—"before my time," as I was always being told.

And often I resented it: being turned into an old person ahead of schedule, as I thought. Still, I found in the past a kind of safety too: it was all dead and over and done with, I thought, and couldn't hurt me in any way. I could continually remake it and reshape it, reassessing its significance as I went. The present wasn't like that: it turned and twisted and was full of surprises and disappointments, even dangers. The past involved no risks. Of course, I know now it was all different from this. The past is never dead but continues to extend itself into the present, shaping and influencing what we do and say right here, right now, and never really letting us go—as with Tennyson's Ulysses, who forever remained a part of all that he had met. And if we live long enough—last long enough, I might say—we become survivors; and it is to this group that I would like to turn my attention now.

Survival certainly isn't just a physical affair, a matter of who lives longer or who buries whom, as we say. Some are survivors at forty; others never will be, even at eighty. Survival has to do with who endures, who finally may even, in the words of Faulkner's Nobel Prize speech, prevail. It has to do with what you've come through, what you've learned, what you've lived to tell, which isn't necessarily a matter of age. Maybe *tell* is the operative word for my purposes here because it presupposes that having really "come through," you're not going to keep your experience to yourself. I am reminded of some lines from the first hymn I ever learned, "Amazing Grace": "Thro' many dangers, toils, and snares / I have already come." And, as a survivor, you're ready to bear witness, give testimony, in the best evangelical tradition, to your ordeal and subsequent victory—hence the Ishmaels, the Ancient Mariners who constitute our finest artists, whether writers or otherwise. (Are all artists survivors of a sort?)

Survivors, of course, aren't always easy people to have around the house—any more than are artists or saints, for that matter. The very qualities that made them tough enough, even prickly enough to "come through" aren't usually the ones that make for the most congenial and harmonious personal relationships or the easiest social intercourse. As a rule, in fact, they aren't. Often, therefore, we're inclined to hold them at arm's length except of course when they're performing, telling their tales, which discipline, by definition, provides its own distancing. And they continue there to instruct, perhaps to delight, even rebuke us by their examples. But we don't want to come too close, perhaps just as we don't want to sit too near the stage or go behind the scenes after the performance is over, which is not to suggest that their art or their artifice is all an illusion but, on the contrary, that it's awfully tough and businesslike, all too real.

When I was growing up I used to hear my mother say, often of someone who I had thought "didn't have a care in the world," that he was such a fine man, he had had "so much trouble." I even wondered whether having had "so much trouble" automatically insured your being a fine man and whether such a history guaranteed my mother's approval. I know now, of course, that it didn't: my mother was simply paying her own characteristic tribute to the survivor, who had indeed earned it by the very fact of his having "come through." He hadn't merely endured; he had prevailed, albeit sometimes scarred and battered. And he had earned the right to talk about it too: he had indeed lived to tell it. Finally, he had lived "a useful life"—always her ultimate encomium for such folks.

Does this all suggest that the nonsurvivors are weak, even unworthy of our notice? Surely not. One doesn't write them off in any Darwinian sense. Some natures simply don't seem constituted to endure, much less prevail. But they're no less worthy of our interest or deserving of our pity for all that. Perhaps, in one sense, they're too fine for the rough and tumble of this world; perhaps, in another sense, they don't have the guts. So we bestow on them a tear and a sigh. Do we think the less of them for having hearts and bodies that break? After all, aren't there some sorrows, some misfortunes so deep, so catastrophic that one shouldn't survive them? A teasing riddle, to be sure.

Nevertheless, we *go on* to contemplate the survivors because always, I think, we have to side with life, not just life on any terms whatever but life that lives, persists, endures, and yes, prevails. We can't not side with it, really: it's what keeps us—and the arts—all in business. And it's often greasy and sweaty and hairy and smelly, sometimes even horrifying in its purest form, the sheer determination to survive. But it's real and, well, it's life. And it's that, I believe, that all the arts finally celebrate—crazy, mixed-up thing that it may be, with its principal actor himself the glory, jest, and riddle of the world. But the artist, the writer says *yes* to it all—not in the sense that he necessarily *approves* of it but in the sense that it's rich and strange and, in the strictest sense, *wonderful,* not to mention the greatest gift that any of us is likely to be given. For what it's worth, this seems to be the fundamental impulse behind all the arts.

But let me speak more particularly now of the survivors among the old, bearing in mind that much of what I say about them applies as well to their kindred spirits less stricken in years. Since I have become middle aged, I have been able (more or less) to catch up with myself: the world I grew up into I am now a part of and not as a stranger, you might say. I've left youth behind and am now a member myself— though only a beginning one, I'm quick to add—of the group I was always associated with earlier: those who have reached the autumn time and now look forward to the winter season, the white country after the harvest. As I look around me, I feel that I'm beginning to realize what it was that I somehow admired, was somehow fascinated by in the aging and the old all those years of my youth. I was fascinated by the fact that they were survivors, who were still there and able to answer to roll call. Though they might be, and often were, temporarily exasperating in their concerns with what seemed to me the irrelevancies of past matters, often tiresome in their complaints about their bodies and the lives they were now forced to lead, and frequently so much circumscribed compared to what they had known earlier, I could not but wonder—even marvel— at what they had come through, say "Amen" to the fact that they were still in business, still able to kick, though perhaps not very high; and finally I had simply to say "hurrah" for their being still alive. For always, we have to honor life, however disturbing its particular forms and manifestations may appear. That's why we often relish the vulgar, even the grotesque: it's life, often excessively or perversely so. A doctor friend has told me that his elderly patients worry mostly about two things— their money and their bowels. Why their bowels? Well, he says, they can't worry about sex anymore! And of course we laugh at his interpretation, but our laughter is not unmixed with a kind of delight in and wonder at the old folks' persistent vitality and unblinking realism.

Often the old people of my youth had survived a great deal, whether the loss of goods and chattels, the loss of strength and health, or the loss of friends and loved ones. Diminishments all around, no question about that. And yet they clung—often fiercely—to life and, despite their age and changing times, were often all too much at home in the world. Few of them wanted to quit it anytime soon, I might add. And in all this there was a sort of triumph: "Look what we've come through, look what we've lived to tell! And it's not over yet," they might well have proclaimed.

They did proclaim it, too, in the wonderful tales of past times they told, even when they seemed to be comparing, to its great discredit, the modern world with the one they had known so well in days gone by. In all this there was a sort of backhanded compliment to life and vitality, however diminished it might be. It never occurred to any of them—these old folks—that they might bore the younger generations with their memories: why, it was all a vindication of the life force itself, to see and hear what folks could come through and live to tell. And you ought to be proud to think you had such survivors, such doughty warriors in your life because that's what it was: a triumph for life and the spirit of man. And, finally, it had all been a lot of *fun:* the battle, the struggle to stay afloat, to prevail. You often did have to laugh to keep from crying. But they *had* endured and their experience ought to be worth something, and they were glad to pass it on to you; and you would be glad to hear it too if you knew what was good for you.

Naturally you can't know all this when you're young, even if you've grown up with the past, as I did. But get a little age on you, as they say, and you'll come 'round. And you'll listen more attentively than ever as the old folks, the survivors, talk. The archetypal survivor in literature is surely Coleridge's Ancient Mariner, with his wonderful

and sobering tale of guilt and expiation. No one of us can ever hear it
without becoming, like the Wedding Guest, that always-perfect listener, a sadder and a wiser man. Or there is Wordsworth's old leech
gatherer, who refuses to give in and go under, so old he seems almost
inhuman, inanimate, yet still persevering, as he says, in his occupa-
tion. Even King Lear, purged finally of his pride and his folly, is a survivor who has lived to tell a very great deal before his final dissolution.
Otherwise, there would be no catharsis for any of us.

All these I recollect along with the more immediate witnesses
from my own culture and my own life: the old men sitting on the
benches in the courthouse yard, too far along now for anything much
except recollection and perhaps a wry thrust at the folly of the younger
folks who think they know it all, or the aging checker players in my
father's and uncle's hardware store, still full of beans but already, some
of them, beginning to feel the winter chill coming, already beginning
to think and to talk out of the past and their experience therein, as
though it might have something more than useful to say to modern
times. ("When I was a boy . . .") I think also of the old women—maybe
even more than the men the traditional keepers of flames and inter-
preters of oracles—and the rocking chairs on the front porches where
they sat. (What has the loss of the front porch and the rocking chair
done to the quality of our lives, even the quality of our art in the modern world?) Brave indeed was anyone who ventured to run the gauntlet
of the front-porch rockers: you could never get by them unscathed, always had to listen to some anecdote, answer some probing question.
And often you passed by not without some blood's being drawn: you often
had to account for yourself and your doings to those good ladies, whose
questions weren't really impertinent when properly considered. After
all, they had earned the right to pry: they were veterans, they were survivors. And they could tell you a lot if you would listen.

And so, as I've entered middle age myself, it's the survivors—
the old and the not-so-old—that I've found myself concerned with more
and more, writing about more and more. They always had been there,
in my life; but I suppose, like all younger people, I couldn't properly
appreciate them. And, as I observed earlier, survivors are not always the
easiest people to have around. As in the Book of Job, they may seem all
too fond of saying, "And I only am escaped alone to tell thee." And
that *can* be difficult to live with. I'm sure that I thought I'd had entirely
too much of that sort of thing in my life when I was younger. But then

I grew up, grew older, sometimes still resenting the past but knowing full well I could never escape it, so perhaps coming to exist in some sort of uneasy truce with those old memories, whether of joy or of sorrow. And later, as time laid its hand more firmly on me, I began to think again about the survivors, to find in them more than just memory and reflection. I began to think of them as some sort of veterans of an old and unending campaign, maybe even, if this doesn't sound cheap and vulgar, as some sort of cheerleaders, always urging me and everybody else on by their own precept and example, always saying *yes* to the struggle, *yes* to life and not ever, ever giving up without some sort of fight. Surely they could be prickly at times. (I remembered my grand-father, who hadn't been at Appomattox for nothing: he often refused to bathe and insisted on eating peas with his knife.) Again, the very qualities that make for survival aren't always the social ones. And the nature of old age works against some social qualities too: old age is often a series of deprivations for body and spirit, and very often old age is spent alone. (The Ancient Mariner was perhaps the solitariest man who ever lived.)

But just as the survivors keep on saying *yes* despite all their di-minishments, I think we who are their heirs also have something of the same responsibility: life, as terrible as it can be, must be served, must be honored. And so I suppose that's why, as I look about me now in mid-passage, I've come to see what the survivors are all about and come also to see that they must be cherished, must be celebrated. We're all in this together, young and old alike, you know. It's the survivors who have already lived to tell a tale or two, already shown us the way; and we must do something about them right now.

I

WANDERERS, WARRIORS, ORACLES

The Birthday Picture

---•●•---

Years later every time Bill Craddock looked at the photograph of his fourth birthday, he would have to stop and think. Even now he remembered something of the events of that day, back in the 1930s, when times were hard and people made their own amusements, at home or elsewhere. He remembered his mother had sat up late the night before, making little airplanes for the party favors: for each one there was a roll of Lifesavers (for the fuselage) and a stick of chewing gum for the wings (or was it two sticks for a biplane?). She kept it all together with a rubber band, and Bill thought it was very ingenious of her. Then his aunt—his mother's sister—made and decorated a birthday cake for him herself. There was a photograph of him sitting on the front porch, with the cake resting before him on a low table; and he was all braced back in his chair, as though trying to restrain himself from jumping into the cake too soon. Anticipation, glee, all sorts of emotions were written on his face there; but the principal one seemed to be a kind of self-congratulation for his having actually reached the age of four.

He even remembered asking his mother, the day after the party, whether he was still four years old; and she replied, with some amusement, that he was. But he knew there was a great difference between three and four, even then: you weren't a baby anymore, for one thing, you were a child. And it was very important to him that he had reached that new status. He wouldn't have gone back to the other for anything. In two more years he would go to school; in just one more he would be allowed to walk downtown to his father's store, all by himself: his father had promised that.

But the picture that Bill always remembered and was still drawn to look at years later was the picture of the whole party itself. He was in the center, of course, and all his friends were seated around him on the front steps. In fact, you could even see a part of his mother's foot,

as she sat in the porch swing while the picture was being made; and
there were several other mothers lurking on the side of the porch (it was
a long one that went all the way across the front of the house). But of
course it was the children who were the real subjects. In this picture the
cake was absent, nor were there any other signs of just what the occasion
was all about. Of course anyone from a small town could have surmised
in a minute what such a group of children, all dressed in their Sunday
best, were assembled for. And it would not have been hard to spot the
honoree, with Bill planted firmly in the exact middle of the group and
looking awfully pleased with himself, awfully pleased with being four.

The picture had been taken by Mr. Ed Fields, who was the only
real photographer in town. He had been making pictures in his studio
since the Year One, everybody always said. A lot of the time he was
mildly drunk, though the children weren't supposed to know that: they
just thought he had a red face and was usually very cheerful and jolly
to be around, like Santa Claus. And why he took to drink nobody probably could have told you. Did he have—or had he had—aspirations of
being an artist as well as a commercial photographer and then found
that a small town such as Woodville (only fifty miles north of Memphis)
afforded little scope for such expectations? Did he feel wasted in such a
backwater? Nobody ever knew. He made a good living, photographing
high school graduates and brides and weddings, sometimes even funerals (the flowers on the grave after it was all over, as a rule). And there
were always the birthday parties, for which he charged more since it was
a "house call" and he had to venture outside his studio, which was up
over one of the dry goods stores down on the square (and right across
the hall from Dr. Henderson, the dentist).

But anyhow Mr. Fields was always fun; and he seemed to know
how to handle children who, many of them, were sometimes afraid of
having their pictures taken. For one thing, Mr. Fields would always
spend forever getting his camera set up on the tripod; and then he would
disappear under that black cloth to see whether everything was in focus.
And though Bill and the other children knew it was still only Mr. Fields
under that black cloth, they sometimes feared that he might be doing
something mysterious and awful under there (they didn't know what
exactly) such as turning himself into somebody else or even disappear-
ing altogether, as Bill had once seen at the tent show when it came
through town. Even when Mr. Fields got everybody posed, he still took
a long time, being sure that everything was just right for the *exposure*

(which always sounded like a very terrible word to Bill, with its connotations of the diseases his mother always said he might be *exposed* to if he didn't change his shoes when they got wet or else played with the dirty children who lived in the old house down the street). But what was even worse were the times when it was too cold or rainy for Mr. Fields to make an outdoor picture at one of the birthday parties of the town (and he was almost a fixture at all of them). Then he would have to make an indoor *exposure,* which Bill and a lot of the other children found almost terrifying because of the flash that Mr. Fields had to use for such a picture. There was a sort of contraption that looked like a shortened version of one of the things you used to wash windows with (a squeegee, was that its name?); and Mr. Fields would load it up with flash powder, which was white and resembled flour or lime. Then when he snapped the shutter of the camera, he would trigger the flash gun, as he called it; and there would be a big "poof," almost an explosion, with a big light going off simultaneously and powder and sparks flying everywhere, and the picture would get taken. And Bill was almost afraid of that—not like he was of Mr. Fields going under the black cloth but more just like he was of being shot at or of something in the cowboy movies he had seen on Saturdays. There was no mystery about that, just plain old shock.

But Bill and the other children had all gotten pretty much used to the black cloth and the flash gun; and if they weren't *hardened* to it all, they just accepted it as fact. They knew, finally, it wouldn't any of it *hurt* them. And you couldn't very well have a birthday party, back in those days, without Mr. Fields on hand for the pictures. Why, Bill wasn't altogether sure except that his mother and all the other mothers said it was all very sweet and would all give them something to remember in the years to come. At that stage, of course, Bill wasn't spending too much thought for the future except in the most immediate way, like what they would have for dessert tomorrow or whether—if he thought far enough ahead—he might get a new tricycle for Christmas. Oh, there was school in two years; but that was so far off, he could hardly even imagine that he would really be going there. It was just mainly something you thought about. But the *future* as such wasn't something he seriously considered; on the whole, he was pretty much locked into the present. The *past* wasn't anything he could think about at all.

Bill never forgot that fourth birthday party. It was the first one of his he could really remember. In fact, he wasn't even sure he had had a third birthday party. If he had, he had certainly forgotten it. But the fourth one he remembered all his life. The favors he never forgot, nor did he forget the decorated cake (did it say "Happy Birthday Bill"?—he couldn't remember) his aunt had made him. And also there was homemade apricot ice cream, the kind his mother always served at her book club, when she entertained it, and Bill got to lick the dasher as well as pass the napkins. He never could understand why they didn't have apricot ice cream at the drugstore or why Fortune's, which made the best ice cream in that part of the country ("All Cream Ice Cream"), never tried their hand at it: no other flavor was so subtle to him. But when he asked his mother about it, she said maybe everybody didn't like apricot ice cream so much as they did: it wasn't everybody's dish of tea, she said—not like chocolate or strawberry. Bill found that hard to believe, though: apricot wasn't as *strong* a flavor as those others, that was true, but it was not like any other flavor in the world once you got into it. Anybody who didn't know that was a *fool,* which was a word his mother would wash his mouth out with soap for saying if she ever heard him.

For days ahead of time Bill had started getting ready for the party. Oh, he had been to others, and he pretty well knew what form the entertainment would take: pinning the tail on a donkey, playing "Red Rover" (if it was warm enough to go outside) or else "Ring Around the Rosy" (which could be very embarrassing if you were the last one to sit down and therefore had to tell your sweetheart's name). And sometimes, when there was really a fine party on hand, Miss Rosa Moss, who had taught the first grade in Woodville for as long as nearly anyone could remember, would come and tell the children at the party a couple of stories. And then the mother of whoever's party it was would present her with an embroidered handkerchief or a bottle of toilet water as a way of saying thank you.

But for the first time he could remember, Bill was now going to be the *honoree,* as they called it; and *he* would be the one to receive the presents and the congratulations of "many happy returns" and so on. That was always tricky—the presents, of course. The honoree had to pretend that was the last thing in the world on his mind, when the guests came swarming in with their gifts, though of course he knew and they knew it was the main thing everybody was thinking about at that point: what would the presents be, would they be the right size if it was something to wear, or would they be something embarrassing (like silk panties for the girls)? And how would they be wrapped? Some of the mothers were really skillful at doing that—devised artistic wrappings with lots of loops on the bows and so on. Bill's own mother wasn't very much turned that way herself and just mainly used a single strand of silk ribbon (red, as a rule) and plain white tissue paper. And always she wanted Bill's present to be something "practical," something the honoree could really *use,* not just play with. So his present was often some plain white handkerchiefs (not too fine for everyday) or else a good solid story book. It never was a toy or anything you could just play with. Of course, some of the guests simply brought something they had picked up at the dime store at the last minute and had had wrapped there too. And it usually looked like it—just cellophane ribbon and no real tissue paper but plain brown wrapping paper from the store. Bill's mother said that was because some of the mothers were just too mortally lazy to do it themselves. And that was almost the worst thing his mother could say about another woman except for one other thing—that she *wouldn't* cook; and that was the worst of all.

So Bill got bathed and dressed an hour ahead of time, with some help from his mother, and stood right behind the front door, impatiently waiting for the guests and trying to remember what his mother had said about its not being good manners to stand there with your hand out (for the present) when a guest came in the door. And before long the guests did begin to arrive, and Bill then tried to remember what his mother had said about not being so greedy to open the presents as soon as each guest had come but to wait until they were all there, both presents and guests, and then do it all. And it was hard, but he managed, and there were some good things there (his father said that night, with some dryness, that Bill had made "a good haul") like a new Uncle Remus storybook and a cap pistol. So Bill was very happy, with some toys as well as "useful" gifts. And after the presents were all unwrapped, it was time for the games, which were fun; as the honoree, though, Bill couldn't win any of the prizes, which were mostly small bags of Hershey's silver tips.

And then, just before time for the refreshments, Mr. Fields arrived to take the birthday pictures; after all, he had to get there before the cake was cut so he could photograph Bill with the whole thing before it got eaten up. And the day was fairly warm (it was October), so they all were able to sit out on the front steps for the group picture. And Mr. Fields did what he usually did: disappeared under the black cloth (but nobody was too much afraid of that now) and then came out for air and then went back under for what seemed an hour until he got everything the way he wanted it. And then he took the rubber bulb that tripped the shutter in his hand and said, wiggling the fingers on his other hand back and forth above the camera, "Now watch the little birdie, tweet, tweet!" And everybody did (though Bill thought that *was* a silly thing to say: where was the bird?); and Mr. Fields squeezed the bulb and snapped the shutter, and the picture got made. But that was not until a little girl in the front row looked behind her just at that moment, and so Bill in later years never knew who she was though he tried figuring it out by eliminating his friends who were there and looking straight at the camera.

And that was all really. After Mr. Fields had left (having declined some of the refreshments), Bill cut the cake (first he made a wish—an electric train—and blew out all the candles in one breath) and everybody had ice cream and cake. And then it was time to go home. But as each of the mothers (some had come with their children, which Bill thought a rather babyish thing to do) left, Bill's mother would say, "I'll see that you get one of the group pictures when Mr. Fields has them ready." And of course Bill had to thank everybody for their presents, just as they had to thank him and his mother for the good time they had had at the party.

And when the birthday pictures came, Bill thought they were all right, with everybody more or less looking like himself—and acting that way too, with some of the guests giggling and others almost on the point of making faces (not the ones whose mothers were there, though). But he didn't see what all the to-do was about: the group picture was just what it was supposed to be—he and his friends on his fourth birthday. So what? But his mother said she was so pleased with the way the pictures had come out and that, in later years, Bill would appreciate such things more than he knew. And that was pretty silly: grown people were always taking the starch out of you by telling you that you were too young to know something or else saying you would understand when you got older. It almost made you mad.

But several years later, after Bill had started to school, he came across the group picture of his fourth birthday party, which he hadn't seen for some time: his mother had packed it away with his baby book and his first pair of shoes, and he was almost ashamed to look at them. But he took out the picture and looked at it and saw right off that one of the little girls (sitting right behind him on the steps) was now dead (a terrible disease called leukemia, where, they said, your white corpuscles ate up the red ones). And he wondered who would be the next one to drop out of the birthday picture. Would it be his best friend, Joe Green, who sat on his right, or maybe Helen Gilmore from next door, who was sitting right in front of him? Maybe it might even be Bill himself. He sat down and held the picture in his hands a long time while he thought all these thoughts: he hadn't so much realized before what could happen to people at a party, in a group—his party, his group. And so every year or so Bill would rummage around in the old cedar chest where his mother had packed his baby things and get out the fourth birthday picture again and see who else might be gone. And by the time he got to high school there were several: a ruptured appendix (before antibiotics) and a car wreck accounted for two more. And after that came the Korean War.

Years later, after Bill had left home and was living in Memphis, he still had the birthday picture with him. And whenever he gave a party where some of his old friends might be, he would threaten to get out the picture and show them how awful they had looked as children: blackmail pure and simple, they called it! But every now and then Bill would get the picture out, when he was all by himself, and look at it for a long time and try to remember that birthday party as well as he could and fix both it and his friends firmly in his mind so that none of them could ever leave him again.

First Date

———————————— • ● • ————————————

"Now, son, remember you're not on your own anymore; you're escorting a young lady tonight, and you're responsible for her welfare. And you must never forget that fact." That was what Eddie Williams's mother said to him as he was getting ready to take May Belle Sanders on Billy Johnson's hayride. He was in the eighth grade, and it would be his first date ever. And he was nervous enough as it was, what with all the teasing he had to take from the older boys about him being so fat and May Belle being so fat, they would both fill up the front seat of his father's truck, with no room for his father to drive.

That was one of the great shames of Eddie's life: the Williamses didn't have a car, they just used the pickup truck Mr. Williams had for his feed store (fortunately, it wasn't painted in the Purina checkerboard pattern). And of course Eddie didn't have his driver's license yet (he was only thirteen), so his father had to drive him everywhere. The older boys had all assumed his father would take that truck to pick up May Belle for the hayride. And for a week ahead of time, they would come up to Eddie in the cafeteria at school and make out like they were measuring his backside, to find out whether it *and* May Belle's (they said they had already measured hers) could fit into the front seat of the truck.

Naturally Eddie wouldn't have gone to pick up May Belle in the truck for anything on earth: it was bad enough not to have a car, bad enough not to be able to drive himself, to say nothing of being driven to his first date by his *father*. But he had already determined simply to walk down to May Belle's and get her; then they would just walk from there to Billy's house, where the hayride was to begin. Eddie hadn't gotten around to figuring out what he would do if it rained, but it was September and school had just started so he thought the weather would be all right. And anyway, that was the purpose of a hayride, wasn't it— to go out under the harvest moon that would be shining high in the autumn sky and have romantic thoughts? It simply *couldn't* rain.

Eddie didn't know how he felt about girls yet. He sometimes thought they were fun to be with, but then they would break out into unexplained giggles and even squeals of laughter and run off into corners with each other and look knowingly at him and the other boys and whisper in each other's ears. And it all made him rather tired, even nervous. Yet there were other times when he thought they were nice to be around, sweeter than boys, and more comfortable. But this was his first date, and he felt all mixed up about them and himself and everything else. And that was bad enough without his mother having to say what she did about being responsible for May Belle and giving him just one more thing to be worried about—in addition to being fat and May Belle being fat and having no car. At any rate, he at least hadn't yet broken out into acne the way a lot of his friends had: he could be thankful for that. But exactly how was he supposed to be responsible for May Belle? She was at least as big as he was, if not bigger, and he couldn't imagine that anybody would ever *do* anything to her, like carrying her off on a horse right off the streets as he had seen in the picture show on Saturdays. (For many years, Eddie thought that was the reason a man was always supposed to walk on the street side when escorting a woman: so no outlaw or desperado could come along on horseback and scoop her up and carry her off.) Well, he didn't think anybody would do that to May Belle.

May Belle was something of a tomboy, and she didn't have many friends either—no more than Eddie had. She was fat and ate all the time, but she was also just *big*—big-boned and all. His mother said May Belle's grandmother had been a Luckett and all that family were just big, period. Why, when her great-uncle, Mr. Charlie Luckett, had died, they had had to hunt all over West Tennessee for a coffin big enough to bury him in. (He was nearly seven feet tall and weighed three hundred pounds.) But May Belle could also be a lot of fun: you could even tell her dirty jokes, and she could hold her own in any kind of contest there. Maybe, Eddie thought, May Belle felt she was an outsider too—just like he did—because of her weight and generally unattractive looks. But she was fun, and for some time he and she had formed a kind of private club—just the two of them—that got together and compared notes about what all their friends were doing and what girls were being chased by which boys and vice versa. And they often worked their arithmetic over the telephone together at night. Really, they were quite fond of each other; but neither had apparently ever had romantic feelings about the other. Somehow May Belle didn't count: she wasn't a girl, but she wasn't a boy either. Maybe she was neutral, so Eddie felt somehow safe with her. At any rate she never made fun of him because of his size or the fact that he took piano lessons or anything like that. In fact, there had been a time when May Belle played the accordion herself and had even been persuaded to play it for Sunday school. But she gave it up after one or two tries: some of the other children referred to her as Old Juice-Box, and that was enough for her.

But Eddie didn't think of himself as a coward, certainly not a sissy; and he didn't think such things about May Belle either. It was just that they felt comfortable together: neither one had to prove anything to the other, and they weren't any kind of rivals either. They were simply *alike* and drew together for that reason. But as for romance, that was the farthest thing from Eddie's mind. You just couldn't have romantic thoughts about May Belle—not the kind you had about Vivien Leigh or Greer Garson or even such a commanding presence as Bette Davis. But May Belle was about as romantic as an Irish potato, and really Eddie didn't think he wanted it any other way.

The hayride, which was being given by Billy Johnson's parents, was the first time any of these eighth graders had been paired off as couples, to have dates and all that. Really, Eddie heard his mother saying to his father, she didn't see why the Johnsons had to rush things all that much: why not let the *children,* as she called them, remain innocent for a while longer? But that was just like the Johnsons: they had only moved to Woodville from Memphis five years ago, and she supposed they thought they had to show that small town a thing or two and wake them up. She didn't know but what they'd better let sleeping dogs lie, from things she had heard about Mrs. Johnson's past doings in Memphis and some of Mr. Johnson's business dealings in Woodville (he was in the supermarket business—the first one ever installed in Woodville). But Eddie's father had just told her to hush, not be so suspicious of people, even if they were "brought on," a "foreign element" in the town. But that was just it, his mother said: nobody knew much of anything about them before they moved to Woodville; they didn't seem to have much *background.* And Eddie knew that his mother was a powerful big believer in background. The worst thing she could say about anybody—or any lapse on his own part—was that he didn't act like he had any background at all—nothing behind him, you might say. And that's just what she thought about the Johnsons: no background to speak of, so all they could do was to get some attention (Eddie's mother called it *notoriety*) by doing things before anybody else and hence the hayride, the dates, and all the rest of it. Why, they'd be throwing a dance before long, she said. But Eddie didn't see how that was all that bad, and he didn't feel all that innocent either. He certainly knew where babies came from and also about girls having bad days every month. Indeed, he had already talked a lot of it over with May Belle, who knew as much as he did.

So Eddie looked forward to the hayride, despite some initial misgivings and despite his mother's seeming attempts to turn May Belle into something other than what she was—a good buddy. He didn't intend for any of it—the hayride, the dates, the attempted romance, any of it—to change his life. So that night he put on his new sport coat and got all slicked up and walked down to May Belle's and picked her up, and they walked all the way down to the Johnsons'. (He wondered whether May Belle's mother had given her a "talking to" beforehand of the sort his mother had given him, but he thought he'd better not ask her now.) It was a mild September night and it didn't rain, and there was a real harvest moon up in the sky. Everything looked promising for a good evening. They got to the Johnsons' all right and found a lot of their classmates already there. There were a few snickers at Eddie and May Belle; and somebody even said, under his breath, but not completely, "*Two* fatties for the price of one!" But neither Eddie nor May Belle took any notice of that.

Soon the truck that was to take them on the hayride down to Long Lake drove up; and they all piled in the back, some twenty-odd young people. Mr. Johnson drove, and Mrs. Johnson went along too, sitting beside her husband in the cab of the truck—to be "chaperons," she said—a word Eddie had heard before only about high school dances. Somehow it sounded more formidable—and not nearly so nice—as *parents* or just plain *grown-ups*. But that was just one more of the Johnsons' city ways, Eddie supposed; and he reckoned it was all right. But he wondered, in the back of his mind, whether his mother might not be right: the Johnsons were trying to force things too soon.

But they were all in a high good mood when they left for the lake. Already they were singing the songs they had learned at church camp and Boy Scout meetings—songs such as "John Jacob Jingleheimer Smith" and "The Bicycle Built for Two." And there were even a few people who wanted to sing "Let Me Call You Sweetheart," but they were shouted down with the comic version: "Let me call you sweetheart / I'm in love with your machine." Once or twice somebody even started singing "There's a Long, Long Trail A-winding"; but nobody else took it up. Really, for all the talk about harvest moons and romance and all the rest, nobody seemed to want to get romantic. They just wanted to be good friends a while longer, it would seem. Certainly, they were all dressed more for comfort than for romance: the girls all wore old school dresses and the boys, corduroy knickers. (It was during the 1940s; nobody then would have dreamed of wearing blue jeans—certainly nobody in town: that was for farm people.) And there was a good deal of rough and tumble horseplay in the back of the truck: boys and girls throwing handfuls of hay at each other, threatening to rub each other's faces in it and so on. Nobody even held hands. Sometimes they did— the boys and girls—at the Saturday matinees at the picture show. But as a rule they sat separately there, boys with boys and girls with girls. And the show was the main thing then anyway: you had to see the whole program (cowboy western, Three Stooges comedy, and the latest chapter of the current serial) at least twice to have any social standing at all; and, if you were really enterprising, you could manage it three times.

Anyhow, this was the mood of the hayride. It was just another Saturday picture show, nothing romantic about it at all. (They didn't even like romance when it intruded there: the singing cowboy was the first step down, most of them thought. And it was altogether right for the hero's horse to come between the hero and heroine at the fadeout: westerns were no place for such foolishness.) A few of the children such as Billy Johnson, whose party it was, might have had something else in mind: his date was Janice Carroll, who still boasted about the three boxes of candy she had received from three different boys last Christmas. But again, Eddie wrote that off to Billy's being "brought on" from the city though he had lived in Woodville for five years.

When they finally got to the lake, it was full dark; but Mr. Johnson had already been down that afternoon and arranged a pile of wood for the big fire they would build to give light and also to roast wieners and marshmallows. And that was soon lighted now, with the flames leaping higher and higher and casting alternating lights and shadows over the group. In the distance they could hear the lake waters rippling in the slight autumn breeze, and over it all hung the harvest moon now high in the sky. Mrs. Johnson said it was a scene right out of a novel and wasn't it romantic? And Mr. Johnson grinned at her knowingly and said maybe these kids didn't know much about romance yet and would have to be taught. But first they had to have some refreshments, and so out came the wieners and marshmallows and lots of potato chips and other picnic food and great jugs of cider.

Mrs. Johnson said, when she was pouring the cider into paper cups, that some kinds of cider were "hard" but this was not. And the hard kind could make you drunk, but they were a little young for that as yet. And Eddie thought that was just as well because he had about as many new things happening to him right then as he felt he could manage. Not that he had any particular misgivings about alcohol when he thought about it (which wasn't often); mostly it was a subject for ridicule, like at the picture show when some man in the comedy came home drunk at night and couldn't find his way into the right house. And really, that was all pretty silly, Eddie thought. His father had already cautioned him about ever thinking it was "big" or "grown up" to drink and smoke, but right now Eddie didn't think he would ever be particularly tempted that way. It all seemed rather pointless to him, so it was just as well that the Johnsons' cider wasn't hard.

After everybody had eaten, Mrs. Johnson said it was now time for them to play games; what did they think of Post Office? Well, Eddie knew all about that from some of the things the high school crowd had let out around him, but he didn't think he was ready yet to start kissing girls or letting them kiss him. How would it *feel* to kiss May Belle? Really, he'd never thought about it before. And his stomach got all tightened up as it did on Saturdays when Hopalong Cassidy was getting the worst of it from the Indians and it looked like the U.S. Cavalry might not arrive in time. There were a few giggles from the other boys and girls, a few sidewise, sheepish grins at each other. But at this point there didn't seem to be any real enthusiasm for Mrs. Johnson's suggestion. So instead she proposed a riddling game, where the losers would have to pay forfeits and then redeem them by performing whatever tasks she assigned.

Well, Eddie never had been any good at guessing games, and he knew he wouldn't now. Games and contests just weren't his thing, he had decided; also he had something very like contempt for those whose whole lives seemed to revolve around them. Okay, so some people were smarter and quicker than others, just as some were stronger and better looking. And some horses could run faster than others, so what about it? As to who and which ones could do all this, he decided he really couldn't care less. And besides, he was fat and slow and awkward, but he knew he wasn't stupid. So the riddling game began; and, just as Eddie had foreseen, he lost out and had to pay a forfeit, which he decided would be the music-club pin he always wore. (Some of his friends did make fun of him for taking piano lessons, but he wasn't going to pay them any mind. And wearing his music-club pin was one way he could prove it.) So now he hurled it down as though in an act of defiance at Mr. Johnson's feet (he was assigned to be the keeper of the forfeits). And then he could start thinking about what he would have to do to redeem it.

The game continued for an hour so that, when nearly everybody had forfeited something, it was time for the redemptions to begin. And that was a ceremony over which Mrs. Johnson was to preside. Mr. Johnson would take the forfeited article and hold it over her head so she couldn't see it and say, "Heavy heavy hangs over your head." And she would ask, "Fine or super-fine?" ("Fine" meant that the forfeit was a boy's, "super-fine" that it was a girl's.) And Mr. Johnson would reply accordingly, and then Mrs. Johnson would set the person concerned some task according to his sex. (Of course age didn't have to be considered; they were all more or less twelve or thirteen.) And Eddie noticed that most of the tasks imposed by Mrs. Johnson involved some sort of pairing off of couples, something to take them away from the firelight into the darkness that surrounded it for a couple of minutes, something that somehow might lead them into romance. But Eddie noticed that, when they returned, they all seemed somehow uneasy with each other and mostly kept their eyes on the ground. And he wondered what on earth would happen to him when it came his time and how he would handle it.

He had to wait a good while. It seemed as though Mr. Johnson was deliberately saving his music-club pin for the very last one; at any rate it took a long time. So when he did hold up the pin over Mrs. Johnson's head, the hour was getting late and the harvest moon had set. And Eddie's stomach was churning away furiously indeed now. Again Mr. Johnson repeated the formula, again Mrs. Johnson asked the sex, and again Mr. Johnson replied "fine." (Did he prod Mrs. Johnson in the back when he said it? Eddie couldn't be sure.) But somehow Mrs. Johnson looked rather sly and knowing as she responded with the forfeiter's prescribed task: "The young man must take the hand of the young lady he brought as his date, look into her eyes and recite the most romantic poem he knows, then kiss her right here before all of us."

Eddie thought he would die of embarrassment. He had never had a romantic thought about May Belle in his life, never dreamed once of kissing her, much less reciting a poem to her. And the only poem he could think of now was the one they had all learned in the seventh grade about the rainbow: "My heart leaps up when I behold / A rainbow in the sky." He couldn't think of anything sillier or more inappropriate now. But there was nothing else for him to do but take May Belle by the hand now and recite the poem to her, for them all to hear, which he did, feeling more and more like a fool all the while. And then he darted forward and kissed her smack on the lips, making a louder noise than he would ever have thought possible. He then jumped backward, spitting and wiping his mouth, as did May Belle hers also. Several people in the group laughed; and then Eddie and May Belle looked at each other, and there was an emotion in their eyes that neither had ever seen there before: shame, outrage, perhaps even hatred. But he stumbled forward and received his music-club pin from Mr. Johnson and then slunk over and took a seat all by himself on the other side of the fire from May Belle.

After that it was soon time to go, and Mrs. Johnson suggested they all sing "Shine on Harvest Moon" in the back of the truck on their way home. But most of the children were now shy and diffident about singing anything at all, certainly not that kind of song, though one or two of them put a bold front on it and forged ahead. But Eddie and May Belle didn't open their mouths, either to sing or to speak to each other, all the way back into town.

Tennis Whites

The first time I ever saw Donald Prescot, he bounced—almost leapt—into the room really, all 6′ 2″ of him, clad in impeccable and immaculate tennis whites and almost bursting with vitality and youth. And for a moment, I thought he was going to strike up a stage pose and ask, "Tennis, anyone?" But of course I soon learned that the tennis whites weren't in preparation for a game or anything else: he just knew he looked good in them, along with his blond hair and fair skin and the long legs that made him automatically *stride* even when he wanted only to walk.

So he sat there now, in his classmate's room at the university, legs stretched out in front of him as though they were simply too long to worry about, and eyed me through half-closed lids, as though he could see me without my seeing him, and started firing away with questions. His classmate, Bill Davis, was a cousin of mine, though considerably younger; and I had stopped off to have lunch with him en route back to my job in the city from a visit down home. Bill, I suppose, had told Don a good deal about me—how we both came from the same small town in West Tennessee, but I had gone off to school in the East, managed to get to Europe a few times, and now worked for a newspaper, which all sounds more glamorous than it actually has been. But I don't doubt it all made me sound rich and strange, if not downright exotic and foreign to Don, and I supposed now he had come to see the sideshow.

I liked him at once, of course. You had to, really. Yes, he was good-looking; and yes, he knew it. And I could imagine he'd been told that he was good-looking a great many times too. He knew the tennis whites didn't detract from the golden-lad image either. But at the same time there was something terribly innocent, maybe even vulnerable, about him that kept it all from degenerating into nothing but a kind of narcissism. For one thing, though he was bright enough, he really didn't know very much; I could tell that right away. And he had the good sense not to parade his ignorance but rather to ask all the questions he could think of, as though he were literally trying to educate himself thereby. And really, I believe he was; furthermore, I thought he was *educable* (Matthew Arnold's word, remember). "What made you want to go into journalism?" he said. "What was it like going to school in the Ivy League?" "How did you feel in Europe?" It was as though he couldn't wait to ask all the questions, pose all the riddles. And I'd been asked them all before. But of course I was only too glad to have the opportunity to speak—my cousin Bill might have said show off. On the other hand, there's nothing in the world so exciting as teaching somebody who really wants to learn: I knew enough, in or out of the classroom, to appreciate that. And here was an eager pupil; I could see that too.

But all the time I was talking, I had the feeling that Don was not only dutifully listening here and now but somehow also filing it all away for future reference. (Was he filing me away? I didn't suppose anybody quite like me had ever crossed his path before. And that wasn't vanity, just an acknowledgment of the limitations of time and place.) At any rate, whatever show I was putting on the road for him was not going unattended. And let's face it: an audience is always flattering, even at times absolutely necessary. And a young audience—especially for older performers—can be the most flattering of all. So I went on from strength to strength, Connecticut to Italy, books (I had written a couple of novels, not very successfully) to newspapers.

The white wine helped of course: I was taking Bill out to lunch later, so we were having a social glass, in which Don joined us, beforehand. But somewhere along the way, after I had gotten off on music ("That was the summer I went to Vienna and went to the opera every night for five nights!"), I realized I had lost my principal auditor. Don sat there staring into space—not just inattentive but also involved in some private drama of his own for which my travelogue provided the background music. But I wasn't offended or angry: I was interested and wanted to know more.

Bill had told me, in his letters, a fair amount about Don already: how he was bright enough but didn't "apply himself," as we used to say; how he was quite a lad with the girls, but somehow his heart never seemed to be in it, whatever the state of his glands; how in some ways he ignored the world, not always happily, in the case of deadlines and papers due. And yet he somehow always seemed to fall on his feet. The game was never played all the way out for him and no chickens ever quite came home to roost. An only child, he had had every so-called advantage that fond (though not blind) parents could provide; and he wasn't impervious to his obligations in that quarter. But he wasn't weighted down by neurotic guilt either. Now I didn't know when I had met anybody who seemed so healthy, mentally and physically: it made me feel better just to talk to him, to say nothing of look at him. (The older you get, the more the young can affect you that way, I've found.)

And yet there was something else there too: he had a private story, some sort of drama of his own going while I was talking. Because in the middle of my Italian travelogue (I had just remarked that I wanted in due course to die in Venice: it seemed *made* for that), he interrupted with, "I'd give anything to go there; but I'm afraid I might be disappointed, I've dreamed of it all for so long." And when I asked what he meant, he said, "It's like the movies. When that's all you see, growing up, you get spoiled because they condition you to expect perfection, like in a dream, which of course you're never going to get in this world. And that's true, whether it's with seeing the sights or falling in love or anything else."

He wasn't being impertinent either: I could tell that. But I thought he was awfully young to know what he knew. And all of a sudden my heart warmed toward him in a way it hadn't before. I said, "Yes, of course, dreams work that way. But we've got to have them, even when they're larger than life, maybe even vulgar, don't you think? Because even then, they're better than no dream at all. And the great thing, you know—or perhaps you can't know this until you're older—is that so often dreams come true, they really do. And one of the greatest things about travel—or any other goal or dream—is finding yourself there, really and truly, and all the way from Tennessee or wherever your dream began. But of course, you know, dreams don't just drive up to the front door and blow the horn: you have to work to make them come true. And that's part of the fun too. Thoreau—or maybe it was Emerson— put it all very well when he said there was nothing wrong with having castles in Spain: that was where they belonged; but it was up to you to put the foundations under them."

I looked over at Bill, and he was eyeing me speculatively over his wine glass. Was this an old story to him now? Had he seen others besides me falling for Don's charm, playing up to him, even performing for him as I didn't doubt I was now doing? Doubtless, he would have something sharp to say to me later on. Or perhaps he hadn't known I possessed such strong convictions about the life I'd been leading and was surprised now at my vehemence if not my eloquence.

And then Don said, "I've been a dreamer all my life, and sometimes I've gotten into trouble that way. When I was in the fifth grade, my teacher was Miss Virginia Perkins; and I can hear her right now saying, 'Donald Prescot, quit looking out the window and daydreaming. The class is in *here*.' And of course she was right, but I always wanted to tell her that I had a point too. And I felt the same with whoever or whatever else was always telling me the action was all *here,* whether it was my parents or my teachers or the football coach. They were all knocking dreams, I thought; but then what did *they* have to offer in their place—grades, goals, championships, scholarships? I didn't see that they had much to tempt you with either if these things didn't somehow *mean* something. And that was where dreams came in: you had to imagine beauty and glamor and romance first before you really knew what you wanted to dream about, what you wanted to work toward. Otherwise, you were just taking it all secondhand from older people—like everything else in your life—who would tell you what you *ought* to want."

I had heard most of this, in one form or another, from frustrated young people before; but in Don's case I now felt more intensity than usual behind the conflict. And he was more articulate too, though I wasn't altogether sure why. After he had left and I had taken Bill out to lunch, we spoke of him, just the two of us. And I told Bill I had been very much taken with so much youth and innocence so obviously in conflict with itself. And Bill said, "Well, don't let it get you down or go to your head. I'm fond of Don, I really am; and we've been good friends ever since we came here as freshmen almost four years ago. But he can drive you out of your mind if you don't watch out. One day it's this, and another day it's that, dreams and all the rest. 'Why don't we take off for a year and work our way round the world on a tramp steamer?' Or 'why don't we hitchhike our way to California?' He's bright enough of course, but he never gets a paper or anything else in on time if he can help it. And the girls all love the sleepy eyes and the blond hair and the long legs, but God help them if he ever undertook to *provide* for them. I can't see him committed to anything, much less married to anybody. Sometimes I think part of the trouble is that he's been told once too often how 'cute' he is, and clearly he is a good-looking devil; but you can't make a life work out of being a lily of the field, even in tennis whites. There may be other things involved in his hang-up too, but I don't know about them."

And I said no, you couldn't live on capital forever; and what was Don going to do when he got out in "real life," where most of us have to earn our bread? And Bill said, "God only knows, and of course he doesn't really have to do anything because his folks are very well off. And he's the apple of their eye, naturally. But he's got to do *something* if he's going to have any self-respect; I'd certainly feel that way myself. Sometimes I think he's completely irresponsible, and I hate to think dreams do that to you. After all, I've had one or two of them myself. And don't be mistaken, by the way, about the way he reacted to you: he's never met anybody quite like you before—you know, 'down-home boy turned Ivy Leaguer and glamorous traveling journalist.' And you've impressed the Hell out of him. But you're just going to end up right in his collection along with everything else."

"What on earth a collection of?" I asked. "And my life hasn't been all that glamorous, you know. I've had to work and sweat damned hard to get where I am, if indeed I've ever gotten anywhere."

"Yes," said Bill, "but Don doesn't know that. Did you ever read a story by Willa Cather called 'Paul's Case'? No? Well, it's about a boy who had dreams that were too big for him or else he was too weak or too lazy to do anything about them. And he came to a tragic end. Well, I'm not suggesting that Don's situation is exactly like that, but he is a *collector*. And now you'll go into the collection in his head, where he makes up his dreams. Really, he'd almost rather think about you than see you, once he's got you safely in his head. That way, he can turn you into what he wants; but if he had to deal with the real-live you every day, the glamor might fade and the dream as such might vanish. Real people can talk back to you, you know; dreams can't. That's what the boy in Willa Cather's story never learned, and I don't think Don has either. Sometimes I wonder if he ever will."

I told Bill he was far too young to be so cynical or maybe so wise, and then we parted. But in the weeks ahead I couldn't get Don out of my mind, and the golden figure in tennis whites gleamed from time to time before me as I sat at my desk in front of the beat-up old Royal portable I had cherished for literally thirty years. (It was outmoded and inefficient, said my friends; but I was devoted to it.) What was it about

Don anyhow that fascinated me—just youth and beauty and a kind of innocence, only that? No, leave all that for old maids such as Henry James. It was energy, and it was hope; it was the future. Above all, it was *life*. Also, of course, it was the dream, all dreams. We had to have them or we would die. In middle age I had come to believe that very strongly. And yet, of course, I knew Thoreau or Emerson was right; you had to work to put the foundations under them. Jay Gatsby had done that for even such a vulgar dream as his; Thomas Sutpen had done that, God knew, for such a nightmare as he had conjured up. You couldn't just sit around in tennis whites and look pretty. I knew that as surely as I had ever known anything in my life. I had been a great dreamer in my day myself, but I had never been pretty. And I *had* worked.

What would become of Don, this golden boy in tennis whites I had met so briefly but who had grown now, more and more, into some sort of symbol in my mind? And what did he mean to me anyhow—a suggestion of myself when young, the self I might have become but didn't? And how much better off was I for not having done so, assuming I ever could have? These are questions I've been pondering a good deal of late. Perhaps I'm having some sort of mid-life crisis, as they call it: I just turned fifty a few months back. Anyhow, the other day I had a letter from Don, out of the blue, asking me whether, in the course of my travels, I would be good enough to drop him a postcard from time to time: that way he would be traveling too, by proxy. He said it would mean so much to him to know someone like me, who was leading the life he had always dreamed of leading. And the next time I was through town, we really must get together and have dinner and talk things over. He still couldn't make up his mind what he wanted to do after graduation, he said; and maybe I could help him decide.

The Moon-Fixer

"That boy's going to be a moon-fixer." That was what my Uncle William used to say about his grandson, Andrew. At first I didn't understand what it meant: I wasn't all that much older than Andrew myself, just five years, really. How could anybody *fix* the moon; better still, why would the moon ever need fixing? I supposed it was just a saying, as older people usually dismissed their more extravagant flights in daily conversation. But then, so what? Did it refer to the fact that Andrew clearly was going to be quite tall and so might be able to reach the moon, or did it go further and suggest that Uncle William thought Andrew was so wonderful, there wasn't anything in this world he couldn't do, nothing that went wrong he couldn't *fix*? Probably the latter because I learned very early that Uncle William, who had been widowed years ago and whose only child was Andrew's mother, my cousin Alice, was enormously proud of this, his only grandson. Even now I can see him seating Andrew in his lap, hugging him tightly, whispering some secret term of endearment in his ear, and then proclaiming for all the world to hear: "This boy never did anything wrong in his whole life!"

And then Andrew would blush and duck his head into Uncle William's ribs and act as though, if he could, he would absolutely *drown* in his grandfather's body, though whether from delight or embarrassment I never knew. But though Uncle William's affection for his grandson was absolutely unconditional, it wasn't completely blind. Day after day, that summer when Andrew was ten and was learning to roller-skate (using a broom to keep his balance), Uncle William would sit on his front porch, watching Andrew negotiate the long concrete stretch of the front walk, only to collapse into silent laughter as Andrew took each predictable tumble. And you could tell that Uncle William was fighting manfully not to wound the very apple of his eye with such levity, only to lose every round. He did the best he could to conceal his mirth: he didn't guffaw but rather heaved silently, with tears streaming down his face all the while. Andrew, of course, saw none of this: he had his mind purely on the challenge at hand. But each time he fell, he would rise shakily, dust himself off, grit his teeth, and begin again. And Uncle William would begin heaving again. He told my father (who was his brother) that if Andrew hadn't looked so solemn, it wouldn't have been so funny; but the combination of Andrew's posture and his demeanor was just too much for him. You had to admire Andrew's determination, he said, and his seriousness; but it *was* funny. The one time Uncle William did lose his composure about Andrew occurred when Andrew was six and playing the cymbals in a "kiddie band." Uncle William and my father almost broke up the recital because they said the sight of Andrew, straight as an arrow and absolutely poker-faced, clashing those *stove-lids* together was "just too ridiculous for words."

There was never any doubt, of course, Andrew repaid Uncle William's devotion: always he deferred to "Papa's" judgment, whether in fact or in opinion. Andrew's own father, Cousin Alice's husband John, had been killed in the Korean War; so Uncle William was the only father Andrew had ever known—and Uncle William's house his only home. Cousin Alice had one other child, Frances; but she was a good deal younger than Andrew and born after the death of her father. So she comes into the story only incidentally.

Except that she was another member of Andrew's admiring audience—what in time I came to call Andrew's stargazers because, the older he got, the more they tended to combine into a sort of fan club. And certainly, by his very definition a *moon-fixer* required something like *stargazers*. It did seem as though Andrew was born to be admired and finally adored; and, in due course, I think he was. Handsome as the devil, of course—tall and dark, brown-eyed, and just faintly brushed with roses in his cheeks. And to see him grow up—from cherub to lightfoot lad, you might say—was to understand better a great deal of English poetry—and classical too, for that matter. But there was more to Andrew than just looks; he was *alive,* you know, and he had *joy.* Joy in life, I supposed, but finally just joy in being Andrew. He walked just like one of Sir Walter Scott's heroes ("He trod the ling like a buck in the spring"); and when he talked, he would arch his eyebrows and his shoulders excitedly, and you thought of a young dolphin surfacing, playfully disporting himself in the briny deep.

A born leader, a natural athlete, and all the rest, he easily made Eagle Scout early; and his grades at school were always excellent if not the highest in the class. He even played the piano—a little, not too much to lose standing as a real boy. There really didn't seem to be anything he couldn't do, anything he couldn't fix, or so I thought. And I early began to view Andrew's achievements with some skepticism if not downright misgivings: after all, he was only five years younger than I. And young people are not all that generous about one another's accomplishments. One thing I did notice pretty early: Andrew rarely laughed out loud though he often smiled. And his smile was extremely engaging—as though you and he had some secret that nobody else would be told. But laughter somehow eluded him: was there something too public, too risky about that? Because all along, Andrew was essentially a very private person, and you felt he wasn't *telling* anything.

Of course, I couldn't appear to let Andrew's victories dishearten me: he should, as a junior, have been beneath my notice. And it wasn't as though either Uncle William or Cousin Alice sang his praises twenty-four hours a day: they were tremendously proud of him, of course, but they were both extremely sensible people and not about to spoil him more than could be helped. It was just that Andrew was simply always *there*—handsome, talented, strong, intelligent, and all the rest. No one could—or ever would—forget him. He would always be included; he would never be left out. He hiked the farthest, dived the deepest, ran the hardest, and always smiled the broadest. And he wasn't really spoiled either. If you had wanted to be unkind, you could have said he didn't have to be: he had it all already. But there was always something essentially sweet about him—generous and warmhearted. And I had to admit that. It was just that Andrew had seemed to take it all on as a right, not a privilege, the way the rest of us had to. Indeed, he often seemed to lead a charmed life. And I *was* five years older. That didn't help. If his story were a real *romance,* Andrew should have been fated to fall in combat with some mortal disease or else die heroically in the next war, whatever that was. Then he would have been propelled right on into legend: too good, too beautiful for this world and all the rest, compounded of equal parts of Keats, Byron, and Hollywood. But the actuality was at once more real and more true.

I used to puzzle about Andrew and all his perfections as I grew up, and indeed it almost made a Calvinist or a determinist or something out of me: some people just had it and others just didn't. And you were born that way and you died that way, and nothing in between really changed things. It was something I had worried about all my life, and I thought I had reason: fat, awkward, shy, I never saw myself as winning many hearts or turning many heads. My looks and personality would never be my fortune. But after a while, I decided just to relax and become one of Andrew's stargazers too. My own life (I was in my early twenties by then, out of college and earning my living) hadn't been all that electrifying; and I had about decided to just sit back and watch other folks for a change. Andrew was always worth watching. What happened to him in life would always be of interest, even concern, to me.

Not that he was any kind of show-off, but I knew now that he had what we call *presence,* and he was always *there.* You knew that at once. No one would ever ignore him; no one could ever forget him. He was the sort that people always referred to, almost without thinking, as "such a splendid boy," the model of what every young man should be. And I should have been green with envy. But somehow I never was. He was just *Andrew;* and all the good fortune, all the good looks—everything—went with that. He never acted as though he had any of it just coming to him either—automatically. But he *was* used to it: you could tell that. It never seemed to cross his mind that he might fail, that somehow, somewhere he might not always be the handsomest, the strongest, the brightest, or whatever. And everybody expected him to do great things.

I suppose that in my stargazing, in my Andrew-watching, I was all along halfway hoping that he would sooner or later get his comeuppance: it simply wasn't right that someone should indefinitely proceed from strength to strength, glory to glory, world without end, amen. And I was young, and young people are dreadfully moral. So I waited to see what would happen. Surely, reality, the world, *something* would catch up with him in due course. It wasn't that Andrew was a faker who would be *found out,* a charlatan who would be unmasked: the Andrew you saw was the Andrew for real. But in many ways, it was all based on luck: the looks, the brains, the charm just *happened* and, for him, they happened right. No wonder he might be a moon-fixer: it all seemed fated, in the stars, which shows how little I knew then, how young I still was myself. (And maybe this story is as much mine as his.)

But then Andrew went off to college, and for the first time he was off his home turf. This is not to say that he had necessarily been spoiled rotten or overly protected at home; but, as I said, he had been

Andrew there and everybody had known it. Now he had to be not only Andrew but something else too, and perhaps that something else wasn't a moon-fixer. He did all the right things of course, but now they weren't fraught with any particular glamor: many others were doing just the same. He didn't go out officially for a team: he obviously couldn't take it all on. But he did join a fraternity, throw himself into intramural sports, declare a major (economics), and begin his inexorable and—I didn't doubt—inevitable progress toward Big-Man-on-Campus status by the time he graduated. After graduation he would become an executive of *something:* you knew that right away. I should have said earlier that the girls were, as usual, wild about him; but then you would know that too, wouldn't you? There never seemed any special one for him, though: Andrew always played the field.

During the Christmas of his senior year when he came home— as handsome, as clever, as *winning* (maybe that was the key word about Andrew) as ever—I began to see him more dispassionately. (And by that time he had had his share of college successes: Phi Beta Kappa and Big-Man-on-Campus too!) And it all began now as innocently as possible. Andrew and I were going to a Christmas dance that somebody was giving at the country club, and he was putting on his blue flannel blazer. We were going together from Uncle William's, and he stood there arranging himself before the long mirror in the front hall. I was trying to hurry him because I was afraid we would be late to pick up our dates. But Andrew was not to be rushed, and he inspected himself meticulously before the long mirror—not to primp but to get it all correct, as he did everything else. He straightened his tie, brushed some imaginary dandruff off his shoulders, and then turned his attention to his coat, the blue flannel blazer. And I saw something that I've never forgotten. The gesture with which he snapped its brass-buttoned, double-breasted folds together was one of the most unconcerned ones imaginable, yet it was somehow dramatic and revealing. And I realized all of a sudden that that was just it: *that* was Andrew—the right gesture, the *winning* one, the gesture of someone who had never been without a blue flannel blazer ("the glass of fashion and the mold of form"). And what's more, he never would be without one, never would entertain that possibility, any more than he would entertain the possibility of not being asked to some function where blue flannel blazers were the appropriate thing to wear. And it was all instinctive but extremely limited: *it was all in the world he knew*. He had never been left out; he had always been there, in his place. But then what was his place? And why had I never asked the question before? Had I, despite my reservations, been as bedazzled as all the other stargazers, all the other Andrew-watchers?

Before him now, in the future, I could see unrolling a long vista of inevitable blue flannel blazers, inevitable promotions, inevitable successes, onward and upward in every way—the right wife, the right house, the right children and, I didn't doubt, the right dog and cat. But there would be no stars at the end of the climb, much less a moon— certainly not a moon that he could *fix,* in his well-ordered, airtight world. The realization made me sad, but then I looked at Andrew again as he finished buttoning his blazer and reflected that he probably hadn't given it much thought one way or the other. (Who had been the real romantic here all along anyway?) Being Andrew, being the moon-fixer was simply his *job;* and I had been foolish to expect anything else. But I had no more time then to pursue all the implications of my insight. Because right then Andrew looked up and grinned and said, "Now, son, let's don't keep the girls waiting any longer." And I followed him on out the door.

Shoot, Child,
What You Talking About?

———————————— • ● • ————————————

"Shoot, child, what you talking about?" That was the way my cousin, Emma Jane Powell, always emphasized whatever she was telling that might seem farfetched or incredible, a way of assuring you that though what you were hearing might seem to border on the fabulous or apocryphal, it wasn't a patch on what she *could* tell if she put her mind to it. Or it might also have been her way of beginning a tale, as though she was assuring you that though you *thought* you knew the ins and outs of the matter, this was the way it really was and she was going to set you right or, in her words, *straighten you out.* And, as you see, I naturally think in italics when I remember some of her utterances: they were like stage directions. And indeed, that's just what they were, in more ways than one. Like so many of her family before her and like so many of her friends in the world around her, she was a *performer* and loved every minute of it too. (And I might just interject here that, as time goes by, I no longer marvel that people from the South write stories and novels and plays. The real marvel would be if they didn't—so rich are the resources for drama in the talk that continually engulfs them—perhaps even threatens to drown them at times!)

But back to Emma Jane. She was about ten years older than I was (and that makes a vast difference when you're growing up, but of course is just nothing when you get to be an adult); and we weren't all that close kin either. But she was the niece of the cousin I always called Auntee, who was one of the great people, great loves of my life. Part of the original fascination Emma Jane held for me lay in her being just that—Auntee's niece; and I studied to discern the resemblances between her and her aunt. In some ways they were nothing in the world alike, Auntee's perceptions about the more delicate feelings and affections being something of a closed book to her, I always thought. And yet the more rip-snorting side of the aunt was clearly visible in the niece, from time to time. Neither one of them was anybody ever just to sit down and hold her hands and wait for something to happen: both of them well knew how to ride the whirlwind and direct the storm. And indeed, I can't right now see either of them as ever playing a passive role in anything.

When Auntee's husband died and left her more or less penniless (he had been a well-to-do farmer and had had reverses but mainly just "run through everything he had in no time at all," as they said), Auntee didn't do a thing but come back home to live with her old-maid sister, Cousin Rebecca; and then, when she got tired of more or less being Cousin Rebecca's chief cook and bottle washer (and, I suspect, hearing from Cousin Rebecca that *she* was "keeping her up"), she just went out and got a job as manager of the high school lunchroom. And when Emma Jane's husband left *her,* she knew that she might have herself and three children—all girls—to feed, so she up and went back to teaching kindergarten, which she had been doing before she married. And she said, while she was at it, she was mighty glad she had held onto the little farm her folks had left her. Her father, who had never approved of Emma Jane's husband—whose name, by the way, was Travis Latham—had told her that was where they would end up all along—though of course Travis was stepping mighty high in those days. Big construction firm running around all over West Tennessee and adjoining areas of Mississippi and Arkansas putting up *everything.*

But the thing was, her father told her soon after she and Travis were married, Travis didn't do a thing when they moved into town but go stick his letter in down at the First Baptist Church and transfer from the one where he belonged out in the country at Mt. Nebo. And then he proceeded never to darken the church door—out playing golf every Sunday of the world if he could manage it. And Emma Jane's father, Cousin Lee Powell, was like most of the other men of his time and place: *hunting* was the only sport a man ought to have. And *golf* was something bankers in knickers played after they had been clipping coupons and foreclosing on widows and orphans all day long. He said, in fact, that if Emma Jane had been a boy and ever come home dressed like that, with a golf stick in her hand, he would have *worn her out.* So, from the beginning, Cousin Lee wasn't too hopeful about Emma Jane's marital future. But he and her mother, Cousin Ola, always *stood behind her* (Auntee's words), no matter what. And that went for her marrying a

Baptist (all of us were Methodists, of course) from out at Mt. Nebo who
was trying to come up in the world by playing golf.

But anyhow Auntee was always partial to Emma Jane, who had
been the first grandchild in the family and who had been frail when she
was little: for a while, they even thought it might be her *lungs*. And so
because Emma Jane had given them trouble and concern, she got the
attention. Why, Auntee said she never could forget one time, when
Emma Jane was staying with her and her husband out in the country,
as a little girl, Auntee woke up in the night and discovered Emma Jane
missing from the bed she had had made up for her right there in their
room. So of course she screamed and woke up her husband with the
blood-curdling words, "The baby has fallen in the cistern!" But this
was completely wrong: Emma Jane had simply got lonesome and gone
and jumped in bed with one of Auntee's husband's children by his first
marriage. So they all relaxed and quite literally went back to bed. But
when, many years later, I asked Auntee why she had immediately
jumped to such a horrid conclusion, she just said, "Well, Baby, I've
discovered in life that if anything awful can happen, then it probably
will, and so you'd better get ready for it. And then if it doesn't, you're
just that much ahead. And at that point I couldn't think of anything
worse than finding Emma Jane's body floating in the cistern the next
morning when I went out on the back porch to draw the water to cook
breakfast with."

So all her life Emma Jane had had folks to worry about her, but
she always knew her own mind anyhow. And she married Travis Latham, the Baptist golf player and construction man, purely to please
herself, and they could all just like it or lump it. And that was that.
They flew pretty high for a while, too—trips to Hot Springs for the
races and also for the baths (people would come there on stretchers and
leave there dancing, they said; heavy smokers were supposed to leave
the bath sheets stained perfectly yellow with nicotine that had been
sweated out of them in the process); and there were trips to Knoxville
for the U-T football games too (even chartering a private railroad car
with some friends one time). And when the children were old enough
to appreciate such things, they began to travel and see the places re-
dolent of history—New York and Washington and such like. And
sometimes they would take Auntee with them—"just to babysit,"
Cousin Rebecca would observe, with her eyebrows raised and her lips
turned down. But Auntee loved every minute of it: the only thing was,

they never got up to Lake Louise in Canada, where she had always wanted to go because, as she said, there was just nobody that loved nature—and especially mountains and lakes, which was what scenery was all about—more than she did. Indeed, the great dream of her life, she told me once, was to go to Switzerland one day. And she didn't like it a bit when I told her, after I'd been there myself, that I thought the Alps and the Swiss themselves had been greatly overrated. All you could do was just *look* at them, I said; and then what? And she snapped, "Well, Baby, all I *wanted* to do was just *look* at them, not *talk* to them. I can do that, one way or another, right here at home." And I knew that once again, I "stood corrected" by Auntee, one of the few people I've ever known in my life who always knew exactly what she wanted and why.

So when later on Emma Jane and Travis began having some trouble, it worried her a great deal. She couldn't say too much around Cousin Rebecca, who might have been sitting there twiddling her thumbs, just biding her time till she could say "I told you so." As a retired fifth-grade teacher, she knew the old Adam pretty well; but she never had seemed to realize that the whole world wasn't the fifth grade. And, of course, Auntee was wise enough to know that though Emma Jane was the apple of her own eye, there was another side to things too. It took two to argue, she always said, quoting her late husband. (The other man in her life she always quoted was the great Dr. Livermore in Memphis, who had presided over her husband's last illness and never pulled any punches and told her *just how it was going to be*—and it was, too. And, as though making an unconscious play on his very name, Auntee would always say, "Child, that man taught me how to *live*!") I never knew too much about Emma Jane's "trouble" myself: I was off at school then. But I gathered that Travis had begun to chase around after other women. And I suspected that Emma Jane, who, remember, had been a kindergarten teacher before they married, might have been trying to keep everything in her life as well regulated as the world of preschoolers. And I knew no man in the world was going to put up with that for long.

Indeed, when Travis finally walked out on her (to just up and go live with one of those wenches, right there in your face, Auntee said), he told her, "You know, you're a good woman, but there's just no market for good women!" And after her initial hurt Emma Jane laughed as much as anybody else. She said maybe so, but she hadn't changed her ways for him and wouldn't for any other man she'd ever seen or might see. And if that was the story of her life, well then that was the way it was. Anyway, shoot, child, she said, what you talking about? Didn't you know that all *men* were like that anyhow? Her own dear Auntee had said that, when all was said and done, there wasn't one of them who was a gentleman below the waistband of his pants! Which I thought a philosophical way to look at it. Travis had been making a good deal of money by that time, so she got a good cash settlement when they were divorced, too. So all things considered, Emma Jane was well provided for; but the thing was, she still wanted her husband.

I used to think she talked too much about the whole thing: after all, she wasn't the first woman in the world whose husband had left her. But then she could see the fun in the case herself: why, she said, she did miss having a *man* in the house and if she got raped, way down there in that new subdivision where they lived, why she'd never tell! And when I remarked to her, the next time I came home that it looked as if people's *glands* could sure get them in a passel of trouble, she said the only *gland* she was concerned with was Travis's and somebody ought to operate on that! *That* would cure what was wrong with him! Auntee pretended to be shocked by such talk, but of course she wasn't: she called a spade a spade herself, nobody more so. But then Emma Jane said, shoot, child, what you talking about? It was the truth, wasn't it? And you might as well face it.

But then if Emma Jane was anything in the world, she was a *manager*. And she said there wasn't any man in captivity that was going to ruin her life: she was going to survive and live to tell it too. So she didn't do a thing but go back to teaching kindergarten, though she probably didn't really have to. Both her parents had died several years ago, and she had been renting out their home place on very good terms to one of the neighbors out there. So her circumstances were fairly easy, I think. And she did her best to raise the children without Travis on hand. He never moved any farther away than Memphis, so he was always pretty much available for such events as Christmas and Father's Day and graduations and would, I supposed, be on hand to give away the girls when they were married. In due course he went through more than one new wife—some several, as I recall. And Emma Jane said she didn't think he had any money left by that time: all those divorces must have taken their toll, and she was thankful she had gotten hers all in a lump sum. She never forgot that love and romance, as wonderful as they might be, had to be financed.

She said she'd tried to teach her girls that too, as they were coming to be grown. On the other hand, she'd also told them not ever to refuse their husbands *anything,* and if a man's home wasn't pleasant, he was certainly going to find his pleasures elsewhere. And any woman in the world ought to know that. When she said this to me, I remarked that, from all I had heard tell, she was certainly out of step with the modern world. But she just said, shoot, child, what you talking about, any woman was a fool to worry about being *equal* to men: women had always had the real power if they only had the sense to use it right! Anyway, they all had more sense than men anyhow, and a woman was a fool to let any man on earth ruin her life. (In general, I thought this all sounded a lot like Auntee, who was one of the greatest realists I've ever known.)

And on the whole, Emma Jane said, you might as well call things by their right names: a slut was a slut and a whore was a whore and if a man didn't know the difference between them and a wife, he deserved whatever he got. (Auntee always said that, when it came to speaking her mind, Emma Jane was Joan Blunt herself.)

Pretty stern philosophy all this, but Emma Jane could—and did—take her own prescription when the time came. She never quit loving Travis either, I always thought. Once, between wives, he even asked her to take him back; and of course the children were clamoring for her to do so. But she wasn't about to do that, she said; it would be just the same thing all over again and he would start running around with somebody else. Anyhow, she said, Travis didn't really want to be married to anybody. What he'd really have liked was simply to have her living next door so he could come over whenever he got ready. And maybe that wasn't peculiar to Travis but was just the nature of the beast, but she couldn't spend the rest of her life trying to figure it out. So they never remarried, but I don't think Emma Jane was ever about to marry anybody else either. And that's the way it all stayed.

I always go to see Emma Jane when I go back home. Auntee obviously is gone now, and that may be one special reason for my wanting to see her: she reminds me of Auntee. But always, too, there's the sense of being in the presence of somebody who has *managed* in life and is still in the game, enjoying every minute of it too—even the "trouble" because, after all, that's life too; and neither Emma Jane nor Auntee before her was ever about to be left out of that. Shoot, child, what you talking about?

A Cool Day in August

———— • ● • ————

I have seen their wedding "write-up" in the Woodville paper of many years ago. And it says there that Miss Sally Currie and Mr. Marcus Windrow, "two of the most popular members of the younger set," had "stolen a march on the old folks" and decided to surprise their many friends with a quiet wedding ceremony at the home of the bride's parents, after which they had taken the night train for Chicago. And naturally everyone "rejoiced in their union" and wished them every happiness in the years to come. My mother, who was a cousin of the bride, said the newspaper account left out the most amusing part. Sally—or, as I grew up calling her, Cousin Sally—always said it would be a cool day in August when she agreed to marry Marcus, he'd asked her and she'd put him off so many times; and the funny thing was that the day they married, it was just that—one of those cold snaps you can get in the late summer that let you know that fall is coming, though not right away, the kind of weather my mother always called "real fallified."

But anyhow, I gather that everybody in Woodville thought that was quite appropriate, that Cousin Sally and Marcus should get married on a cool day in August and thus start their married life on a joke, you might say. Because they were both of them quite a pair—perfect monkeys, my mother used to say. Marcus must have been a regular small-town "card," from all I've heard, with a quick wit and instant repartee and of course a discerning ear and eye: he was certainly an institution in Woodville by the time I came along. One reason I knew so much about him was that he worked in Sinclair's, the men's clothing store right next door to my father's and uncle's hardware and staple grocery store; and he was in and out of there several times every day—at least once in the morning, to drink a Coca-Cola with everybody else who was on hand, and usually again sometime in the afternoon, just to see what had happened there since his morning visit. In fact, the store itself was a sort of informal clubhouse for many of the people down on the square, clerks and customers alike; and it was a prime place to hear—and tell—the news of the day and exchange views on the state of the world and the condition of the cotton crop. And Marcus was certainly a principal actor on that stage.

There wasn't any malice in his wit, I think, though of course I've gotten to know most of the tales about him only in later years, after they might have been gentled by time. But even as a child, growing up in the store, I thought he was funny; and he was always very kind to me, never condescending, never "talking down" to me, and always winking at me when he first saw me, as if we were contemporaries and there were some sort of private joke between us. He certainly wasn't the sort of dirty trickster you might encounter in the small-town world of Ring Lardner, though, or in that of William Faulkner, for that matter. But he didn't mince his words either. To Charlie Banks, a little bantam rooster of a man who was never backward about coming forward, as they say, he administered something of a rebuke when Charlie came charging into Sinclair's one day and demanded some sock supporters *right that minute:* "Hell, you're down there where they are. Hold them up yourself!" And to a brand-new father bursting with pride in the new arrival, so much so that though he described the baby's looks in great detail and whom it took after and so on, he never seemed to be concerned with its sex, Marcus said, "Well, friend, now tell us the most important thing of all. Is it an open-face or a stem-winder?" And all the audience guffawed, including the new father. But no one took it amiss: they knew that Marcus never meant harm, but he did mean sense. His jokes never turned ugly or nasty either. Like many men of his time and place (I think particularly of my own father), he was a bold talker but never really smutty, certainly not in "mixed company." When women's skirts went higher in the 1920s, I heard he had a little fun at Cousin Sally's expense (and they had been long married then) by observing that a new dress she was very proud of was so short, every time she put it on he could practically see Fisher's Crossing—that little wide place in the road the trains always whistled for just before they got to Woodville! But that sort of comment was about as far as he ever went.

Like I said, Marcus was a Woodville institution, and everybody knew one or more stories about him. I can see him right now, his coat off and his sleeves rolled up, if it was hot summertime, but always very neat in his appearance, and his customary bow tie smartly in place, the suspenders he always wore firmly securing his trousers, and all ready for whatever the day would bring. And there he stood behind the counter in Sinclair's— or, as I usually remember him, beside the drink box in my father's and uncle's store, savoring his Coca-Cola and holding forth to all and sundry. Don't misunderstand me. He wasn't a smart aleck, and he wasn't a show-off. And he never hogged the floor either: there was too much competition for that. He wasn't the only one there who could tell a tale, remember. But everybody conceded he was one of the best.

He and Cousin Sally were well matched, and I suppose now they must have been something of a team. Her humor was slyer, more delicate than his; and they performed in tandem very well, I gather—as complements for each other. In fact, that was the way you usually thought of them—as "Marcus and Sally," almost like an "act," and most always together, hardly ever apart. Whereas Marcus was direct and forthright, she worked more by suggestion and innuendo; but with her, as with him, there was no malice, nothing really ugly. Of a Woodville husband who was known to be something of a philanderer, she observed, "Well, you see, he's a very attractive man, and he travels a good deal, and in his travels he likes to meet other attractive people." And of a local belle who got married with tremendous fanfare, eight brides-maids and all, but was back home with mamma and papa before the year was out, Cousin Sally observed that her marriage "didn't take."

I realize now that I'm not making either Marcus or Cousin Sally sound very amusing; and probably it's one of those things where you "need to know the people" and need to know their world really to appreciate them. Outsiders didn't always find them funny, I know. One time, after I had gone off to school, I had some visitors from out of town and naturally wanted to take them by to see Marcus and Cousin Sally, the delightful couple I had talked about so much. But they were both on their best "company" behavior and so dignified and prim and precise, they hardly "performed" at all. And I gladly could have killed them both. Certainly, they did a lot more than just stand around delivering one-liners, as we would call them today. Perhaps, too, it wasn't what they said so much that distinguished them as the way everybody thought of them—as people whom you couldn't fool about things, people who had the sense God gave them and weren't afraid to use it, and could always be counted on to see through pretense and folly and speak with some kind of sense about it all. And naturally they could always laugh and make you laugh also.

Marcus could definitely laugh about singing in the Methodist quartet, where he made a very good tenor. (He said that was the only way he'd ever get to Heaven.) And he was full of tales about the kind of things they all got into when they were summoned out to the back side of nowhere to sing at a funeral or some big to-do, like when the presiding elder or even the bishop made one of his visits. Cousin Sally, too, was always lending her talents to whatever civic organization was up to something. I remember one time she served as "Mr. Interlocutor" when the P.T.A. put on a blackface minstrel show in the high school auditorium—dressed impeccably in white tie and tails and seated on what must have been the bishop's "throne," borrowed from the Methodist church sanctuary. And I was dazzled by her wit and glamor and also by her wearing *pants,* which few women of her generation did back then, when I was growing up in the 1930s.

I suppose, in those days, I must have thought of both Marcus and Cousin Sally not so much as persons but as entertainers. Because whenever I saw them, they were more or less on display, doing their thing, as we might say now, sometimes separately but usually together. And, of course, they were my parents' contemporaries, even a bit older; and we were thus separated by that gulf too. In some ways they had no age: they knew everybody in town and were themselves known to everybody there and fit in, as we say, with all groups. But who really knew them? I even used to wonder whether anybody ever really saw them offstage. Or were they always doing a kind of act? What were they like, behind the scenes, when they were at home with only each other? Was it always a cool day in August then? It all used to puzzle me as I was growing up. It was obvious of course that Marcus and Cousin Sally had missed out on some things. They had no children, for one thing; and I wondered whether that was ever a matter of regret to them. Would they have been more "humanized" if they had been parents?

Such passions as they had (and I wasn't sure about the sexual ones) seemed reserved, in Marcus's case, for baseball and, in Cousin Sally's, for bridge. Again, they didn't go overboard there either. But you could see Marcus sitting out on the front porch, his radio right beside him, every weeknight and Sunday afternoon of the world, listening to the St. Louis Cardinals' baseball game, whenever they were playing during the season. And sometimes he would even take off and go up to St. Louis for a few days when the "Cards" were playing a particularly exciting home series. Cousin Sally didn't go with him, as a rule. That was when she would go off to a bridge tournament in Chicago or somewhere else. And afterwards when you asked her what kind of luck she had had, she would just smile sweetly and say she had "done right well." And that was all you ever got out of her.

Cousin Sally didn't "talk," my mother said, always adding that people like me would do well to emulate her example. Cousin Sally's father had been a judge, even winding up on the state appellate bench; and my mother said that none of the family ever forgot that "Papa" was a public figure and thus exposed to all sorts of hazards that might be brought on by impolitic conversation. And so they smiled and nodded but didn't ever really *say* much, especially on any kind of controversial subject. As I was growing up, I always imagined that sort of attitude would make for very bland days and very quiet nights and was sure it might all be rather dull; I could only suppose that somewhere, sometime Cousin Sally must let down her hair. (Was that one reason she had married Marcus—to have somebody to talk to?) But I didn't even know that for sure. My mother did say that the only time she had ever seen Cousin Sally "emotionally disturbed" was when her mother, Cousin Melvina, died; and then nobody could do a thing with her. But since that time nobody had ever seen Cousin Sally with her guard down anymore: maybe she had resolved never to let herself do that again.

And so there they were—Cousin Sally and Marcus, very much a part of the community and yet somehow out of it too. And I wasn't sure that it was just the fact of their being childless that made them so. Everybody knew them, and yet I wondered whether anybody really knew them. Nevertheless, they were a Woodville fixture. Maybe you always had to have people like them around—into things and yet out of things, to help you step back out of the picture frame yourself from time to time. After Marcus retired from business, you could see them most any time of day sitting out on the front porch—when it was hot—watching the people go by and always glad to see you when you stopped in to see them. They lived well: Cousin Sally's father had left her well provided for, and Marcus owned a great deal of farmland. He never had *had* to work at Sinclair's or anywhere else. But, again, money was not something you *talked* about, any more than you did your body and its less-public functions. And I realized, more and more, that that was just the way they were. The world was full of unavoidable realities, some of them less pleasant than others; and if you had any sense, you could see them and you knew they were there. But you just didn't say much about them.

My uncle was like that too: he knew the way of the world, but he just didn't think you ought to *dwell* on such things. It wasn't like an ostrich—sticking your head in the sand, refusing to acknowledge their very existence. But it used to worry me until I was older; and then I began to understand that sort of attitude, though it was foreign to my own, which held that it was always better if you could occasionally talk about things, though of course you didn't want to make a life work out of that either because other people would get tired of it all and, after a while, it didn't do you any good yourself.

But anyhow, I began to realize something like this about Marcus and Cousin Sally when he had a stroke about the time I went off to college. Yes, he was partially disabled, though he did make a fine comeback and got so he could drive the car downtown and visit with some of his old chums around the square. But neither he nor Cousin Sally ever alluded to his illness. And it was the same when, a couple of years later, she had to have surgery for cancer. You could go up and visit with them on the porch and talk about everything in the world, and they were both of them sitting there nearly dead, and they never said a thing about illness or feeling unwell or anything of the sort. My mother would tell me, when she wrote, that it was almost exasperating; people felt it just wasn't good sense for them to act that way—like they were hiding something. In fact, people almost resented it. It was sad, too, she said: neither Marcus nor Cousin Sally had any immediate family left and you would have thought they *needed* their friends now. She herself partly understood, she said: she remembered Cousin Sally's reaction to her mother's death and what she had inferred was her determination ever since never to "lose control" of herself again. My mother said she naturally admired such a firm resolve; but of course you always had to take Woodville, Tennessee, into account. People there always expected to share your sorrows as well as your joys. And maybe that was a good thing or maybe it wasn't, but nevertheless that was the way it was. You could be only so private in a place like that. But I thought, well, maybe it's still a cool day in August for Marcus and Cousin Sally; and I hoped they could stay that way right to the end.

And, do you know, they almost did. I was in my first year out of college when Cousin Sally died—after terrible suffering, they said. But they kept her right there at home as long as they could, only taking her to the hospital in Memphis toward the very end: neither she nor Marcus would have it otherwise. And she was buried in one of her own dresses too—none of that sort of negligee stuff they often use now on the female dead. I heard that Marcus insisted on that, also that somebody "sit up" with her the night she lay in state, before the funeral the next day. He couldn't do it himself: he was too unwell. But he said, when one of their friends sympathized with his being alone that night, that it was mighty lonesome for Sally over at the funeral home too. And so several of their friends stayed there with her body that night—an old custom hardly observed anymore, even in small towns.

Everybody wondered how Marcus would get along after Cousin Sally died; but as far as anybody could tell, he was making it all right. I was away working in Memphis by then, so I didn't see him for some time. And when I finally did get by to visit, it was summer and of course we sat out on the porch. Marcus was in a wheelchair now. John Edward Curtis, one of a family of Negroes that had worked for them a long time, was there with him; and I gather he did most of the nursing. (John Edward had been working as a hospital orderly up in Detroit, but I heard that Marcus had sent for him to come back home and "see him through.") We had a good visit too; we didn't talk about Cousin Sally but, instead, about the St. Louis Cardinals and the upcoming election and most everything else. As I was leaving, I did venture to say something by way of sympathy, how sad it made me to think that Cousin Sally was gone, or something like that; but Marcus just shook his head and said, "Oh yes." And I thought about all the good times they had had, all the fun they had had, and wondered why he didn't say more. But by this time I had some idea.

Marcus himself didn't last long after that. And he never left the house again, I heard, and was able to die right there in his own bed, with just John Edward and a few neighbors with him at the end. He had made a new will shortly before he died and, after leaving token legacies to some distant cousins, left everything else to their neighbors and some of Cousin Sally's bridge-club friends. And, of course, John Edward came in for a substantial bequest. Naturally, all of this caused a good deal of comment around town. But of even more interest to me was what my mother wrote about the last months of Marcus's life. She said John Edward told somebody that he never had seen anybody, black or white, more ready to go than Marcus. He said it was true that he always seemed his old self and continued to laugh and tell tales right up to the very end. And he never talked about Cousin Sally either. But John Edward said he never would take another dose of medicine after she died.

Sisters

• ● •

Cousin Serena Cobb was a first cousin of my mother, and she lived down the street from us in a big two-story house that always needed painting. But the thing was, the house belonged to her and her own sister, Cousin Hattie Rice, and a whole raft of half-sisters (their mother, Aunt Jenny, had married again after Uncle Josiah died). And they never could agree among themselves where and when to paint. And then, of course, this was during the Depression years, and ready money wasn't any too plentiful with them or anybody else.

Cousin Serena's husband, Cousin Edmund, had been dead for forty years or thereabouts, according to my mother; and she said she couldn't even remember him very well but, from what she knew of Cousin Serena, he had probably died in self-defense. He had left Cousin Serena a good deal of farmland a few miles south of town, though. And she managed to live off her income from that and the various jobs she had had in Memphis in the years since. But that was the thing about that whole branch of the family, my mother said: they none of them could wait to leave Woodville and run off to Memphis, as if the streets down there might be paved with gold. And their idea of *living,* if you could believe such a thing, was living in *apartments* and eating nearly all their meals out. And when she thought of all the good food their mother, Aunt Jenny, had put on the table in her time, she couldn't help but wonder how on earth any of them could eat in cafeterias and tearooms or anything else downtown Memphis had to offer. However, every one of them—the half-sisters too—had nothing on the brain back in those days but *men* and getting one for themselves as quickly as they could. And when you saw some of the ones they came bringing in, it made you wonder if they couldn't have all taken a bit longer in the act and done better. And who and what they were or where they came from, nobody ever quite knew for sure and was maybe afraid to ask. But when you gave women names like that (and she never could understand what had come over Aunt Jenny), you couldn't think it foretold any good—names such as Wanda and Laverne, to say nothing of Serena; and even Mary (the youngest one) had to spell her name with an "e": "Marye." But they were all like that, my mother said: not a one of them could let well enough alone. And when Cousin Serena kept boarders for a while after she moved to Memphis, she would make them get up before she left for work so she could make up their beds. Or at least that was what they told on her.

But Cousin Hattie was an exception, apparently because, for one thing, she never had married and had always stayed home, to look after Aunt Jenny when she got old. And after Aunt Jenny died, she said she never had had a happy day since because she *loved* her mother. But my father just told her that she wasn't the first one ever to lose a mother and if she had just put a few more red roses on her hats when she was *young and pretty,* she wouldn't be in that fix right then. To which she would always snort and say, "Oh, hush, you old fool you." Clearly it tickled her, though. And you could see her most any time of day going to town to get the groceries—walking since she never had learned to drive and probably couldn't have afforded a car anyway—or buy her ice cream (that she ate for her ulcer) at Harris and Taylor's drugstore. There they sold "Fortune's All Cream Ice Cream" and the soda fountain itself was named "The Mattie Maud" in big curlicue letters up over the mirrors and lights, after the respective wives of Mr. Harris and Mr. Taylor. Of course she stopped and visited with everybody along the way, coming and going, too. And that seemed Cousin Hattie's life—that and taking flowers to the cemetery every few days because she said *she* wouldn't forget their mother, no matter what the rest of them did. Most people around town just thought of her as a sweet old fool that would talk you to death, called everybody in the world "hon," and wouldn't hurt a fly.

This was all substantially correct, I suppose, until Cousin Serena decided to come back to Woodville after all those years in Memphis, where she had lived almost ever since her husband died, and move in with Cousin Hattie. And though she was certainly entitled to do that (like I said, the house belonged to all the sisters), it upset Cousin Hattie's way of life and everything about it. And she would go all over town, saying that Cousin Serena had had a husband and a home of her own and nice things and she didn't *have* to live in Woodville, but she herself didn't have anywhere else to go. Of course, Cousin Hattie hadn't had a husband either and everybody understood *that,* but naturally nobody said it. And anyway, if Cousin Serena was bound and determined to come back to Woodville to live, why didn't she just build herself a house on her own property that her husband had left her out on the edge of town? Everybody wondered about that.

So in due course Cousin Serena did move into the old house with Cousin Hattie, but not before she had effected a number of changes—such as turning one of the big upstairs bedrooms into an "efficiency," a word that Cousin Hattie always pronounced as though it were something vile—or at any rate, brought on from Memphis and so therefore newfangled and suspect. And she had herself a bedroom and living "area"—another Memphis word—and a "kitchenette." But she still had to share the upstairs bathroom with Cousin Hattie, and the downstairs was rented out anyway to a succession of what Cousin Hattie called her "roomers," but what Cousin Serena loftily referred to as their "tenants." And then she would always go on to say that when you had big old broken-down houses like they had, you couldn't expect to attract the best class of tenants anyhow. Cousin Hattie, of course, had always been on very good terms with her renters; but Cousin Serena held herself aloof because, she said, it didn't do to get mixed up with all the kind of people that you didn't know who they were or where they came from or anything about their background. Why, one little couple—rather sweet too—had just moved in; and when she asked the man what he *did,* he told her he was a "body man" and she thought he worked for one of the car dealers. But come to find out, he worked up at the funeral home!

Anyway, it wasn't what she was used to: she remembered when the whole house had been theirs and their mother was alive and had that beautiful rose garden out in the side yard—what they had called their "garden spot." And now they had sold it off to their next-door neighbor some years ago, and the only flowers on the place were those tacky old day lilies that just took over during the summer. (Everybody on the street—unbeknownst to them, of course—called them "Miss Hattie lilies" because they associated them with Cousin Hattie's place.) Obviously you didn't have to *do* anything for them, Cousin Serena said, just stay out of their way till they were finished blooming at the end of the season.

So Cousin Serena moved into her "efficiency" and began to torment Cousin Hattie—to hear Cousin Hattie tell it. She would quarrel with the roomers about using too much electricity, and she would quarrel with Cousin Hattie about who would be the first to use the bathroom in the mornings. And nothing could go to suit her. And Cousin Hattie told it all over town. People would sympathize, but then say, behind her back, well, she was just a poor old maid and she hadn't had a husband and a home of her own and nice things and that was just the trouble. (Old Miss Pearl Hendren, who was the *rankest* of Baptists, said *she* wanted to know, did they really think they were going to Heaven with such as that in their hearts, and they had both better stay home and read the Bible.) Anyhow, Cousin Serena got all the official sympathy because she didn't go from door to door telling her tale, and she did more or less enter into community affairs (nobody had seen Cousin Hattie at church since they didn't know when). But Cousin Serena stopped short of joining a missionary circle, though she said she had come "as near as ace" to doing so. But that would have been too confining: she never knew when she might want to just hop on the bus and go to Memphis for a day or two, to kick up her heels because, child, she would always say, Memphis was in her *blood.*

My mother would always add, after Cousin Serena had left, that it certainly was the truth—and not always for the better, either. For one thing, when Cousin Serena worked as a hostess or something at the YWCA all those years, she was going with a married man from out of town, on the side. And Cousin Serena herself had said that when she applied for a position one time at Goldsmith's department store, they told her immediately that, with her looks and personality, they weren't going to just stick her behind a counter: they were going to put her in the French Room right away. And there were few situations *she* couldn't handle. Take the time the man next door—when she had her own brick home out on Avalon—hid under the bed and so caught his wife in the very act with another man (or rather, came out from under the bed when they went to embrace) and wanted to come use her telephone to call the police or the lawyers or whomever. But she just said no, siree, she had a position to consider; and that was all there was to it. When Cousin Serena got to that part, my mother would always purse her lips and raise her eyebrows as though to indicate that *she* knew what to think of good looks and personality and living in Memphis and all the rest, and it wasn't much either. One time Cousin Serena, who had gotten on a tear about something or other, even proclaimed that if she had her way, there would be three things that would be at the bottom of the Mississippi River, and that was cigarettes and whiskey and mean women. And my mother said right then she had wanted to ask Cousin Serena whether she could swim.

So that was the way it was. Cousin Hattie was something of a nuisance, telling her tale all over town and usually alluding to Cousin Serena as "the other one." But really, she got the private sympathy because everybody knew she more or less *had* to put up with Cousin Serena: she really didn't have anywhere else to go, and Cousin Serena did. My mother even asked Cousin Serena one time why she didn't go on and sell some of that farmland and build herself a house out on the rest of it and be her own boss and manager and enjoy the few years that remained to her while she could. She could understand why Cousin Serena wanted to come back to Woodville, she said. When the years drew nigh, all the old ones that had been away always started heading in home. And that was as it should be, but you might as well be comfortable while you were at it.

At that point Cousin Serena had hemmed and hawed and looked vague, and my mother said she was probably thinking about her grandchildren. Cousin Serena had had a son—her only child—that she never spoke much about; and he had gone to the bad or something in a bank failure and even done some time in the penitentiary and then had gone "out West" when he got out. Nobody, certainly not Cousin Serena, knew exactly where he was. She saw the grandchildren occasionally in Memphis, where they lived with their mother, but she didn't talk much about them: my mother always thought it was just too painful for her. And besides, she didn't look and act much like a grandmother anyway. She was still—though in her seventies then—a good-looking woman, and she wore good-looking clothes. That whole family—sisters and half-sisters alike—had always been real "fixy" anyhow, my mother said. (Cousin Serena never had even taken off the diamond ear bobs her husband gave her when they married.)

She still had men on her mind too: there wasn't a widower or an old bachelor in captivity that was safe as long as Cousin Serena had life and health. Or that's what one of my cousins—the one I called Auntee, who was an even bigger realist than my mother—said. Sometimes when somebody just referred to Cousin Serena in passing—for instance, you would say you had just seen her on the street or something and she looked well or whatever—Auntee would suddenly announce, apropos of nothing: "And would marry *tomorrow* if somebody would ask her!" And most people would say, well, they really hadn't thought about it, but they bet that was the truth. But the eligible men managed to stay clear of her, and she never married again.

Finally she did go ahead and sell off some of that farmland and build herself what my father always called her little love nest out on the highway to Memphis. In those days, it was way out beyond the city limits. But whenever she needed to go somewhere, she would just call a taxi; and best of all, the bus to Memphis went right by her front door. I wondered what she and Cousin Hattie would do, now that they didn't have each other to fuss with. My mother had always thought they got along much better behind the scenes than they made out like: she thought all that quarreling—or the reports of it—mainly just gave them something to do, though she did always say she thought Cousin Hattie was just silly, but Cousin Serena was really mean. In the old days, when we went down there to see them or take them some apples or figs in the summertime when we had all we could use ourselves on the trees and bushes out in the backyard, one of us would have to talk to Cousin Hattie and the other would take on Cousin Serena; but the two of them never said a word to each other. And it always embarrassed me to death, but it didn't seem to bother them at all.

And, of course, that was it: I know that now. The quarrel gave them something to do, gave some sort of meaning to their lives. And when they didn't have it—or have each other—anymore, they both sort of dried up and blew away. Cousin Serena was found dead out by her garbage can one morning, out on the highway: she had apparently gone out to empty her scraps from the breakfast table and fell right there. Cousin Hattie was away in Memphis, on one of her occasional visits to the half-sisters, when they would take her home with them to pet and feed up for a while; so there was no one on hand to take charge. But Auntee, when she heard about it, went over to the funeral home and stayed there while they were "getting Cousin Serena ready," as she put it, until the half-sisters and Cousin Hattie arrived from Memphis. And she said it really "paid off" too because when they all got there, they told her they never would forget her coming to their side when they needed her and they would certainly be glad to do the same for her someday. Auntee said later that wasn't exactly what she had in mind, but *somebody* had to do it; so she had just elected herself, and that was the way it often was with things in this world you really didn't care for but that nevertheless just *had to be.*

So they buried Cousin Serena beside her forty-years-dead husband; and a few years later Cousin Hattie was buried beside their mother, who had been placed next to both of her husbands. And that was the end of the story—except that Auntee remarked, when it was all over and they were both dead and gone, that you could say what you wanted, but she thought the happiest time of their lives was when they were both right there living under the same roof and fussing and fighting with each other all the time. Whoever in the world that knew anything about folks would have expected them to be a *comfort* to each other? The most you could have hoped for, she said, was that they might have lived there in a sort of armed truce and fought out the battle of old age together. But that was all. I was still fairly young then—well, off at school—and I was shocked. I thought that was the most cynical thing I had ever heard in my life. But that was a long time ago, and I'm a lot older. And I think I understand it all perfectly well now.

Mrs. Picture Show Green

————————— • ⬤ • —————————

Actually, her name was Etta Mae Green; but everybody in town called her Mrs. Picture Show Green because her husband, who had been named Charlie, had owned and operated the local movie theater—the New Dixie. And when I was growing up, I thought that was sort of quaint and maybe one of those usages confined to Woodville and places like it in the American South. And in some ways, this was true: Eudora Welty has one of her characters in *The Ponder Heart* known to the community as Mr. Bank Sistrunk because he is head of the local bank. But then later I found Miss Bates in Jane Austen's *Emma* referring to one of the servants at the local inn as "John Ostler." And I knew then it all went wider and farther than Woodville or the South, this distinguishing of characters by their functions, by their trades. The old Romans would have understood: it involved using a cognomen or something of the sort. And, of course, it assumed a more closely knit community than many of us are familiar with today. It performed a very real service, too. If nothing else, in a place where some names were very common, it avoided confusion, as in the case of River Jim Ferguson and Long Jim Ferguson, two other Woodvillians I still recall but not very clearly now—except that they *were* two different men. If one of the Messrs. Ferguson was a big, tall man and the other made his living as a fisherman, that was mainly all you needed to know. There couldn't be any confusion after that: all the rest would follow.

But Mrs. Picture Show Green was a *cutter,* as my mother would have said; indeed, some people would have said she was a *bird.* Long widowed when I first remember her, she still presided at the box office of the New Dixie from time to time and would always make something over me when I was taken to the picture show, even turning a blind eye when my nurse, Louella, would take me with her, in those segregated times, up into the colored folks' balcony. Indeed, the first movies I ever saw, I saw seated in Louella's lap right there. She even taught me to mimic Mae West saying "Come up and see me some time"; and of course there were the Shirley Temple movies, which I didn't like because she (Shirley) was always so brave and sweet (I wasn't either one) when it came to confronting the vicissitudes of life. In her movies one or both of her parents were always dead, too: that didn't help—that was the most terrifying prospect I could imagine for anybody. But the main thing I didn't like was the cowboy movies with all that shooting; I hated anything that even suggested violence or terror. Once I even got up and ran out (from the white section down on the main floor) when a little boy, in the midst of whatever we were watching—I was with one of my older and therefore not very sympathetic cousins—whispered, "They're going to shoot a big fat woman here in a minute." And so my departure was marked with some derision. Later, one of my uncles, as if to explain my hasty exit, irreverently remarked, "Why, he was afraid they were talking about his mamma!" Whatever the case, I had had enough, right then and there.

But Mrs. Green was always sympathetic when the shooting or whatever got too much for me and would always let me come chat with her in the box office till things quieted down. She had other attractions too. Right above her station in the box office was the New Dixie's glittering marquee with the twinkling lights, which so enthralled me when I was even smaller that it almost blotted out Mrs. Green and everything else. Indeed, I remember calling her "Green lights" for a time. But something else she had, more personal and more intimate yet also very public: a hearing aid, usually called an Acousticon in those days (a brand name, I believe). I was fascinated because of the curious noises it would give off from time to time and also because not only did she wear a sort of headphone over one ear; there was also a cord that went down inside her dress where, she told me, it connected with the batteries that powered the whole contraption, as she put it. And when she didn't like what was going on in the world around her, to say nothing of what the characters in a particular picture were saying, she could just *turn them off;* few people in the world around her could do *that,* she went on to say. Even then I began to think she might have an advantage there.

Anyhow, when the noise quieted down—the shooting or the fire and flood and earthquake or whatever—I would sneak back into the theater and resume my seat. And Mrs. Green wouldn't tell on me either—those times when, as Huck Finn might have remarked, things in there got too various for me. I'm afraid I kept it up until about age ten, this timorousness at the movies. *Son of Frankenstein* the summer I was nine proved too strong, and I had to leave the theater altogether and go across the square to the arcade where, during hot weather, my father and his cronies played their endless night games of forty-two (like dominos, only you played it with specially made cards). Even *Gone With the Wind* the very next year got to me, and I had to take a breather during the burning of Atlanta. But what made that cop-out even more embarrassing was that it took place not at the New Dixie but amid the Oriental splendors of Loew's State in Memphis and one of my contemporaries—a girl who lisped—tried to comfort me by whispering, "Never mind; ith's jutht a picthure." My mother never let me forget that, even after I was grown and had made my first trip to Europe and had seen (and applauded) the horrors of the Grand Guignol in Paris.

But Mrs. Green had been a cutter in her day, my mother said. Why, one time she and a couple of other local matrons had even been asked to leave the Peabody Hotel in Memphis. I wanted to know why, of course, but my mother just pursed her lips and shook her head and looked wise and knowing. In due course I asked Auntee, who always told me what my mother wouldn't; and she just looked exasperated, as though *anybody* ought to have known the answer to that one, and said, "Oh, Baby, you know it must all have been something to do with *men*." Auntee didn't suffer fools—or innocents—gladly. And this was all a great fascination because I couldn't then envision Mrs. Green in the role of a femme fatale, even though I suspected she must have been something of a good-time girl in her younger days—before, as my father would have said, Father Time had caught up with her. But she was apparently, in her later days, still saying and doing the things other people would think unconventional, things they would like to do themselves, if they lived away from Woodville. One time she even stood up on a chair when her missionary circle met with old Miss Sarah Howard, who was so sanctified she couldn't meet you on the street without asking you were you saved. But that day Miss Sarah didn't even come downstairs to attend the circle meeting in her own house because she was sewing away for dear life upstairs on an evening dress for her youngest daughter, Felicia—who was supposed to be a very high-stepper indeed—to wear to a dance that night. So standing on a chair was what Mrs. Green thought of *that*.

Mrs. Green did tell me one time, when I was older and became a sort of buddy of hers, as many young people did, that there wasn't anything wrong with Miss Sarah except that she just wouldn't face facts, such as telling everybody in town that her husband, Mr. Alonzo Howard, was just killing himself drinking "that old Coca-Cola," when everybody knew it was really "that old Grand Dad" that was doing him in. Why, one time, Mrs. Green said she herself got up to take the early morning train for Memphis. When it came in, who should get off but Mr. Howard, who told her he had been coming out from Memphis on the late train the night before but had slept through Woodville, and the next thing he knew, he was way up in Fulton, Kentucky, and had to wait there for the early-morning local to come back down! So Mrs. Green didn't see any use in Miss Sarah's getting on such a high horse about sin and such like—mourning over "people jumping in and out of swimming pools half-naked on Sundays," as she always put it, and not pulling her own window shades down at night! When the men who ran the Gulf station across the street (Miss Sarah lived in a big old house right on the edge of the square) asked her to be more considerate of their customers, she replied that they could just turn their heads: it wore out the shades to keep rolling them up and down!

And all these things Mrs. Green would tell me (when I stopped by the picture show to visit with her) in her cracked, loud voice (like many deaf people) as though she was unaware that anybody else might hear her. But I don't suppose she cared either. She had a good while since become a town character, saying and doing the unexpected, and I'm sure she knew it. Young people liked her, of course: she made it plain that she was their ally against what they fancied was the stuffiness and primness of their elders. And she had no children of her own, so perhaps she became a kind of surrogate grandmother for all of us. Young at heart, she always called herself, and I would always then think of the Peabody Hotel and wish her well. But she never said or did anything that was really too out of line; it just made you wonder whether she might not be getting ready to—and it was all the more titillating because she wasn't, despite her age, one of Them but one of You. I wonder now whether she was so "advanced" as I thought her then; maybe you couldn't really have "told her *anything*." She was, after all, a woman of her time; and she lived in Woodville, remember, and wasn't about to leave it for anywhere else. But presiding over the New Dixie box office, seeing so many picture shows, hearing so much (even when deaf) of the town talk, she was bound to know things and to have attained a certain level of sophistication. At any rate, she was the best Woodville had to offer, and I cherished her.

Later on, about the time I was to graduate from high school, there was the MOAT, which was a sort of acronym for the Memphis Open Air Theater, which performed in a "shell" in Overton Park for six weeks every summer—operettas such as *The New Moon* and *Naughty Marietta* mostly. And Mrs. Green would be in charge of getting up a busload from Woodville to go in for one night every week of the season. I was happy to go, of course, and some of my classmates, too, though I think they thought it was all getting too "classical" for them. But Mrs. Green presided over the whole outing (in a county school bus hired for the occasion) as a combination Sunday school teacher and Scout leader, with a dash of Marie Dressler and Laura Hope Crews thrown in, even executing a dance step in the bus's aisle when she got carried away with the excitement of going to Memphis and to the MOAT. I figured she must be in her element then. She even said that if she dropped dead en route (and everybody by then knew she had a bad heart), she wanted us to go right on with the trip—just leave her remains by the side of the road and bury her on the way back.

One special time when Mrs. Green and I were again fellow travelers into the world of music took place when the Metropolitan Opera began including Memphis on their spring tour and one would-be "cultured" lady from Woodville (my mother said she was just plain "new rich" and that's all there was to it) asked us to go down with her to *Aida* as her guests. (And I had always wondered just how much music Mrs. Green could *hear* but figured *Aida* would be no problem, certainly not with all that parading around in the triumph scene, trumpets and all.) To tell the truth, Mrs. Green had said to me, she just liked her music "quick and devilish"; she didn't much care what kind it was—classical, popular, or whatever, though she did have a weakness for Nelson Eddy and Jeanette MacDonald.

Well, parking was a problem that night, as it always was when big events took place at Ellis Auditorium, which fronted the Mississippi. As I recall, the Cotton Carnival was in full swing too, and the king and queen and all the royal court were about to come across the river from Arkansas on the royal barge for their grand entrance into the city. So everybody in the mid-South that wasn't going to *Aida* had come out to see them, and the only parking places to be found now were in

back alleys and side streets far from Main and Front. We and our hostess finally fetched up in her big Cadillac in one of the back alleys, parked
precariously on a slope (to keep the alley clear), with our hostess at the
wheel several feet higher than Mrs. Green and me. But Mrs. Green
didn't turn a hair. When the hostess, said, "Now Mrs. Green, don't
be scared, don't you have a spell, hon," Mrs. Green replied, "Don't
you worry about me; I'm not *about* to have a spell. You just get this
damn car down off this hill." And then she turned around and winked
at me and, motioning toward our driver-hostess, said, in a stage whisper and of course louder than she knew, "Crazy!" But finally we did
get parked in a less hazardous manner and proceeded to *Aida* and all was
well. And Mrs. Green said she heard it all, every bit, just fine.

Mrs. Green was a great bridge player too, and she had a foursome
she played with regularly. I used to wonder whether any of them were
among the other women who had been asked to leave the Peabody that
time, but I never found out. They were all widows by this time, though,
and lived alone and could play all night if they wanted to. Sometimes it
seemed they almost did. When you walked home late at night and passed
Mrs. Green's after seeing the last show (she had "retired" from the New
Dixie by then), you could hear them laughing, sometimes almost screaming with pleasure when a rubber had been concluded or somebody had
pulled off an adroit finesse. And you knew Mrs. Green was in her element
still. I suppose that was the way I had come to think of her—as always in
her element. I wasn't sure just what that was except that it meant she was
right in the middle of things, seeing all, hearing all (even though deaf),
and telling a good deal of it too. (My mother always said she was a "fearless
talker.") But the main thing was that she was enjoying every bit of it; she
wouldn't have missed it for the world.

That was the way I felt, I remember, when I learned some years
later, after I had gone off to school, that she had died. Her next-door
neighbor found her dead one Monday morning, sitting straight up in
front of the television set, volume turned up as loud as it would go of
course, and seemingly absorbed in the morning news. The neighbor said
it all gave her quite a start: they had just finished the weekend highway
"body count" and were going on to give a demonstration of how to make
watermelon rind pickle when she came in. I thought Mrs. Green might
as well have written the script for the whole thing herself. Certainly, I
couldn't have imagined a better way for her to go.

A Husband and a
Home of Her Own
and Nice Things

——————— • ● • ———————

A lot of people in Woodville never knew what to make of Miss Agnes Claiborne; but Cousin Rosa Moss, who was my mother's old-maid, school-teacher cousin, said the main thing was that Miss Agnes's family had sent her off to school up North (she was the youngest and they were tired of having so many of their children—six in all—close around). And so when she came back from Vassar, there was nothing else for her to do but marry Mr. Sam Claiborne, a "new" man who was coming up in the world and probably the finest thing ever to come her way down here. Of course, Miss Agnes had been a Fontaine; and they had always been mighty fine folks in these parts—money, land, ancestors, and all that kind of thing. But Cousin Rosa said you couldn't make a life work out of that, and she supposed Miss Agnes had at least learned that at Vassar, if nothing else.

Cousin Rosa and her sister, Cousin Emma, who stayed home and kept house while Cousin Rosa taught school, were naturally strict about people's conduct—mainly because they were old maids, my mother always said, with nobody ever to cross them, and used to having their own way all the time—spoiled rotten, she said. But my father said it was sad too: there was never anybody around them to smoke a cigar or track mud into the house or rearrange the furniture, nobody ever to mess it up. And that was a shame when you thought about it. But their strictness had some interesting exceptions. For one thing, they could always overlook irregularities in a man that they would never have condoned in a woman—the old double standard still going strong, I suppose, back in the 1930s and 1940s when I remember them. So, when a woman went astray—whether it was to "cross the line," which was their euphemism for sexual misconduct, or just to make an imprudent marriage—Cousin Rosa would say, "Now didn't she lead her ducks to a pretty pond?" And Cousin Emma would nod her head as if in agreement and say, "Women are such fools!" And that would settle that.

But always they were more lenient toward men. Of all the first-grade pupils Cousin Rosa taught, the ones she remembered best ever after were the boys—especially the bad boys, the ones she would say she almost enjoyed spanking because it straightened them out and they went on to amount to something too. Cousin Emma, as usual, was more succinct. "Oh, they're all just *men,* and what else can you expect from *them?*" Sometimes she would even sing "Reuben, Reuben" while she did her housework, which showed what *she* thought.

But Cousin Rosa was always a teacher, and years later she always felt that her pupils—though grown and married and all the rest—were still in her classroom and still belonged to her. When Johnny Howard showed up at the Baptist church one Sunday morning during World War II, all dressed up in his Army Air Corps uniform and decorated with more than one medal (he was just back from overseas), Cousin Rosa said, "Now, Johnny, if you would just do as well as you look, you'd be all right." But Johnny just smiled that old devilish smile Cousin Rosa always said he could pave his way into Heaven with, for all that he got into more fights than any boy she'd ever taught, and said, "Now Miss Rosa, I don't want to be *good.* You know, Mr. Sam Claiborne was *good.*" And Cousin Rosa said she had to laugh, that's all there was to it. Because at that very minute Mr. Sam Claiborne was doing time in the federal penitentiary in Atlanta for being involved in a local bank failure, when everything went *kerflooey,* and nobody in town knew for days whether he had any money or not or whether his children could go off to college or anything else.

It had all nearly killed Cousin Rosa. Miss Agnes was one of her oldest friends; they were about the same age and had more or less grown up together. But, of course, Miss Agnes had married Mr. Sam and had a home of her own and nice things, and they had never seen as much of each other since they had been grown. I used to wonder whether Cousin Rosa could have been the least bit envious of Miss Agnes, even jealous. My mother said she recollected a time when some people had thought Cousin Rosa might marry Mr. Sam; but my father said no, Cousin Rosa was a born old maid and not about to give up her "freedom" or anything else to any man. When she died, it was going to say "Miss Rosa

Moss" on her tombstone and no mistake. In any event, while Miss Agnes
was turning into a fashionable young matron and the mother of a growing family, living in the fine house Mr. Sam built for her out on the
edge of town, Cousin Rosa had gone right along teaching school and
leading her life the way she wanted.

Of course she had a home of her own too, and maybe even some
nice things (her mother's scalloped, gold-band Haviland, for one thing).
But she didn't have a husband, though she did have Cousin Emma. And
there were times when, I suspect, that was a right tall order for both of
them. For one thing, Cousin Emma hated living up on the corner by
the railroad bridge; but Cousin Rosa said if truth were told, Cousin
Emma just wanted to be right in the middle of everything in town and
would be much happier living up over a store building down on the
square. However, their own dear father had built that very house they
had lived in all their lives right there and they weren't about to leave
it till they could both go out *feet first.* And so on. Whenever Cousin
Rosa got on one of what Cousin Emma called her *tantrums* like that,
Cousin Emma would just nod at you and say, "That's Miss Rosa." And
that would be the end of that. It was the same thing she said when she
had gone to the Chicago World's Fair that time and taken a one-day
excursion up to Milwaukee and there was a stop at one of the famous
breweries. Of course, one old woman who, Cousin Emma said, had
W.C.T.U. practically written all over her, sat there straight as a ramrod, radiating disapproval, while everybody else got off the bus to go
sample the beer. But Cousin Emma said *she'd* try anything once; and,
um-huh, there was Miss Rosa.

When the news got out about Mr. Sam Claiborne and the bank,
Cousin Rosa broke down and cried—to think of his shame, and I suppose, Miss Agnes's. But Cousin Emma just said, "Well, anybody as
sanctified as he is—there every time there's a crack in the Baptist Church
door and oozing all over you every time you meet him in the street, to
say nothing of stroking your arm if you're a new widow or a prosperous
old maid and asking if he can't help you with your affairs—may be just
too good to be true. And I told Rosa that when she gave him Papa's
insurance money to invest. But oh no, he was Sam Claiborne and Agnes'
husband and therefore perfect in her sight." And Cousin Emma said
she wasn't about to cry over him or any other man she'd ever seen and,
if she had her way, she'd like to be riding down the street right that

minute, on a big white stallion, with a six-shooter, going after that rascal, just like in the picture show.

And that made Cousin Rosa cry harder than ever. She knew she had to do something, and all she could think of was confronting Mr. Sam Claiborne and asking him straight out what he had done with their money. No, she wasn't a businesswoman, and she hadn't had much knowledge of financial affairs. But right was right, and she was Rosa Lavinia Moss, who had taught the first grade in Woodville all those years; and she knew the world and the folks in it. And when it came to a matter of principle, she wasn't afraid of anything in this world. And she hadn't done a thing to be ashamed of. And this brought on the subject of the little blue Ford.

Cousin Rosa said she must have been born in the saddle: she could ride any horse she ever saw when she was a young woman. And she could drive any animal she could get between the shafts of a buggy too. But she never had learned to drive a car until she was nearly sixty years old, when she decided to buy a little blue Ford so she and Cousin Emma wouldn't always be dependent on somebody else to fetch and carry for them. Cousin Emma and everybody else in the family protested—except my father, who said he thought it would do Cousin Rosa good and, anyhow, everybody in town knew her well enough to stay out of her way when she came down the road. So most any time you could see her and Cousin Emma driving around town or even out in the country, with Cousin Rosa glaring straight ahead and looking neither left nor right and gripping the wheel as if her life depended on it, and Cousin Emma right beside her telling her what she was doing wrong and not to go so fast and, for the Lord's sake, not to drive all *over* the road.

So the sisters got in the little blue Ford, without saying a word to anybody, and drove out to the Claibornes' house, where Miss Agnes met them at the front door and said Mr. Sam wasn't seeing *anybody* (he was out on bond or something). I suppose by that time Cousin Rosa had decided it didn't much matter anymore whether Miss Agnes had a husband and a home of her own and nice things or much of anything else. Because she just looked her right in the eye and said, "Agnes, you go ask Sam what he did with our money." Miss Agnes disappeared and, in a few minutes, came back with the information that Mr. Sam said he had lent it to a man named Mr. Otto Meachum, who lived out in the county, and maybe they could go find out something from him.

So this they did, just the two of them, in the little blue Ford. And it was all so secret, Cousin Rosa said, they didn't want to tell anybody where they were going or what for; and they didn't altogether know where they were going anyhow—out on the back side of nowhere—or whom they were going to see or whether they would know him when they got there or even know where *they* were then either! Then she would laugh through her tears because it *was* funny even if she always cried a little when she thought about Miss Agnes and, I suppose, Mr. Sam. They finally drove up to Mr. Meachum's house, after inquiring the way from everybody in the neighborhood. And when he came to the door, Cousin Rosa stated their case. (And I can hear her right now, looking him straight in the eye and saying, "I am Rosa Moss, and this is my sister, Emma." And that would have been all she needed to tell him or anybody else in the world, she would have thought. The world, when you came right down to it, wasn't substantially different from Woodville and the first grade.)

When she was through with her story, Mr. Meachum told them all he knew was that he had borrowed "two ladies' money" and was happy himself to find out just who they were and, yes, he could and would repay them, principal and interest. And thus it all came out all right; and "the Moss girls," as my mother sometimes called them, came on back to town in the little blue Ford, after what may have been the bravest action of their lives——still innocent of so much and yet lion-hearted when it came to the fundamentals, I always thought.

In a few weeks it was all over: Mr. Sam Claiborne went off to Atlanta and Miss Agnes stayed on in the big house, which by then the bank's creditors had taken over. Finally, she even took boarders, to make ends meet. And she held her head as high as she ever had too: after all, she had been a Fontaine. But she and Cousin Rosa never were very close after that.

A Ticket as Long as Your Arm

———————————— • ⬤ • ————————————

"**I** sometimes wish I had a railroad ticket as long as your arm," was what Cousin Rosa Moss said to me one time when she was telling me about her travels. And she was definitely the traveler in our family because if you had told my mother and father and most any of the others they could never leave our county again, they wouldn't have turned a hair. And I think now my own lifelong love of travel must have been some sort of reaction against that. As long ago as I can remember, I was determined to go places and see things—not just to get away from home, certainly not to leave home for good, but mainly because other places and things *were* different and perhaps also *just because they were there.* In any case, I was forever the young boy watching the Illinois Central mainline trains pounding grandly through our town (few of them actually stopped there) and resolving that someday it would be me on board, a spectator no longer but a real-live actor and, of course, the star of the show.

I've never decided why my parents were so indifferent to travel. Oh, my father would go to St. Louis occasionally on business (he was a hardware merchant and went to market there); and a couple of times he had even been to New York, once even to New Haven, Connecticut— for a Winchester Repeating Arms convention of some sort. But my mother had never done anything like that; and my grandmother, I was told, was never on a train in her life. "I've got more to worry about right here in Woodville than I can attend to," my mother would say, "and I haven't got time to go running around the world to see what other folks are up to." My father was somewhat different: he was glad he'd *been* to New York and such like, but that was it. He'd *done* that and need never do it again. I think now of Thoreau, who said he had traveled a great deal in Concord, and the Concord nights were stranger than the Arabian nights. Anyway, he went on, a great deal of what the world termed *news* (and *travel* and *news* were all the same to him) was mostly gossip and most of them who read it and wrote it were all old women over their tea. It was Emerson himself, remember, who said traveling was a fool's paradise.

But Cousin Rosa Moss was something else. Even as a young woman, around the turn of the century, she had loved to go places—off to school (the Memphis Conference Female Institute), then, after she became a school teacher, off to summer school (once even out to Berkeley, California). Another time she went to hear the lectures and concerts at Chautauqua in upstate New York; and that was wonderful too even if they did put sugar in their cornbread and serve you lemonade made with lemon extract. She was a great one for self-improvement and making the most of your opportunities; but she always traveled "hard," as you might say: when she got off the train in Woodville, they always had the bed turned down for her and she would sleep "straight through" for nearly twenty-four hours to "get over" her trip. Sometime later she was up and about and ready for business, ready to tell everybody all about it.

But the time I first remember, though, Cousin Rosa had to travel for more than just edification and delight: she had to travel for her health because she suffered badly from asthma and needed a much-drier climate than we had in West Tennessee. So every winter or two she would take a leave of absence from her teaching position (she had taught the first grade in Woodville for nearly fifty years—three generations in some families—and few people there could imagine learning to read and write from anybody else) and go out to visit a friend in Phoenix, Arizona, where there was unlimited sunshine and a grapefruit tree growing in the backyard! She started getting better as soon as she got to Texas, she always said; and the farther west she went, the better she felt until, by the time she stepped off the train in Phoenix, she was practically ready to dance a reel and cut the pigeon wing, as she put it—a prospect that always sounded bold and alluring to me, especially since she was one of the biggest Baptists you ever saw in your life and had hardly ever shaken a leg or danced a step. And lips that had touched liquor (or most anything else) had certainly never touched hers.

My mother always enjoyed pointing out that Cousin Rosa stoutly refused the "spiking" for your boiled custard at Christmastime in favor of vanilla extract, which was at least twenty percent alcohol; but Cousin Rosa was adamant. Why, one time on the trip out to Phoenix the air-conditioning in Cousin Rosa's Pullman car had broken down and all the passengers were told they could just move up to the club car ahead of them and be comfortable there (they were crossing the desert at the time). But Cousin Rosa said no indeed, she wasn't going to sit up there and watch "all that crowd" just *swilling* beer all day long—at which point her sister, Cousin Emma, who was a Methodist but didn't let it get her down, would always break in and say, "Sister, if you didn't have any more sense than that, you deserved to burn up." And then she would look over her glasses from her crocheting or embroidery and nod at you and say, "That's Miss Rosa all right: she'd rather burn up alive in Heaven than be comfortable and easy in Hell." And everybody would laugh except Cousin Rosa, who *would* be halfway amused but would usually just snort and say, "Emma, you ought to be ashamed of yourself."

That was the fundamental difference between them right there. Cousin Rosa was always the first-grade teacher and lifelong instructor—always taking her stand on *principle* and always ready to *straighten you out*. Sometimes when she got more exercised than usual, she would pound on the arm of her rocking chair to emphasize a point—or even sometimes wave her arm, even shake her fist above her head. ("I tell you right now, Rosa Lavinia Moss will never do *such-and-such*"—or whatever it was; "she'll *starve* first!") And right then Cousin Emma would usually break in with, "Sister would have starved to death long ago if I hadn't been doing all the cooking—helpless as a baby when it comes to doing anything around the house. But she always acts like that whenever she gets carried away and starts talking up in the air. Anybody in this world would know she was an old-maid school teacher if he'd never seen her before in his life. But I can tell you one thing. Whatever else happens, I intend to be *comfortable* in this world and, if possible, in the next. I'm quite willing for Sister and everybody else to worry about *principle*."

They were as different as daylight and dark, everybody always said; and neither one of them had ever had a beau or even thought about getting married, as far as I know. They were born old maids, my mother always said, and spoiled rotten into the bargain. Their mother, Aunt Sally, was responsible for that, she added, not wanting them to get married and have their husbands die on them early in the day and so be left widows with a house full of children the rest of their lives, like her own sister, Virginia. And so Cousin Rosa and Cousin Emma had grown up fated, even mated to each other; and I couldn't ever have imagined them apart, for all that they spent a good deal of their time battling

away with each other. But, of course, they agreed more than they disagreed, especially when nobody else was there, my mother always said.

Cousin Emma was something of a traveler herself; but she didn't
have to go by train, like Cousin Rosa: that was too formal and stiff, she
would always say. And she was much more venturesome, for all that
she liked her comfort. She preferred a spontaneous expedition too—what
Cousin Rosa would have called a jump-up thing—to a complicated
journey long in the planning. And I'm not certain whether she would
have wanted a ticket as long as your arm either. But then everybody
knew, Cousin Rosa would add, that Cousin Emma had always been
Dick-in-a-minute when it came to travel or anything else. Whatever
the case, she always knew her own mind and then some.

Why, one time Cousin Emma decided to go see one of her old
friends who had moved out to Texas—Houston, I think it was—and
had a daughter who was an artist and even painted pictures "in the
nude" (the models, not the daughter, I gathered, but then Cousin Emma
said what else could you expect in that part of the world). And it just
so happened that both Cousin Rosa and my mother—whom, for some
reason, Cousin Emma regarded as something of an inhibitor of delight
(Cousin Rosa, being a school teacher, was naturally one such)—were in
Memphis for the day. And so Cousin Emma didn't do a thing but con-
sult with my father, whom she very much admired because he smoked
cigars, though not in her house, and was a real *man* who even told her
mildly risqué jokes from time to time. They found a buyer who wanted
to take Cousin Emma's feather bed off her hands *right that minute;* so
they sold it and never told either Cousin Rosa or my mother what they
got for it; and the very next day Cousin Emma went to Texas on her
feather bed, as she put it. And that image always fascinated me: Cousin
Emma sailing through the air, almost as if she were on a magic carpet,
all the way to Texas. And that would have been just what she wanted—
easy and painless and not like having to get all dressed up and sit there
staring at other people just like you in a Pullman car. She always said
that Cousin Rosa thought riding in a Pullman was the next thing to
Heaven because, if truth were told, Cousin Rosa just naturally loved
being *waited on.* But deliver her from all that, she always said: she had
more to do with her time than just sitting there with her hands folded,
trying to look pretty. (Too bad that Cousin Emma didn't live until the
Jet Age, although it was just as well for Cousin Rosa that *she* didn't.)

As a matter of fact, Cousin Emma actually traveled to Texas that time on the bus: that way, she said, she could really see the country and talk to folks—if she wanted to—and she didn't have to dress up for anybody but herself. The line of least resistance was what she always followed except when it came to housework, she said. But then she did that to suit nobody but herself; and believe you me, it was done *right* too. One time during Prohibition when the officers arrested a man out in the county for bootlegging and found the whole cache of whiskey stowed under the kitchen floor—reached by a trap door under the kitchen table—Cousin Emma said she could hardly believe her ears when his wife professed amazement at his activities and said she didn't even know about the whiskey. She couldn't imagine any woman in the world not knowing what was going on in her own kitchen. On the other hand, she said, she did recollect that the woman had been a Spiller from out at Fisher's Crossing before she married and, of course, not a one of them had any sense. . . .

Anyway, I suppose their respective travels were emblematic of their way through the world, their way through life. Cousin Rosa was big and bold, liked to venture out, go places, the farther away the better, and then come home and tell it all. (And how I loved it when I was growing up, hearing her "tell her trips," already then planning my own future journeys!) And she really would have liked to have a ticket as long as your arm too. Everybody should go to San Francisco, she always said, the most beautiful place she had ever seen—the Bay, the Golden Gate, the cable cars, all of it. It made you think of Europe, she said, though of course she never got *there*. She did think of Europe from time to time; but aside from considerations of money, she was always put off by all the popery over there but didn't know how you could escape it unless you did as her old friend, Miss Maggie Evans, and got yourself booked on a tour of Scotland and Scandinavia, including "a side trip to the Land of the Midnight Sun."

But above all, what travel did for you, Cousin Rosa said, was cut you down to size, make you realize there were other people and other places besides you and yours in the world: it opened your mind and let in the light and air. It was the ultimate educational experience; and yes, it really was *broadening*. Because every time you traveled you learned more about the world and, most important of all, more about yourself. Cousin Emma of course didn't take that grand a view. She said travel was fine, in small doses; but she didn't believe in building your whole life around it, and the best part of a trip was always getting back home. In most ways, she went on, the world really was all one, all the same. And anybody that had been born and raised in Woodville, Tennessee, knew enough about human devilment to last him the rest of his life. Still, you had to travel *some* before you could know that, she said. But whatever the case, you didn't want to come back home and bore everybody to death talking about your trip (what *would* she have said about showing your slides?) because nobody wanted to hear about *that;* they wanted to tell you all about theirs! And besides, she didn't have time for all that foolishness: she needed to get back to her own kitchen, which had probably all gone to rack and ruin while she was away, certainly if Cousin Rosa had been there by herself.

When I was growing up, I thought "the Moss girls," as my mother often called them, were disagreeing about travel, just like they did many other things in the world, when they talked like that. But they're long dead and gone, and I'm a lot older myself now. And I don't see any of it that way anymore.

Still Swinging

—————————— • ● • ——————————

There was a big fat man in my hometown named Fred Jamieson (pronounced "Jimmerson" by people who remembered his grandfather, but Fred had come up in the world, my mother said). And he didn't ever make much of a noise in the world, just performed odd jobs for people around town, a sort of superior handyman, you might say. But he was always very genial and obliging, and everybody liked him. His wife, who was named Verna Mae, was a big fat woman who looked as though she ought to be married to him; and everybody liked her too. They were comfortable and easy-going and never went off the deep end about anything: you could almost tell that by looking at them. And even when adversity came, they took it in their stride.

One morning when my father went down early to open his store, there was Fred Jamieson coming down the steps from Dr. Wilson's office, up over Harris and Taylor's Drug Store. (That was the era of doctors' offices in small towns down South being on the square and *upstairs*, often over a drugstore, which of course you shouldn't be climbing in the first place if you were sick, my mother always said.) And my father saw that Fred had a bandage around his left index finger "as big as a baseball," he said; so naturally he asked him what was wrong. And Fred said, "I had a bone felon that had to be lanced. I suffered death all night long with it and got down to Dr. Wilson's as soon as he was up." "Did it hurt when he lanced it?" my father asked, already pretty well aware of the answer he would get. "Hurt? It took two men and one woman to hold me!" And with something of a triumphant cackle, Fred went on down the street, headed home.

My father had great fun telling the story because, he said, it just showed the kind of man Fred was: he didn't deny the reality of pain and suffering and trouble—whatever it was—but rather grinned at it and went on anyhow. Really, he was almost like my father's old friend, Mr.

Joe Andrew Summers, who had served in the Mexican border skir-
mishes of 1917—under General Pershing too, before the general got
pulled out and sent to France. And somewhere along the line, he was
captured by the Mexicans, who cheerfully announced that, at daybreak
the next morning, they were going to shoot him. But it didn't faze Mr.
Summers, according to my father. He just said he was right tired from
all he'd been through, so he just lay down on the bunk in his jail cell
and went to sleep! By morning the Americans had counterattacked, the
Mexicans had retreated, and Mr. Summers was a free man. My father
always said any man who could do as Mr. Summers did certainly had a
clear conscience. One thing, at any rate, was sure: he wasn't ever going
to die of nervous prostration! He just took it as it came—another Fred
Jamieson.

On the other hand, you could be the other way around, he said,
like Miss Eva Pierce, an old maid there in town who was an old friend
of my mother. She had spent her life being scared to death—scared of
ghosts, scared of burglars, scared of most anything you could mention,
he said, but mainly, if truth were told, scared of *men*. And that was why
she never had married. Nothing but skin and bones either, he said: why,
her behind wasn't any bigger than a willow leaf! And she was one of the
silliest women he'd ever seen in his life to boot. Why, back in the days
before everybody had electric refrigerators (which they all called Frigi-
daires, regardless of the actual brand), Miss Eva had called him down
at his store one day and asked him to come down to her house right
away because there was a *mouse in her icebox!* Why she called him, he
never could figure out; maybe it was because he did indeed have the
Frigidaire agency then. But anyhow, when he got there, he found that
it was the chain connecting the lid of the icebox to the chest part that
was rattling every time you raised or lowered the lid; and *that* was Miss
Eva's mouse! (My mother said he wasn't being fair: poor Eva always had
been a nervous child and her mother had babied her since she was the
youngest, so she was naturally spoiled rotten.)

But that wasn't the main thing, according to my father. Every
afternoon of the world— anytime after four o'clock, when most of the
ladies in town had their baths in the summer—you could drive by Miss
Eva's house; and there she would be on the front porch, swinging. That
was all she did all day, as far as he knew; and he couldn't imagine what
she did during the winter, when it was too cold to sit out on the porch.
He said he thought her mother, who was dead and gone now, had told

her that if she'd just sit there long enough, in that swing, sooner or
later some man would ride up (whether on a horse or in a car, he didn't
know) and *carry her off*. Well, she'd been doing just that—she was still
swinging—as long as he could remember; and nobody had carried her off
yet! If truth were told, he said he sort of hoped something *would* carry
her off: it would give her the biggest thrill of her life! And whether it
was a burglar or a boogerbear or a real-live legitimate beau, he didn't
think it made much difference. Or maybe she just needed somebody or
something to *get* her! It would be all the same to her, he said. At this
point my mother would always interpose with "Now, now—"; and he
would hush but, by way of compensation for his enforced silence, then
take a big puff on his cigar and emphatically expel the smoke as if to
say *that* was what *he* thought.

The Pierces' old cook, Martha, who had been with them since
Miss Eva was born, told somebody that, yes, Miss Eva was spoiled and
always had been, but what made her more nervous and peculiar as she
approached old age was that her nature had done went back on her,
which was to say that her sexual functioning was on the decline. And
Martha went on to add that the reason she hardly ever left home was
that she was so "homely." That seemed as good an explanation as any—
if anybody could ever "explain" Miss Eva. But once she practically scared
the wits out of Martha by imagining that she saw her own father, old
Mr. Pierce, who had been sheriff of our county way back yonder but had
been dead for thirty years, hiding under the stairs with his pistol all
drawn and cocked and his sheriff's badge on too! But whether she
thought he had come to *get* her or had come after her to *carry her off,* she
didn't say. Martha didn't stay around to find out either. Miss Eva ran
screaming out the front door, and Martha made a beeline out the back—
and didn't go back to work either until Miss Eva's married sister and
her husband had had the doctor with her. But he was a new young man
in town and didn't know "the case," as people said; and he told the
sister and brother-in-law there really wasn't anything wrong with Miss
Eva except maybe she just needed some excitement in her life. They
didn't appreciate this, though they may have privately agreed with him.
You might *think* it, but you shouldn't *say* it.

But that was the way, my father said. People like Miss Eva got
away with murder because they always had; everybody had known their
papas and their mammas and they had all been there since God knows
when and you had to make allowances for them. Spoiled to death and

selfish into the bargain. Living on their ancestors too—*who* Mamma *was* and *what* Papa was *worth*—but they'd never done anything themselves. On the other hand, there was good old Fred Jamieson, who didn't ask favors from anybody and went through life grinning instead of whining. No education or cultivation, no "background," he said; still, you couldn't help but like him. Suppose Miss Eva and her sort were just picked up by the hair of the head and dropped down a hundred miles away where nobody on earth had ever heard of them and theirs: it would do them all a power of good, he said.

Well, that might be so, my mother said, but then well, you know, poor Eva. And my father said, yes, that was just it: people had always said "poor Eva" and always would, but nobody ever would think of saying "poor Fred." People finally got to acting just as you expected them to—just as you treated them, he said. So whose fault then did it finally turn out to be? It took more than one to spoil somebody, he said. Well, maybe so, my mother said, but think of all poor Eva had missed— a husband and a home of her own and nice things. You just had to feel sorry for her. Why, for all she knew, Miss Eva had never even had a date with a boy in her life! And she well remembered, she said, when she and Miss Eva and the other girls their age began having their periods (my mother had just gone to the pencil sharpener when Lucille Vaughan, just back from the rest room, breezed by and whispered, "It's happened!"). And Miss Eva didn't even know what was happening: her mother hadn't told her a thing. And when she should have been a senior in high school in the same class with my mother, Mrs. Pierce had kept her at home because she wasn't "strong."

So when Miss Eva should have been having dates with boys and going to dances and learning what the whole business was all about, she was shut up in the house with old Mrs. Pierce and maybe even "confined to her room," for all anybody knew. My mother said she didn't think Miss Eva had ever even graduated from high school, and there was certainly never any question of her going off to school later on— but as for Miss Eva's not being "strong," my mother said she fully expected her to bury everybody in her own family and yours too: that kind always did. And my father heartily agreed. Anyway, my mother said she did hear once that, long after Miss Eva was grown, she took a terrible notion one day that she *must* have an evening dress; she never had had one before. What in the world she needed it for, my mother said she couldn't imagine. But anyhow, Mrs. Pierce was supposed to have phoned up to Miss Ada Younger's Ladies' Toggery and asked them to send down an "appropriate" evening dress for Miss Eva. And what she ever did with it nobody ever knew: she could hardly wear it to swing in, my mother said, and that was all she ever really *did*.

Well, I grew up and went off to school, and after that I took a job in a city far away from home. But every time I went back, I would hear that Miss Eva was still swinging on the front porch. After all those years, that was almost her *job*. And everybody in town knew it and would have been surprised if she'd done anything else. But then I'd see Fred Jamieson somewhere along the line, and he was still fat and still cheerful. And I would go back to my job feeling that, in places like this one, nothing ever changes. And, you know, nothing did either—even in death. In fact, it was Fred Jamieson, who had started doing light housework for Miss Eva after old Martha finally died, who found her dead in the bed one morning when he came to work. (He couldn't rouse her, and he had a key to the house for emergencies.)

And yes, you've probably already guessed it: Miss Eva was sleeping in the evening dress, more like a dinner dress really, as people used to call them, with long sleeves and a high neck—black lace, of course. Fred told somebody it looked like it had seen lots of wear and tear; but then, he said, she never threw away *anything:* old magazines, old newspapers, anything. He said he had no earthly idea what it was all about; but then she was a sweet old girl, though a little peculiar and set in her ways. And if it made her feel better to sleep like that, he said, it was certainly all right with him.

Were You There?

In those years, when anybody from home was taken "over to Bolivar," that was more or less the end of him. The mental hospital for our part of the state was there, and the name of the town became pretty much synonymous with the institution. (Did anybody actually *live* in Bolivar? I never knew.) And "mental hospital" was a big step forward, I guess: they had only recently stopped calling it the lunatic asylum. At least now they were supposed to *treat* people over there, not just perform some sort of custodial function. But I hardly remember anybody ever coming home from Bolivar—coming home *well,* that is.

Our county was said to be represented adequately there. Indeed, people even made jokes about its having filled its quota and then some: it was said that somebody from home got "sent" over there one time, but the authorities said they were full up with our folks and wouldn't keep him. That was the way it was then, when I was growing up in Woodville in the 1930s: you got "sent" over there, maybe even by court order or something. And it was halfway a shame and a disgrace and maybe halfway a joke but hardly an illness. So when anybody was "in Bolivar," you didn't say too much about it.

I suspect that many of the patients there were merely senile and there wasn't anything else to do with them: it was always hard to handle such things at home. And who knew much about psychosis or neurosis back then? But from time to time, you would hear of somebody who had gone over to see some relative and found him "belted to the bed" or something of the sort. That conjured up all sorts of visions of the Dark Ages and the sins of the fathers and insanity as a divine visitation for wrongdoing—an *affliction* in every way. And in those days plenty of people didn't hesitate to use that word, whether for a birth defect, a retarded child, or anything else like that. (Had such things been *sent?*) *Insanity* is what it still was for most people, not "mental illness." When the gates of Bolivar were shut on you, it was as though you had been sent to prison—and for life. Perhaps that was why people were inclined to joke about it; it was too terrible to think about otherwise. And unlike crime, it all seemed such a mystery; often there was no rhyme or reason as to who and what were so afflicted and why.

This seemed particularly true of the young—not the old and the senile, but those who hadn't even reached adulthood when they were "put" there. I remember several such cases in my youth—young people somewhat older than I whom I had only heard of, never remembered as active and well. I remember that my father once told me that Mr. So-and-so had a boy only a few years older than I who had been "over at Bolivar" for some years. And I hadn't even known of his existence: he was dead as far as Woodville was concerned, I suppose. When my father was telling me about it, I remember that he hugged me and held me to him, as though thanking God that, at any rate, I was all right. And now I find that memory very moving—though at the time I think I was very much embarrassed, as I always was when older people showed emotion.

But I never saw the young man my father spoke of, and he became something of a myth to me—perhaps an *exemplum,* even a *memento mori;* in any case, he was a sobering representation of what could happen in a world where order and reason did not always prevail. And perhaps all the more present for not being seen: he followed you everywhere in your mind.

What I did see, though, was a young woman from Woodville who was a patient at Bolivar, whom her family used to bring home to visit from time to time—always with a nurse. And that was something very disturbing indeed. Because there was nothing mythical about her: she was herself the very ocular proof of madness. I had heard that when she first began to "go crazy," she had pulled out her eyebrows with tweezers, then threatened to cut her mother's head off with a butcher knife. She was *violent,* they said. And I wondered if they ever had to belt her to the bed. But she belonged to a prominent family in town—and if they wanted to bring her home for a visit, not many people would have been bold enough to object.

My principal memory of her concerns seeing her at the Baptist revival one summer when I was about seven or eight and she would have been about ten years older, in her late teens. My family were Methodists, but we always attended big meetings in other churches—at least for one or two nights, to show our community spirit, I suppose (though I always tried to avoid the last night of Baptist revivals, since some of their more fire-eating evangelists would always feel called on then to preach on the Second Coming—and that usually scared me to death). There was some sort of special soloist that night who had been brought out from Memphis; supposed to be the star turn of the evening, he rendered "selections" during the collection and just before the sermon. And the one I remember was the spiritual, "Were You There?"

I had heard it before, of course—sung by my nurse, Louella, or maybe when I had gone to church with her and her family out at Morning Star. But never before had it gotten hold of me as it did then, the Baptist soloist (a soulful tenor, as I recall) giving it all he had in the way of pathos and "expression." The words I knew already, and they always depressed me. It began, "Were you there when they crucified my Lord?" Then, in the next verse, "Were you there when they nailed him to the tree?" and finally on to "Were you there when they laid him in the tomb?" And those were dark horrors enough—the sacrifice of the Savior, the Lamb of God, perfect God and perfect Man, for the sins of the whole world.

But what made me shiver, even *tremble,* as the song went on to mourn ("Sometimes it causes me to tremble, tremble, tremble") was the suggestion that I too had had a hand in it all; I too had been guilty of this greatest of all crimes. I too, like Peter, had denied my Lord, maybe even gone to sleep on him when he needed me. I too had watched idly as they crucified my Savior and was perhaps no better than the soldiers dicing for his garments beneath the cross. I too, afraid and ashamed, had hung back when they buried him, and it had finally been nothing to me. But even then I knew that it was more than just me that the song was indicting. Every one of us had stood aside; we had all been traitors, all mankind, because to be such was in our very nature. It was simply the way people were, and there wasn't a thing in the world you could do about it.

It was at that point that I remember looking up at the "crazy" young woman, sitting there with her nurse (a stout-looking matronly type who could handle her in case she got violent, I supposed) in the midst of her family. Tears were streaming down her cheeks, and there was such misery on her face that it seemed to me I had never seen such sorrow before—the oldest, deepest grief in the world. And I was both shocked and incredulous. Could she really know what was going on, both in the world around her and in the song? Could she really grieve for this greatest of all sorrows that humanity could endure, the sorrow of the self? Did she know what had really happened on Calvary, and did

it really speak to her and her condition? I wondered. Did she have some
glimmering of what was her own miserable lot as part and parcel of it
all—the fallen world, the madness that lay in every human heart, sane
or insane, the ultimate sorrow of the world? And would she have liked
to talk about that, would she have liked to ask other people, myself included, where they were when she had suffered her own affliction?

I remember seeing several older people shake their heads when they
saw the young woman's tears, as if to say that it was all too much for them—
madness, grief, the universe itself—some terrible puzzle that they simply
couldn't figure out and would really prefer to ignore. And I wondered
whether any of them there would understand the feelings I was groping
my way toward articulating. But it would be a very long time before I
could do that, I somehow knew even then. Who could reach the young
woman now, behind her tears, lost as she was in what they sometimes called
mental darkness? Who could do anything for her, who could help her now?
Finally, as her sobbing became more violent, her nurse had to take her outside, no doubt fearful that she would disturb the congregation or even interfere with the service itself. I suppose many people wondered why her
family had brought her there in the first place.

And that's all. I don't know that I ever saw the young woman
again; I just knew that, as the years went along, she was still the same
and still "in Bolivar." But then about the time I went off to school, I
heard that they had performed a new—and, it was said, very daring—
operation on her, a lobotomy. And it had turned her into a different
person altogether. Now she was calm and quiet, never inclined to be
violent, and sometimes even talked about things that had happened before she got sick. She never worried about anything now, they said, never
seemed disturbed by anything that happened.

And her family, who had insisted on the operation when they first
heard of its possibilities (not without some reservations on the part of
the doctors, I understood, because of its "radical" nature), were all delighted and even spoke of sending her out to California to live with an
older married sister and perhaps get some sort of job. They said she never
cried at all now, didn't seem to let anything bother her one way or the
other and, as my mother would have joked about anybody who didn't
sweat *anything,* was just as happy as if she had good sense. In any case,
everybody in town said it was simply a miracle, and nobody was afraid
to be around her at all anymore.

Mrs. English

—————————— • ● • ——————————

Actually, her name was Mrs. Garrett; but one of the more formidable matrons in our town started calling her "Mrs. English" soon after she arrived there from England at the beginning of World War II. Mrs. Garrett had been living in London with her only son—a bachelor who worked at the American Embassy—for twenty years; and people at home had almost forgotten about her until she arrived to stay with her sister, Mrs. Haskins, "for the duration." And then it was "English this" and "London that" with her until some of the neighbors rather wore out on it, especially since Mrs. Garrett had originally hailed from Barton's Crossroads over in the Forked Deer bottom: they thought she had gotten above her raising by a good deal.

And then she was such a contrast to Mrs. Haskins, who was, as they always say, plain as an old shoe and hadn't been anywhere or done anything except go to Memphis a couple of times a year and read detective stories (in bed) nearly all day long, in that big old house that hadn't had a breath of new air in it for God knows how many years. Oh, Mrs. Haskins had some roomers who lived in a back bedroom-and-bath apartment. But Mrs. Garrett, fresh from London and the incipient Blitz, burst into that house, much as she did into our town, as something very rich and strange indeed.

First of all, all her clothes were English; so she went in for dipping hemlines and the most fragile of slippers, preferably high-heeled with both toes and heels out. She had a very worn-looking fur coat of some sort (I never could tell what the animal was) that she wore on state occasions, as well as for warmth (presumably) during the winter. It was one of her few concessions to grandeur and its claims, I suppose, because she couldn't have had much money to spend on herself, the way I figured it. And she didn't improve matters any by dyeing her hair henna and using so much face powder it made her look as if she had been plastered all over with flour. The whole effect was one of decayed or maybe even abortive elegance: whatever she had been, you knew she no longer was. But she tottered around on her high heels, and every time you met her on the street, she would have to get right up to you and squint to recognize you (because she was nearsighted and too proud to wear her glasses unless she was reading, my mother said). And then she would wave her hand in your face, as though hailing you from a mile off, and chirp, "Hello there! Howar ya? So glad to see ya!" And the "are" was accented and run together with the "how," "glad" had the broadest "a" ever heard off the stage, and "you" scarcely got any attention at all. Of course, it was stagy and "English," after a fashion— just as one would expect from someone who had lived there for a number of years and was determined to have something to show for it.

So it was easy enough to make fun of Mrs. Garrett. My mother even used to call her "Birdie" because of the way she chirped around the house and picked her way around town on those spike heels. A lot of people claimed that if she didn't watch out, she would forget and talk without her accent some day; and they wondered whether she would sound like Barton's Crossroads or what. They certainly didn't believe it came naturally to her to talk so "English," though of course all their ideas of talking "English" had been formed by picture shows and the radio. But anyhow, nobody really minded or took her very seriously: if she was so important or had had so interesting a life (as she implied her London years had been), what was she doing living in *our* town?

I, for one, was inclined to take her pretty much at her own valuation. And I think even then, as an adolescent, I had some idea that she had come to live with Mrs. Haskins mainly because all the foreign civilians had been ordered out of London and she really didn't have anywhere else to go. I didn't think she had much money either, though of course I was Southerner enough to have seen a good deal of the "shabby genteel" in my day and understand and respect it very well. But I took to her right away, mainly because I could talk to her about England, which I was beginning to realize was more and more the most important country in my imagination.

Mrs. Garrett didn't have anything else to do, except read all the books in the public library and listen to her little radio, to get the war news; and I suppose she was glad to have some diversion, even that of a teenage boy who was scarcely more than a child. But the wonders she did reveal! Why, she used to pass Buckingham Palace every day of her life (their "flat" had been a few streets over behind it); and often she would see Princess Elizabeth and Princess Margaret Rose playing in the garden: really, she could have actually spoken to them through the big iron fence if she'd wanted to. And I ached at the thought: I had fancied myself in love with Princess Elizabeth for a number of years, even dreamed of strolling with her across the green lawns of Windsor while we talked of our love and she promised to be mine. And to think— those two worlds, England and West Tennessee, weren't so abysmally far apart after all, though joined together now by the extremely unlikely medium of Mrs. Garrett. Who ever would have thought it, in our town? The little bird with dyed hair. And she had lived for music and art too. Hardly an evening had gone by that she and Martin, the son, hadn't gone to the theater or to a concert: she'd heard Caruso and Paderewski, seen Noel Coward in his own plays and, of course, Sir Gerald Du Maurier, father of the Daphne who wrote the enchanted *Rebecca*, everybody, everything. It was almost too much.

I would go over to see Mrs. Garrett every few days, especially in the summer when school was out; and, as soon as I called from the front door, she would begin bustling about her room (she had Mrs. Haskins's former guest room, on the right just inside the door) setting things to rights, combing her hair (which was always in the process of growing out, snow-white roots and all), and meanwhile whistling some sort of nontune that fascinated me because I wondered what it meant. Was it to reassure me that she was readying herself for my arrival, or was it a signal that she was *there* but not ready to receive visitors and not to come in till she threw open the door, or what? I never knew. Yet it seemed to fit with Mrs. Garrett's theatricality and her Englishness and all else that seemed to go with her. She was foreign to our town yet still one of us too, just enough, really, to let you know there *was* a difference.

But when Mrs. Garrett threw open her bedroom door, she stood there as though welcoming me to the grandest English country house imaginable (she'd had wonderful weekends in some of them, she said), and I would pass into what might be an audience, a gossip session, or perhaps even a combination of both. The gossip was always all on her side: she didn't seem to want the news of local events. But she loved telling me about her years in London, her two trips to the Continent (once to Paris, once to Brussels). And I was insatiably curious: how much did things cost, what was the London Underground like, how about the English trains, and what about the history behind everything? I couldn't ask enough, from my reading and my dreaming. Oh yes, England was a dream, along with what I had imbibed from the movies about gilded halls in Hollywood or elsewhere. Yet England didn't seem the false romance that I was begining to suspect Hollywood offered more often than not. (I had even quit writing to movie stars now.) After all, it was real and it was there, with a real king and queen, and real palaces and real history; and it still had Knights of the Garter and a beautiful countryside and villages and stately homes. It was a dream that wasn't a dream.

How I yearned for it, I who already knew then, I think, that I would study English literature and history when I went off to college. And how I looked up to Mrs. Garrett, even if she was the silly "Birdie" who seemed scarcely to know she'd ever left England, much less that she was living in Mrs. Haskins's house. I suppose that's what a lot of people at home resented—the way she seemed to come in and take over Mrs. Haskins's house (though Mrs. Haskins had never been very sociable) and receive her own callers but always on her own terms. She never entertained, never went to see the neighbors but mostly stayed inside the front bedroom as if it were a cocoon of some sort, with her dyed hair, her memories, and her radio. I know one time my father went over there, to deliver something Mrs. Haskins had ordered from his store. And he came back laughing because he said both the ladies had their beds turned down even in the daytime—so they could crawl in and pick up the novel they'd just put down, get up to eat or go to the bathroom, and start right up again. He thought it was very funny.

And yet I wondered. What kind of life did Mrs. Garrett have there? Mrs. Haskins and she could never have had much in common; Mrs. Haskins was good as gold but dull as ditch water, and the farthest she ever got—or wanted to get—from home was the First Baptist Church. So what was there for them to talk about? I didn't think Mrs. Haskins would want to hear about opening nights at Covent Garden or being close enough to the handsome Duke of Kent at a palace garden party (think of it!) to touch him almost. He was the one that had married the beautiful Greek Princess Marina, had a little boy born on 4 July and so named for President Roosevelt, and then died in a plane crash only a few weeks later! Oh, there were tears for that, I can tell you—from both Mrs. Garrett and myself. God knows what my classmates would have thought about that, but England my dream had taken far too great a hold on me to worry about them now. And wasn't the dream, funnily enough, at least halfway incarnate right there in Mrs. Haskins's house—in the person of Mrs. Garrett? I marveled at it yet accepted it too, without a great deal of thought.

I know my parents, who were certainly more sympathetic to Mrs. Garrett than most people, used to ask what we talked about when I went over to see her. And I would reply, "Oh, just *things*" and never go much further. They never pressed me either: they respected our strange relationship, I think. I know Daddy used to go out of his way to give Mrs. Garrett a ride home from town, as she struggled with a big sack of groceries, feeling "just like a charwoman," she said. And they would exchange comments on the war and their joint admiration of both President Roosevelt and Winston Churchill. Mamma was more inclined to resent Mrs. Garrett, I suspect, for more or less taking over Mrs. Haskins's house and appropriating almost all visitors who came to see them as exclusively hers. But she made no attempt to interfere with my going over as often as I wanted, and once I heard her tell Daddy, well, Mrs. Garrett was affected and all that but you had to feel sorry for her, in a way.

I know I did. I thought, goodness, what she had given up (of course unwillingly, I felt), just to come live in our dull little town, with Mrs. Haskins, and all the novels, and her little radio—she who had actually trod the streets of London and taken tea on the terraces of English stately homes. About all she had to look forward to now were Martin's rare visits (he'd been transferred to Washington), when she would go down to join him at the Peabody Hotel in Memphis for a long weekend. He scarcely ever came to see Mrs. Haskins, and I suppose some people might have resented that—that and his not coming to our town. Anyhow, when Mrs. Garrett returned, she would be full of Memphis and Martin—almost as full of them as she always was of England. So the next week the local paper would carry, in its columns, an item that she had been visiting her son in Memphis, naturally at the Peabody. And always, Martin was spoken of as "formerly of the American Embassy in London." I never knew what he did there: he might have been a glorified clerk, for all I knew. Nevertheless, he actually was—or had been— there; and he was now in Washington at the State Department. And it all sounded perfectly grand—another dream come true, I supposed.

Between Martin's visits, though, there were long, uninterrupted stretches when Mrs. Garrett would have to make do with her own resources. And sometimes I used to wonder whether I minded her present situation, really, more than she did. She never complained directly; she would sometimes say that she and her sister never went out and how strange that was after her life in London, when she was out every night. But she didn't repine, though her eulogies on her adopted land were apt to be more pronounced at such times. And it was during those periods, I suppose, when she was hard for some of the folks at home to take. It wasn't that she rammed England down your throat all the time or extolled the virtues of everything British at the expense of all others. It was just that she couldn't comment on the weather or any fact of everyday life without making some sort of comment on how such matters went in England. And people naturally assumed that if she did make comparisons, they would not be in our favor.

One thing I did notice was that Mrs. Garrett never had any new clothes; I didn't think she'd bought any since she first arrived from England. But whether this was because of straitened finances or loyalty to British merchandise, I didn't know. Naturally, I was curious though I never dreamed of asking her about it. And after all, she or Martin or somebody had some money if they could stay at the Peabody for the weekend. I know one time she spoke of having to have some shoes repaired and airily dismissed the matter with the statement that it was no wonder since she hadn't had any new ones since she came from England. Was she somehow trying to freeze permanently her whole English experience, to preserve it unspotted from the world; was that why she dyed her hair? Did she have some sort of dream too, even as I did, that she was determined to hold fast? Still, she had had her dream. Couldn't she make some compromises with the everyday world now?

Of course, I could tell that I was idealizing, even romanticizing Mrs. Garrett and her English experience. *Romance* was certainly the last word you thought of when you took one look at her. Yet, in another way, she proved something about romance for me: it really could happen, right in my town, where there was somebody I knew who had journeyed abroad and seen the world. And you didn't have to be a movie star in either looks or purse to do it. That's what I suppose Mrs. Garrett proved.

Our conversations stayed mainly in the romantic realms too: geography and history, sights and sounds. They didn't go very deep: Mrs. Garrett would never have been called a student, certainly not a thinker (some people would have insisted she was shallow); and, after all, I was still a boy. But one time I know we came as close as we ever did to having any argument. (Usually, of course, I was like a big blotter, ready to soak up, without question, whatever she cared to give.) But she began extolling the virtues of English "public" schools, which I already knew were not really public, for being so exclusive and for teaching their boys "discipline" (accented, of course, on the second syllable). And I began to question her about their exclusiveness, whether it was a good thing or not (after all, suppose I couldn't afford them or they wouldn't take me if I applied). I wondered whether it was right or good for boys to be so closely watched and carefully kept in check. She replied that it was certainly all as it should be: not everyone should be in school anyhow, and people had to be taught manners and morals (I think she probably said respect and obedience) sometime. In short, it sounded to me as though she might be trying to ally herself with a system that might see fit to exclude people like me, a world that might even disallow my dream. And I was frightened and angry and made bold to disagree with her. It was at that point that she turned on me, as any other adult (I never thought of her as one, so gay, so light-hearted), and more or less told me I wasn't old enough to know what I was talking about.

I was stunned and hardly knew what to think. Was Mrs. Garrett, Mrs. English really, deep down inside, just like everybody else? Yes, I had been willing to concede that she might be ridiculous—as ridiculous as my ever meeting and marrying Princess Elizabeth. But I had never thought of her as just another older person, another adult, so I was both puzzled and troubled. I didn't go back over to see Mrs. Garrett for a week after that; but when I did, she seemed as glad to see me as ever, perhaps even more so. And I wondered whether my visits were as important to her as they were to me. After all, who else around town could she speak to about her realized dream that was now gone? Of course, I couldn't have told you all this at the time. Indeed, I might have been very much surprised, even shocked, to think an adult could need me or find me important. But such, I suppose, is youth.

In due course, I went off to college and didn't get home very much anymore. When I did, I hardly had time to go over to see Mrs. Garrett, and I used to feel guilty about not going. The war was long since over, and Martin was dead—killed in an automobile wreck in Washington. Mrs. Haskins had died and left Mrs. Garrett the house, so at least she had a roof over her head. But I thought, poor Mrs. Garrett, all her dreams gone now—and not even England to go back to. I felt very sorry for her and grew to feel even more guilty for not doing something for her, to show I hadn't forgotten her, indeed hadn't altogether outgrown her. But I never did. I would pass her on the street and give her a lift home from the library, and she still spoke the broad "a" sound and all the rest. She still hadn't bought any new clothes that I could see, and she still dyed her hair. But you couldn't condescend to her, certainly couldn't patronize her: she wasn't asking for anybody's pity. And she tottered along on these unsuitable, even dangerous heels, as birdlike as ever.

The last time I ever saw her, I had made my first trip to England and went over to tell her about it. I had gone without desserts, having economized for a whole year, to save up enough money to go. I had had a wonderful trip and had found England to be all I had hoped and perhaps more—a dream come true in every way and my real home that I was coming to at long last, after many years' probation, even wandering. And I wanted Mrs. Garrett somehow to know all this, and I wanted to show her, tell her that I appreciated the part she had played in helping to share and give substance to my dream. Young people talk easily, but I wasn't sure I could put all this into words. But anyhow, I went over and tried. But before I could get very far, indeed before I got anywhere near the part I felt Mrs. Garrett had played in my history, she put out her hand, now almost clawlike, as if to stop me, and said, "Yes, my dear, I know. Martin always said England was like a well-kept golf course, but I always preferred to think of it as one of the few dreams in my life that ever came true. And I'm very grateful for such an experience. The memory of that, along with my radio and my reading—that's what I live on, that's what keeps me going now that so much else is gone."

I didn't, couldn't say much after that but soon got up and went home, and I never saw Mrs. Garrett again. She died the next winter, mainly from old age and just being worn out, the doctor said. And I thought, well, that might be part of it but not all. Oh, I didn't think she had died of grief either—nothing so melodramatic as that. Maybe she had simply lived with her one dream long enough; or maybe not even her dream could finally hold all else—time, the world, life, death— at bay. It was a powerful one, though, encased as it was in a fragile, even absurd vessel: it had kept her going for a long time. And I wondered whether anybody could ever ask for much else.

June

Pop wide open, you son of a gun;
Pop wide open I say;
Pop wide open you son of a gun;
You haven't popped open today.

Years later that was how the old-maid cousins would remember her, fresh out of finishing school (Ward's Seminary in Nashville) and visiting her sister in Woodville, now standing on top of the dining room table in her high heels and blazing out these verses (did they border on the scandalous?) while accompanying herself on the guitar. Was that what it meant to be "finished," they wondered? At any rate, Woodville had never seen anything like it before.

Her name was Julia Calloway, and she came from Brinkley, Arkansas, and she had kinfolks all over West Tennessee; so she always loomed large in conversation there, both before and after her visits. It wasn't a question of her deliberately trying to scandalize them, they finally felt—after considerable deliberation. It was just that Julia had so much life, perhaps even so much joy, that some of it had to boil over. And thus her songs, her jokes. Once she even dressed up to look like a disreputable tramp, and went round to the back door at the old-maid cousins' house and asked for a handout. They were completely taken in; not until the next day did they learn the truth. And at first they were inclined to be angry, but then Julia could never be judged by the rules of ordinary mortals. She was quite literally a law unto herself.

Her sister, Harriet—Mrs. Abernathy, who lived in Woodville—would always tell you that. She would say, "I don't know what in the world is going to happen to June"—she always called her that instead of Julia—"when Papa and Mamma are not there to hold her down. She doesn't mean any harm, and there's not a really mean or self-ish bone in her body. But a lot of people are such fools that they don't know it. Anytime you get near them with *life*—to say nothing of sing-ing and dancing—they get scared to death. And suppose June scares off all the good boys that want to marry her—and I know there're some two or three—what will she do? I tell you, I worry about her. The youngest of us all and spoiled to death, though I do say so myself. But then who could refuse her anything she wanted? I know I never could."

The old-maid cousins weren't so lenient. "June probably doesn't mean any evil; but she ought to know that, in a place like Woodville, you have to take other people's opinions into consideration, whether you want to or not. Dancing on the dining room table may be all very well for a time, but what man is going to want that in his wife? June had better watch her step." Years later, though, she still hadn't changed—at least outwardly. Driving down the road in her first car, she hollered to the man approaching her, in the dusk, "Dim your lights, you son of a bitch!" And he apparently heard her and did. But Wood-ville was not amused.

Always she was skating on thin ice—at Ward's and then out in the world. In those days, young ladies in Southern seminaries were expected to be just that—young ladies. And Ward's preserved all the proprieties from an even older era—before the turn of the century—fetching and car-rying the students to and from the railroad station when they arrived or left and of course providing them with a chaperone every time they left the grounds of the school—certainly every time they went to a dance over at Vanderbilt. And June must have found this all very heavy going because every time she came to visit in Woodville, she would regale her sister and the old-maid cousins—or anybody else, for that matter—with the strat-agems she made use of to circumvent the rules at Ward's. Signing out for early mass—she was a Methodist—on Sunday was just one of them: she could then spend the rest of the morning flirting with the Vanderbilt boys at the drugstore. What would become of her, finally, they all wondered? And a woman's first duty then—back around the time of the First World War—was to get married and "be at the head of a home," as some of the Woodville ladies would have put it.

But did June really want that? And what could she do if she didn't marry and "be at the head of a home"? Mrs. Abernathy worried about it more than she liked to show. She was an unconventional soul herself—just enough older than June to view her as something of a child but not too old to relish June's fun either. When June first smoked in public, during one of her Woodville visits, Mrs. Abernathy had to pretend to be shocked, if only for Woodville's sake. But of course she wasn't really. She just told June privately that it all seemed like a tiresome habit to her and did June really *enjoy* it? To which June replied that that wasn't the point; what really was the point was that she did do it, just to show Woodville that she could. And Mrs. Abernathy could see the point of that. Not for nothing had she herself pulled up stakes for a couple of years and moved to Memphis to run a very select boardinghouse there: her husband, who was a lawyer, could just do without her for the present, and the children needed to have better schools, she said. But then as suddenly as she had left, back she came from Memphis, settled down (without boarders) to keep house in Woodville; and for all the world knew, never had any doubts, any regrets one way or the other. And her husband, Mr. Abernathy, hadn't seemed to mind: he always viewed her as something of an exotic tropical bird and seemed never to be surprised by anything she did or said. For all the world knew, the Abernathys picked right up then where they had left off and lived happily ever after.

Perhaps Mrs. Abernathy was all the more indulgent toward June because she thought June was doing and saying everything she herself had missed, was still missing. At any rate, June would breeze into Woodville several times a year, going to and from Ward's Seminary; and even after she "finished," she still kept coming. Her parents were dead by then, so she looked more and more to Mrs. Abernathy for some sort of stability, some sort of home life. And Mrs. Abernathy was, of course, delighted to have her.

But again, when and whom was June to marry? There were several Woodville boys who would have been glad to oblige—Tom Johnston, for one. But June didn't seem to have marriage on her mind. Flirting, teasing, laughing, dancing—yes, all that and more too. But never did she seem to want to settle down. It was all a puzzle to the town—and to Mrs. Abernathy also, to some extent. Didn't she want what every woman was supposed to want back then? Didn't she want a home and a family? Really, sometimes, Mrs. Abernathy told her, she thought June would like nothing better than being an *actress*. And June's dark brown eyes flashed fire, and she said she would indeed like nothing better. But then was her heart in it, did she really want a career that bad? She couldn't have told you herself, and certainly nobody else could.

Finally, as if almost in desperation, she married a man over in Arkansas—one of the Stovalls—with a lot of land and a lot of money. And she let him try to turn her into the mistress of a great plantation, to say nothing of a wife and mother. But she wasn't happy. Always she would be going into Memphis, even Little Rock (which she hated as being nothing but an overgrown town) to shop, even up to Woodville, whenever she had the chance, to see Mrs. Abernathy and get away from the fireside, as she put it. (There were no children.) No, she wasn't happy in marriage; but what were the alternatives for her then? And what would happen to her if she were free all over again? Wouldn't she make the same mistakes as before? What did she really want from life? Could she have told you herself?

Finally, she left her husband—not for another man—but went out to Texas, where she and Mrs. Abernathy had an aunt—Miss Annie Keller—living in San Antonio. In those days Texas—and the whole West—was considered a cure for most anything, from a broken heart to a considerable overdraft at the bank. And people were always going "out" there to get over something, to start all over again, to try something *new*. June said she didn't know what might happen to her in San Antonio, but it was better than being buried alive in Arkansas; and Mr. Stovall was agreeable to a divorce. (What did he think *he* had gotten for his money?) So out she went, to visit Miss Annie, who should have been sympathetic to June's situation: she had been the family wanderer, the hoer of wide rows in her day. But perhaps she and June were too much alike because, after only a few months with her, she told June to pack up and leave. Furthermore, she said she had five nieces and five diamond rings, but the day she died she was certainly going to pitch June's down the sewer. (This was the same Miss Agnes who had gotten mad at her husband—Uncle Bob—one day and burnt up his wooden leg while he was asleep, so she had to go downtown and buy him another one!)

So what was June to do then? With no training of any sort, she was hardly fit for the job market, though she did have enough to live on as a result of her settlement from Mr. Stovall, who had behaved very generously indeed. But what was she to do in order to fill up her days? She couldn't laugh or talk or dance forever. Didn't she still want a home of her own, a family, to be a *matron?* That word always made June laugh. She said it suggested dowagers with large bosoms and behinds (she had neither) and was altogether too staid and sober for her taste. And didn't she want children? Not especially, June said: she was too much of a child herself.

Oh, she wasn't any silly young woman—now no longer so young—trying to hold on to being a belle: June was no fool, and she knew the clock and the calendar were taking their toll. Really, then, there didn't seem to be a place for her in that world.

Finally, still out in Texas, she married again—this time a Mr. Burdine from Austin—and went to live there, where she seemed to fit in very well with the life of a small university city. It was just bohemian enough for her—and she for it; and Mr. Burdine, who was also very well-to-do, didn't seem to want her to "be the head of his home," have children, or otherwise turn matronly on him. Apparently, he was quite captivated by her—a "free soul," he told somebody once, just like himself. And so they spent their married life traveling: Europe of course, after they'd crossed and recrossed the American continent many times, and even the Orient, which in those days—the 1920s and then the 1930s—was still considered pretty exotic. June even got photographed in India, riding on an elephant, which caused some tongues to wag in Woodville when the picture appeared in the Memphis *Commercial Appeal*. As a divorcée she then couldn't be presented at the British Court, but she and Mr. Burdine moved in pretty exalted circles in England nevertheless. He had been very active in the cotton, then the oil business before his early retirement; so there were always plenty of country-house weekend invitations for them when they were there. And then there was always Mexico, which June claimed more or less to have "discovered" before it got fashionable for Americans to travel there. And despite her earlier unconventionality, she got soberer as the years went on, took fewer chances: in Mexico she always used bottled water, even for brushing her teeth.

Was she happy then, did she really love Mr. Burdine? No one ever really knew. From time to time she would come breezing into Woodville, to visit Mrs. Abernathy for a few days—first on the train, later by chauffeured limousine. It was all pretty grand for Woodville back then. And she and Mrs. Abernathy would laugh and talk and carry on, just like old times. But Woodville always had its reservations about her, didn't think she could really be happy: she hadn't done any of the things a "normal" woman should do, indeed should want to do. And she had done many of the sort such a woman wouldn't dream of doing either.

For the town she thus remained an enigma and also something of a symbol. Still the rebel, still the loner, she still didn't seem to be able to let Woodville alone. Did she have to have an audience for her high jinks, did she have to have somebody to shock? Did Woodville mean more to her than she liked to admit? Would even she have been shocked by such knowledge? Would she have admitted it?

Restless, wandering, money in the bank and houses (one in Austin, another in Mexico) to live in, plenty of clothes (always the highest of fashions, which she could wear, with her still youthful figure), what ate at her? What drove her on to do as she did? Even Mrs. Abernathy wasn't sure. In any case, if she was, she never told. When anyone would ask her about June's comings and goings now (there were more of them because she was a widow, with nothing at all to hold her down), she would always just smile and shake her head and say, "Well, that's just June." And nobody ever knew what she thought.

On beyond World War II June went, graying frankly now (she refused ever to dye her hair, said if the Lord meant it to stay brown, He'd have intervened), still beautifully dressed, miserable during the war when she couldn't travel ("I've always hated the Germans since we visited there for the first time in the 1920s: all that 'rebellion' or 'decadence' or whatever you want to call it was planned, regimented, which is all they know to do about anything"), more and more she would drive herself from Texas to Woodville (very few people had chauffeurs during the war). Somehow, she always got enough gas to drive to Tennessee. But no sooner had she seen Mrs. Abernathy and had a good talking session with her than she was ready to leave for Texas again. And still people all wondered what she did with her time. She was now a rich woman, so perhaps she spent some time looking after her investments. But what then? She wasn't a club-woman born, by any stretch of the imagination; and she couldn't have sat around discussing the supreme themes of art and song for any length of time. She never had been learned enough for that, though she could talk very amusingly about the arts, for a time. Of course there were no children or grandchildren to take up her time. Whatever else she might have, she didn't have discipline: that might have been the trouble all her life. But she was too old to change now, and even Mrs. Abernathy would admit that.

She still liked to shock too, but in the time after the war there were fewer and fewer folks left to shock. Anything racy she might have to say now was left over from her own youth, from before the *first* war, and the young folks of the new era found that all passé, though not without a certain period charm. Once she even heard a Woodville boy, just back from his first year at Vanderbilt, refer to her as a "good old gal." And that made her very sad after she had gotten over her anger.

Everybody still took notice of her, though: you couldn't not have because when she came into a room, business still picked up. You knew that life had arrived and was ready to do business. Conversation, anecdote, laughter still flourished around her. But now there was more and more speculation about what she would do when Mrs. Abernathy was gone, what she would do with herself then and, above all, whom she would leave all her money to. Certainly, nobody in Woodville had any designs on it; and Mrs. Abernathy, long a widow, had enough to keep herself on, in case June died first. She didn't need June's money— or even want it, most people felt. And finally the Woodville people wondered—though they perhaps couldn't have put it into words—what June would do without Woodville to shock, if she couldn't return to be talked about there. What did she really think of the town anyway?

As it turned out, people didn't have to wonder long because one night in 1970, June died peacefully in her sleep at the St. Anthony Hotel in San Antonio, where she had gone to live after giving up her big house in Austin. And when they read her will, which she had instructed her lawyer to do before her funeral, they found that she had left all her money (not so much now as there had been, but still a substantial fortune) to the University of Texas, to endow some traveling fellowships for graduate students (they didn't even have to have scholarly projects to work on, just want very much to travel and widen their horizons). And they found that she wanted to be buried in the Abernathy family cemetery lot back in Woodville. So that was where they brought her. A lot of Woodville people said they were surprised at that: they said June had never liked Woodville when she was alive, so why would she want to spend her death there? Some others said maybe it was one last tease on June's part; one thing was certain, they said, for all her teasing of Woodville in the past, June could never let it alone. Mrs. Abernathy was still alive, confined now to a nursing home and not always in her right mind; but when somebody told her the speculation that had been going on about the reasons for June's being buried in Woodville, she came to herself for a moment and said, well, maybe they were all of them right. "That's just June," she said.

If She Knowed
What I Knowed,
She Never Would Woke

——————— • ● • ———————

On D-Day—6 June 1944—a friend of ours, Sara Anderson, had to have her appendix out. There was no hospital in Woodville, my hometown, then; so she had to be taken to Memphis, where hospital rooms were scarcer than hen's teeth in those war times. But a good friend of hers was on the hospital board, and I believe he pulled some strings so they accommodated her. But even then it was a near thing, as the English would say; or perhaps a tight squeeze (American usage) would be more like it. Sara had been taken sick "way in the night," as people always said, which made it all more lonesome and frightening than it already was. And then she had to be "rushed to the hospital for an emergency operation"—more terrifying still; and she would have had "nurses around the clock" too except there just weren't any such animals during a time of national emergency. But anyhow, she survived and lived to tell it all, as I'm going to relate.

I understand they took her almost directly from the ambulance—there was no time to waste—to the operating room, where the operation was speedily performed. But what to do with her then? There was apparently no other bed available except one in a ward with two old women from "over" in Arkansas. (Mississippi was always "down," but whether this was better or worse I never knew. The main thing was that they were both usually lower down on all the economic charts—the only states that were—than we were in Tennessee; so we always said "Thank God for Arkansas" or Mississippi, as the case might be. In the old days, too, both states had more liberal marriage laws than we did—no waiting around for a blood test. So people were always eloping to Marion, Arkansas, or Hernando, Mississippi—names I thought positively fraught with glamor and romance when I was growing up.) Anyhow, the room with the old women was where they put Sara; and she was, of course, still out stone-cold from the anesthetic. (No recovery rooms then, remember.) There was one chair available beside her bed; and occupying that was her sister, Miss Clara Davis, who had taught me in the sixth grade and could have ruled the British Empire if necessary. Sara's husband was dead; and her only child, Henry, who was a teenager only a little older than I, had to find a seat out in the hall in an idle wheelchair. And that was the lineup.

And so there they sat during the late-night hours and on into the early morning, with Sara still "under the influence" and both of them much concerned about her. The two old women from Arkansas were thriving, though, and having a field day talking to each other and anybody else who would listen. ("Jim cleaned out the hog pen the other day, and it was *that* deep. God, how it stunk!" Or, "What do you reckon we're going to do to them Germans when we catch them, now that we've got them on the run? Or for that matter, the French and all the rest of them foreigners? What we *ought* to do, of course, is just build a wall around the whole place over there and let them all fight it out— and not keep getting us into it all the time to settle for them. And they don't think a bit more of you for doing it either.")

Finally, one of them raised up and looked over at Sara and asked Miss Clara, "Has she woke yet?"; and Miss Clara shook her head, no. Then the woman looked at Sara a long time and slowly nodded her head and said, "If she knowed what I knowed, she never would woke." And that seemed to settle a lot of things because it wasn't long after that until the old woman rolled over and went to sleep and Sara woke up, full of postoperation discomfort and all the rest. And indeed, when Miss Clara told her later what the old woman had said, Sara said she was about right: if *she* had "knowed" beforehand what she came to experience then, she might indeed have been tempted not to "woke."

It didn't help matters for any of them later on, when Sara was recuperating, that the old women turned out to be nonstop talkers, day *or* night, whether about foreign affairs, the cotton crop, or the state of their bowels. And, of course, they had a constant stream of visitors from over in Arkansas and naturally kinfolks unto the third and fourth generation. At one point, late at night, Miss Clara even said tactfully, "I'm going to draw this curtain in front of my sister's bed and keep the light out of your eyes," whereupon one old woman replied, "Naw, honey, I can't sleep anyway, so I'll just lay up here and watch you all."

But anyhow, it was all of it grist to Sara's and Miss Clara's mill. They came from a family of glorious tale-tellers, if sometimes inclined to exaggeration: one of them years ago had even said that he had shed barrels and barrels of tears over that very failing! And they didn't mind telling tales on themselves either. Above all, they liked to tell tales about vicissitudes or hardships (always amusingly recounted) they had triumphed over, as though to say: look—or listen—what we've lived to tell or else look—we're still here and we've *survived* too and aren't about to do anything else. And it was always funny even when the hardships skirted disaster.

Miss Clara would tell about when she had her first school out in the county—a young woman only just out of school herself. And it was a one-room *concern* (her term for any kind of mechanism, organism, or just plain organization) with grades one through eight. She had to teach and also be able to do most anything else on the side—up to and including heal the sick and raise the dead. Why, one time when there was a big revival going full speed ahead out there (during laying-by time, in August, when there was nothing to do but wait on the cotton crop and the children could all go to school), the woman that played the organ was sick; so the old preacher turned to Miss Clara and asked, "Miss Clara, will you please *tromp* the organ for us tonight?" And she said yes, she would *tromp* it. And they went to it right there with "We're Marching to Zion." ("Come ye that love the Lord / And let your joys be known—") But Miss Clara said before it was all over, *she* was about *tromped* out! Still, no matter; she'd lived to tell it and a good deal else besides.

The main thing was to teach those people out there some geography and history so they would know where they were *at* (as they would have said) and some arithmetic so they could *figger* (as they also would have said); in any case, they would know more about themselves and their world, which would help, though she said she didn't know that *facts* as such ever made people any better or any happier. Sometimes, indeed, it seemed almost a mixed blessing to teach people like that anything at all because if they really found out where they were *at,* they might also find out what a hell of a fix they were in! But she said this many years later, after she had taught the sixth grade all those years in Woodville, and by which time she said *she* was an *authority* on Original Sin. (I always remembered her geography classes—her specialty, where she said you ought to know not only about where other folks lived but also how they made their living and what they thought about things, especially if it was different from the way you thought: *that* was education, she said. I also remembered how she would straighten up and pull her corset down just before she launched forth into the lesson, just as though she were girding for battle, which in many ways, of course, she was.)

Anyhow, times moved along, and Sara and Miss Clara moved with them, though not without a backward glance now and then toward the old days. Once during Kennedy's presidency, when civil rights and welfare issues were dominant—especially the situation of colored people in the South—I heard Sara hold forth on what she had said to her (Negro) cook, Viola, about her "good for nothing" (Negro) yard man, Percy. She said, "I looked out the window, and there was Percy, who called himself weeding out my flower beds, just lying out under a shade tree during his dinner hour, lazy as the devil and not a care in the world and just as happy as if he had good sense. *I* ought to be working for *him*. And if truth were told, I already am: *I'm* the one that takes all the trouble and does all the worrying, and I'm supporting him into the bargain. Anyhow, I turned to Viola and said, 'Just look at that. Now do you reckon Mr. Kennedy—or anybody else on God's earth—could do anything *for* Percy?' And she said, 'No ma'am, Miss Sara, I don't reckon he could.' "

And then she continued, "And that's the same way I feel about all this *demonstrating* and what all. Why, do you know the other day, there were four of *them* down in Memphis that laid themselves down in front of one of the bulldozers that were just getting ready to start a new housing project—all for *them,* of course—because they didn't think there were enough of *them* hired by the construction company for the job? And I mean to tell you, it's a good thing I wasn't driving that bulldozer, or there would, sure God, have been *four flat niggers* in Memphis that day!" And then Miss Clara, who was present, remonstrated, "Now Sara, you know you wouldn't do anything like that." And Sara said, "Maybe not, but you sure can have fun talking about it!" And for Sara, that was the end of it: she would survive this as she had survived everything else, including Woodville's conversion to dial telephones. ("Why, if you call up Central in the middle of the night and say you're sick—like I was with my appendix that time—she won't know anything about you or who to call or what to do or anything else. And the worst thing of all

is that she won't give a damn either.") Anyhow, Sara implied, whatever it was, you might not like it (nobody could make you); but you
sure could have fun talking about it. Indeed, she hinted, that was mainly
how you did survive.

Sara even took that view when she was literally on her deathbed
years later. They had her down in Memphis, of course; and the doctors
went over her from A to izzard with a fine-tooth comb and still couldn't
find anything wrong with her though she kept telling them, among
other things, that she had lumps in her stomach. And the young ex-
amining doctor duly noted "lumpy stomach" on her chart. But finally,
when the senior medical man got around to her, he said, "You know,
Mrs. Anderson, we can't find anything really wrong with you. Even the
lumps in your abdomen are perfectly normal. The main thing is, you've
just had too many birthdays, and there's not anything any of us can do
about that." And Sara said, "Well, what should I do—just sit around
and hold my hands and wait to die?" And he said, "No, indeed; keep
on living as long as you can and enjoy every minute of it too. But one
piece of advice I will give you: stay away from doctors because they'll
kill you if you let them! They sure don't know it all, and the cemeteries
are just full of their mistakes right this minute." And Sara said that was
the best piece of medical advice she'd ever had in her life. And that was
the last she ever wanted to hear from *them.* The truth was, doctors wer-
en't any use unless you were sick. They couldn't do anything for well
people! But she was ready to go now because she had gotten to where
she was no pleasure to herself or anybody else. Honestly, she said, she
was just *tired.* And she didn't last long after that: there was nothing else
for her to survive *for,* she implied.

Miss Clara, long retired from teaching, lasted a few years longer.
And she was always a great favorite when she was called on to substitute
at school because she still read *Uncle Remus* to the class after they had
had their lunch. (God knew what the people in New York or Washington would say if they found out she was reading such "racist pro-
paganda," she said. But the main thing about Uncle Remus was that
he had folks' number, black or white; and there wasn't any real difference. One set was just as ornery as the other. It was just *folks;* that was
all.) She was still as strict a disciplinarian as ever: no back talk and no
impudence, or she would whack you over the head with her pencil. And
she still emphasized geography: more than ever now, she said, it was
important to know about other folks in other places because if we didn't

try to understand something about them—and vice versa, of course—
before long we were all going to blow each other up, and the whole universe too. And then where would we be? But meanwhile, we had to
work hard and do right; we had to *behave*. And that was good advice for
the sixth grade and everybody else too.

From time to time, toward the end of her life, somebody would
ask her to tell about the time Sara had her appendix out and what the
old woman from over in Arkansas said. And she would tell it all with
as much gusto as ever, though of course lacking Sara as the other half
of the team. And when she got to the punch line—"If she knowed what
I knowed, she never would woke"—she said she understood it better
every year she lived. In fact, she said, she wasn't too good to have it put
on her own tombstone because it might just be the story of her life. And
then she would laugh just as much as anybody else.

On the Side Porch

———————— • ● • ————————

"I didn't have a bit of business in this world going off to college or having a career or anything else because I was born simply to move furniture, entertain my friends, and sit on the side porch and look out the window." That was what Evelyn Henning down at Barfield said to me the first time I went to see her after many years away from home. "And I don't suppose there are many porches—front, back, *or* side—left in captivity down here, with air-conditioning now the universal order of the day," she continued. "Really, that's done more to change the quality of life in the South than integration or segregation (I never can remember which is the one we didn't want) or television or supermarkets or most anything else in the so-called progress line. You don't see anybody sitting on the front porch in the swing just watching the folks go by: a lot of new houses don't even have front porches. For that matter, I suppose some benighted souls now would want to know what you wanted to sit on the front porch and watch people go by *for*, which I think is all the same as asking what is life for. People that ask a question like that—well, there's just no answering them. They'd probably ask you where you expected to *get* in a porch swing, too! And of course there's no visiting in the side yard on Sunday afternoon anymore: we had to move off the porches to our yards then because so many of the neighbors came, especially here, where we're right on the corner and can see the whole world coming from more than one direction."

"But, Evelyn," I said, "You're not exactly public yourself now because this side porch we're sitting on is just that—a *side* porch. You can't see anybody pass by; and you've got it all enclosed as part of the house, not open to the outside, as in the old days. And as for 'progress,' don't forget that Memphis, which has been the great city in all our lives down here, would give its very soul now to be another Atlanta—you know, 'the city that is too busy to hate'—and with, God help us, an even bigger airport!"

"Yes, I know that," she said, "and my idea of hell has always been an enormous cocktail party in the Atlanta airport. I'm certainly not trying to stop the clock or empty the ocean with a teaspoon in such matters. And if you can't lick them, join them, is what I always say. But I tremble at some of our future prospects. Incidentally, do you know that I just recently sold off the last of our farm property out on the edge of town to some 'developers' that want to put in a shopping center, right here in this one-horse town? I guess we're just lucky they didn't envision a full-blown *mall*. (Of course, that seems to be the wave of the future: life in towns and cities has become so dangerous, you have to move as much of it as possible indoors and then lock it all up.) But the quality of our life down here is certainly altered these days—just like everywhere else—and I don't know that it's particularly an improvement. And maybe it's all somehow tied up with the rise of air-conditioning and the decline of the front porch."

"Anyhow, to get back to what you were talking about, you said you were born to sit on the side porch. And I'd like to know more," I said.

"Well," Evelyn replied and sat there looking out the window at her garden—not much in bloom there because it was late fall—"I think what I was born to be is a *hostess* or a bringer-together of people or a presider over meetings or something like that, a sort of *facilitator,* if there is such a word. Most people in the world today—and, I suspect, maybe it's been true always—don't really have enough get-up-and-go to reach out to other people or get in touch with anybody else about anything. Really, most of them would just sit there all alone in the dark and starve or freeze to death, whichever came first, if you didn't do something about it. Everybody *needs* everybody else really, but some people say they're really too timid or too shy or something to make the effort. But I don't buy that for a minute because some of the biggest rascals I've ever known in my life were always being let off the hook by supposedly being 'shy.' I don't doubt that someday, somebody somewhere will decide that that was Hitler's trouble: he was just 'shy.' And the more fool they if they do! Most of the time it's nothing but pure-down laziness. They don't want to take the trouble and make the effort. And that's nothing either but another form of selfishness."

"A lot of people today would say it's all because of the domestic help situation—or rather, the lack of it," I said. "You just can't get it. And that puts a crimp in anybody's entertaining or 'facilitating' or whatever, now or any other time. The times *have* changed, you know."

"That's partly true, of course," she said, "and we have in our own time seen the end of the seated dinner, though I will personally die before I come to paper napkins or cake mixes. But if you're smart and plan ahead and do a little along the way every day beforehand, you can manage, help or no help. Again, most people simply don't want to take the trouble, whether it's food or drink or anything else. And anything in this world that's good is trouble. You can just count on that."

I wanted to stay and hear more, but I had another engagement so I had to leave then. But from then on I became a regular visitor at Evelyn's, every time I came back home. It was as though she had thrown down a sort of gauntlet then—an explanation or vindication of her life, maybe more than just her own life—a whole way of life. And I felt called on to keep going back, to see whether she had changed in any way and also, I should confess, because I felt Evelyn was a good counterirritant to much of what I was exposed to in my job and my life away from home. She *was* a great joy-giver, and she was always *there.* She said, "All my friends know that from four o'clock in the afternoon on I'm always at home to them on the side porch, with bourbon or Coca-Cola or whatever else they want. Really, in a way, the side porch is the center of my life."

And this became more true as the years went by, even when Evelyn became increasingly debilitated by arthritis. She couldn't go to her friends so much as she had before: now they had to come to her. Her husband had been dead for many years, and both her children lived in Memphis: so there was no one else to be considered in her domestic arrangements. Somehow she always managed to have some help in the kitchen, usually some of the Negroes who had been born and raised on the Henning place. But as everybody always said, Evelyn worked harder than any of *them.* And when she could no longer move furniture (because of some idea she'd just had about rearranging things) or stand on a ladder to straighten a picture frame or squat down in the garden to work in her flowers, well, she said, she could always polish silver. And it always shone too.

What she had done, of course, when she and her husband moved back to Barfield after some years in Chicago, where he had practiced law (not too successfully, I understood), was take the old Henning house and renovate it so they could live there and not in some brand-new "home" in a "development"—the kind of house she always described as being fit for nothing but to watch television in. This was a tall order because all the Hennings except her husband were long dead, and the house had been rented out for years to what Evelyn described as "the wrong element or, to tell the truth, just plain white trash, so you can just imagine the state it was in." Then on top of that, her husband had died shortly thereafter and she discovered there was by no means so much money on hand as he had led her to believe. About all there was left, really, was the farm property. And that was along in a time when land was worth very little: everybody you knew was land poor.

That didn't stop Evelyn, though. She just called in all the people, black and white, who were making crops on the Henning farm (yes, there were real-live sharecroppers then) and told them they'd have to stand by her: she was new to the business, but she was going to learn; and they'd have to be patient with her and she wouldn't ever forget them. It all worked out well too: Evelyn treated her hands right and they responded in kind. But not everybody could have done it, I can tell you. Most people would have tried to bluff it out, to get away with knowing more than they did. But not Evelyn: she told the truth, had sense, and worked hard. Most people usually respect that combination. And so both she and the hands on the place did pretty well in those years.

I had heard of her all my life, nearly, but usually as a rather exotic bird of passage: people down at Barfield (I lived six miles away in Woodville, the county seat) often didn't know what to make of her. Because, without batting an eye, she came back there from what they could only assume was a glamorous life in Chicago and seemed perfectly content to exist in a town so small that people were still going down to the drugstore to have a Coca-Cola every morning at ten o'clock—and meet all their friends there—and, later on, watch the two I.C. streamliners meet (on the double track) in mid-afternoon because Barfield was just about halfway between Chicago and New Orleans. On top of that, Evelyn didn't always observe the local caste lines. She even entertained first families ("Papa always said . . . ") along with comparative newcomers—folks who had lived there only ten years, say, and had gotten no further than selling insurance (accented, of course, on the first syllable).

But Evelyn never crossed the color line, as it were. She had grown up in the Delta down in Mississippi even if she had lived in Chicago; and whatever she may have thought privately (and I always suspected that she was at once more conservative and more liberal than people thought—if that makes any sense), she wasn't rocking the boat in public. I once did hear her say that some Negroes were about as trifling and sorry as white people and worse, she couldn't say; but she was also a worldly woman with a very long head, who knew how the world wagged. She was fair and honest with everybody: no one ever suggested otherwise, and she was respected, if not always beloved. And you never heard of any of the colored hands on the Henning farm leaving either. But Evelyn believed in *society* (sometimes with a capital "s," sometimes not) just as she believed in any other reasonable organism or machine; and she wasn't about to tamper with its workings.

But anyhow, Evelyn was different: Barfield had to concede that and finally respect that. And though they may have thought of her privately as a high-stepper, they were forced to admit that nobody could be more down to earth when the time came. It was she who decided that it was high time the Barfield Methodist Church was equipped with rest rooms. ("Think of all those little children at Sunday school!" she exclaimed.) And how else to finance it but "throw open" all those "gracious historic homes" down there ("old houses at any rate," she said), with only an old maid or some other leftover living in them, to the public in a sort of "pilgrimage" ("like marked-down Natchez") and charge admission? (One thing they did have plenty of down there, she said, was antiques—folks included—and they might as well get the benefit of them.) Starting with her own house, of course, and she did have some handsome things—including a magnificent bed that some Confederate general or other was supposed to have slept in the night before the Battle of Shiloh. Evelyn said that was perfectly all right with her, but she wasn't going to make a life work out of it. The main thing about the past, she said, was that it reminded you that the world didn't begin and end with just you and that it hadn't been planned altogether for your own convenience either. Such knowledge was always good for anybody.

Evelyn didn't go off the deep end about the future either. She liked young people, and she liked having the grandchildren come to stay with her: she said it all kept her young. But she never tried turning back the clock. ("The young of any species are engaging, but youth is really wasted on them.") And it was she who really taught the grandchildren their manners. ("The older you get, the more good manners mean to you. Really, that's about all that separates folks from animals; and even then, sometimes it's hard to tell the difference. At the very least, manners keep the works greased; and I'm certainly all for that.") What it all came down to, I think, was *behavior*. Evelyn didn't really much care *what* people did, but she did like for them to believe in what they were doing and do it well and *enjoy* it. ("I'd rather for one of my children to be a first-rate bootlegger than a jack-leg preacher! I want people to be *professional*, to be *businesslike*, no matter what they do.") And again, that might have been a little too high-stepping or, paradoxically, a little too democratic for Barfield. But, as I've suggested, Evelyn was a kind of law unto herself down there: she spoke her mind perhaps too freely for some of them, but she always *behaved* and expected everybody else to do likewise. Of course, there was also the suasion of what we now call the bottom line: she was solvent, and she always paid her bills.

As I said, it was sometime after I had left home that I really got to know Evelyn. But thereafter I made her house one of my regular ports of call on visits back there. There were few enough of the old faces left for me now; so Evelyn became, in addition to everything else, a sort of touchstone, a landmark by whom I judged not only the world of my youth but also my present life and, indeed, myself as well. The years went by, and she began to show her age more and more; but always she was at home to her friends on the side porch from four o'clock onward every afternoon. And I got so I would drop by unannounced—something else that was going fast, she said. Now people in small towns—your own kinfolks, even—wanted to start calling you up before dropping by. And what was the good of their whole way of life if you had to start acting as if you lived in a city and worked in an office from nine till five? ("If you've got to ask whether it's *all right* to drop by your friends' houses, they can't be much friends. And if you don't *know* whether it's all right to drop by without asking, you can't be much of a friend yourself.")

Sometimes I wondered about her health. I had heard she had everything in the world wrong with her insides, though the only outward sign of infirmity was her arthritic condition. But she wouldn't quit going, walking finally with a cane. And she wouldn't quit entertaining on the side porch or even elsewhere. Nothing could stop that. It was no surprise to her, she said, that the central service of the Christian religion was a meal, even a sort of dinner party; indeed, didn't even Methodists sometimes refer to *celebrating* the Lord's Supper? That's what it was finally all about anyway—love, life, friends, everything. You were a fool if you didn't see it. Did you think it was all just three hot meals a day and double-entry bookkeeping?

So the last time I was ever in her house, she had invited me (it was Christmas and I was home) to one of her famous Sunday brunches, where she had everything in the world to eat, all set out buffet-style—on the old mahogany dinner table that had been in the Henning family as far back as anyone could remember—along with a regular bar set up in the front parlor. There were some Negroes who used to live on the farm to tend the bar and help serve; and nearly everybody from that end of the county was there, wandering all over the house and spilling out onto the side porch in due course. More and more, that was where Evelyn lived, only a step from the kitchen and where she could look out at the garden. Now Evelyn, even with her cane, was all over the place, urging everybody to have more food, another drink (though she was no friend to intemperance), asking everybody about his family or the friends who, for one reason or another, weren't there. And throughout it all, she never forgot a face or a family connection. ("When you live in a place like this, you have to remember that, in the old days, the roads were all mired up with mud half the year and nobody could get out. So they just stayed right here and married each other. And everybody's kin to everybody else, and so you'd better be mighty careful what you say to whom.") A lot of people said—and not always kindly either—that Evelyn was "in her element" on such occasions. ("She'd rather go to a party than be in Heaven.") I thought so too, but I meant it every bit in admiration. And as she moved among her guests now, she reminded me of a queen dowager making a royal progress, dispensing good will, cheer, even grace, and perhaps receiving in return more than admiration, more than thanks—the knowledge that she was following her profession too as a hostess, a facilitator, and ultimately, a life-giver. And she blessed and thanked us all for our friendship.

I'm glad that's my last memory of her, albeit her death only a month later was not out of keeping with that occasion. One of the cousins wrote that some friends were going by to take her out to dinner: it was somebody's birthday, I believe. When the friends arrived, they found her all dressed up, sitting in the big easy chair where she usually received guests on the side porch; and she was dead. A heart attack, the doctor said, the result of more than normal wear and tear. But then she'd always told me and everybody else that she'd rather wear out than rust out.

At the funeral two days later, my cousin wrote, the Methodist preacher said that Evelyn had always given her friends joy, had always celebrated life. And I thought that was a good way to put it: she had been a party-goer all right, but even more she had been a party-giver. Maybe that had been her true calling, her real vocation all along, more than anything else. And I liked to think that she died very much as she had lived: when her ultimate guest had arrived, Evelyn, all dressed up for a party, was right there waiting for him on the side porch.

Now, Baby,
Do You Know One Thing?

———————— • ● • ————————

"Now, Baby, do you know one thing?" That was the way Auntee always began her most startling revelations, her signal that something extraordinary was coming. Never did the dramatic *slide* into her conversation: she heralded it from afar. She knew what it looked like too, the color of its eyes and the smell of its breath; and she called a spade a spade, though there might occasionally be euphemisms for the sake of her younger, more innocent auditors. ("Oh, he's just got his 'pizzum' sprung," she would remark about someone who was suffering from the "old man's complaint," prostate trouble. Again, "men are *weak;* and if it weren't for women upholding the morals of the community, there just wouldn't be any! And that's why people expect a woman to keep her skirts down." That was her watered-down explanation of the double standard.) But she would immediately nod her head perfunctorily as if to indicate that she had observed the proprieties and knew she had; and now that she had gotten *that* out of the way, she would proceed with the conversation, "go ahead on," as she would put it, to the scandal of her old-maid sister, Cousin Rebecca, who thought that was a tacky expression. "Common" was what *she* called it.

And in some ways that was the story of Auntee's life: scandalizing Cousin Rebecca or someone like her, whoever was too refined or genteel or, finally, dead. Because that was what Auntee stood for—*life* and lots of it. You could even tell it from the way they looked, those two: whereas Cousin Rebecca was tall and thin ("poor as a snake," their cook, old fat Florence, used to say) and all sharp edges and angles, hair firmly swept back into a "club" behind her head, no excess baggage for her in either body or spirit, Auntee was short and stout, almost dumpy really, and everything about her was round and comfortable. Her hair was naturally curly and very difficult to control, but she took that in her stride, too. "I just can't worry about it," she would say. And so it usually looked as though it were in various stages of exploding, in a mass of pepper-and-salt ringlets, from her head. After I learned something of classical mythology, I even thought of comparing her to the serpent-haired Medusa—a benevolent Medusa, of course. Also, though she wasn't ugly, Auntee wasn't by any stretch of the imagination pretty or even attractive: she was *plain.* But then *beauty* wasn't high on her list of commendable attributes: "pretty, pretty," she would observe with disdain, of some highly touted beauty, implying of course that pretty was as pretty did and anyone could *look* good. As for her fully developed figure, she would say that that had never held her back: why, her husband used to say when he reached out to hug a girl, he wanted a *handful.* And then she would nod, maybe even wink; and Cousin Rebecca, if she were present, would purse her lips and look stern and reproving. But then she would sigh and set her eyes on the ceiling as if to say there was just no controlling Auntee.

And of course there wasn't, and I don't suppose there ever had been. Auntee was really a cousin of my mother; but I had never known her well till her husband, Mr. Campbell—who had been a well-to-do farmer over in the next county but then "lost everything he had"—died and she moved back to live with Cousin Rebecca. Auntee's given name was Helen, but I never thought about that because "Auntee" seemed to suit her so much better: she *looked* like an Auntee ought to look—comfortable and indulgent but by no means undiscriminating—so I must have given her the name very early in the day. I certainly can't remember ever calling her anything else. She accepted it quite naturally too; and one of my earliest memories of her is of snuggling my head into her very ample but firm bosom (she thought women who didn't wear brassieres were no better than they should be). I was full of some childhood grief that I can't even recollect now, and she hugged me very close and said—as if it were all a great wonder, some sort of miracle—"Baby, Auntee *loves* you." And that was the only thing that mattered. Truly it was indeed such a wonder and such a miracle—and still is. And I'm not too old either to enjoy thinking that there was once somebody for whom I would always be a child, always be a "Baby." Perhaps it's significant that I now have no memory of my sorrow, only Auntee's assurance of her love, which was complete, unconditional, and forever.

Because that was what it was in her nature to do—to love. Unfortunately, she and Mr. Campbell had had no children; so she had been denied that outlet. But she had been devoted to him, and now she was devoted to Cousin Rebecca. And in both cases that might have taken some doing. Mr. Campbell was a good deal older than she was and had been married before; and, I gather, in addition to suffering the bad luck of hard times, he had also been something of a profligate. ("He just ran through everything he had in no time at all," I once heard my mother say.) Cousin Rebecca was also a difficult object of the affections. An old-maid school teacher for most of her life, she was now retired on her savings and her very modest pension, with nothing to do but boss the whole world as though it were just the fifth grade all over again. She would have been more than willing to boss Auntee too, but of course Auntee wasn't having any of that. That might have been difficult too at first because I suspect now that Auntee was financially dependent on Cousin Rebecca—at least until a couple of years after she came to live there when she just went out and got herself a job as manager of the high school lunchroom, a job that she loved and performed very well. (Florence, the cook, had no such graceful deliverance from Cousin Rebecca's bossing: she finally had to die in self-defense, my mother always said.)

For one thing, Auntee's job kept her out in public with people; and, as she put it, she *loved* people though—she said—she still knew a knave or a fool when she saw one. And she got to be around young people and perhaps adopt them, in her mind, as children of her own. Certainly, the feelings were reciprocated; and "Miss Helen" became a fixture at the school: listener to teenage sorrows and complaints, dispenser of advice, healer of wounds incurred in the line of duty (the football team always adored her), fine cook and comfort-giver—ultimately, everybody's aunt. And so she found further objects for her affections. She kept on loving Cousin Rebecca too—when Cousin Rebecca would let her. Cousin Rebecca had led a life really swept and garnished, with few human entanglements along the way; and I think she secretly—perhaps not always so secretly—harbored some resentment against Auntee, who had *gotten away* and been married ("had had a husband and a home of her own and nice things," as someone always put it) but then had had to return home as something of a prodigal daughter, whose husband at least had wasted his substance. And so Cousin Rebecca may have behaved to Auntee as something of the elder brother in the parable: after all, she had been a good girl and stayed home and *behaved,* so why should there be such a fuss about the bereaved Auntee? Perhaps she even thought there ought not to be any more cakes or ale for *anybody*. But once again Auntee had gotten away—this time only as far as the high school lunchroom—but that was far enough.

I'm sure now that she knew, in the normal course of things, that she would have to care for Cousin Rebecca in her last years. But there was no point in taking on that burden, certainly in withdrawing into old age along with Cousin Rebecca, until she had to. And even then, Auntee wasn't promising anything. She certainly wasn't going to let Cousin Rebecca turn *her* into an old woman before her time. As matters turned out, she didn't have to make any difficult choices. Cousin Rebecca went into a long physical decline, fortunately never becoming senile; but in those days (back before World War II) you were still able to get enough domestic help with such affairs on your own. And let's face it: it was a case of *necessity.* There were few nursing homes or such like then. You simply kept your sick folks at home and *managed.* So Cousin Rebecca died and left Auntee her modest estate, and Auntee could have quit the lunchroom right then. But, of course, she didn't want to: it would have meant withdrawing from a good part of her life. And she wasn't about to just sit at home and hold her hands.

She was always on the side of life; indeed, soon after her death, years later, one of her friends (not the most alive one, as you may imagine) said to me, in some sort of wonder, almost amazement really, "Helen got so much out of life." To this comment I replied with, I fear, ill-concealed exasperation, "She put so much *in!*" And I don't know what my rejoinder did for Auntee's old friend, Miss Susie Larrimore, who I always thought was too lazy—and too stingy—to do much *for* anybody, good or bad: in any case, she certainly wasn't *giving* anything away. But it did me a lot of good to say that to her: I thought she had it coming, for one thing, after a lifetime of leeching off her friends, both in substance and in spirit. Further, it did me good in another way to begin putting Auntee together in my mind. What had she meant to me, what did she still mean to me—and why?

What she meant, for one thing, was absolute realism in facing what had to be faced: no whining, no complaining, and no Pollyanna smiling through it either. She could suffer fools gladly but only just so long, and she didn't always have the soft answer that turneth away wrath either. Once when I interrupted her in the middle of one of her best stories, she snapped, "Now, who was telling this anyhow?" And she didn't call me "Baby" that time either. Then once when I was "taking dinner" with her and was so thoughtless as to ask *what kind* of pickle that was on the table, she replied, with some heat, "The best pickle in the world! I made it myself." And I knew that I stood corrected. (She always said it was the worst manners in the world to be so persnickety about what you ate: anybody like that, well, you could just put it down every time, he'd been raised on branch water.) But temper rarely colored her judgments about matters of faith and morals. Concerning the possibility that she herself might be an invalid in her last days, she told me, "For goodness' sake, Baby, if I have to be 'put somewhere' "—her contemptuous reference to the modern distaste and consequent euphemisms for ultimate necessities—"see that I'm at least kept *clean* because I've certainly washed many a butt in my day." Another time, when a couple of our town's leading citizens had to serve time for embezzlement, she said, "Now it's all very well to say they are *hypocrites* who ought to be *ostracized* (two words that fascinated me when I was little) if they ever come back here. But that's beside the point. They just got in over their heads and tried unsuccessfully to get out, and anybody else might do the same. And if you think different, you just don't know human nature." When the Presbyterians had to get rid of their preacher because he was too openly affectionate toward the young boys in the church, she said to me, "There's no use getting on a high horse about all that. Now, Baby, do you know one thing? That sort of thing is just like anything else: it's a *disease*." And when the doctor-husband of one of our cousins left her for a nurse he had met during his tour of duty in World War II, Auntee silenced comment with, "There's nothing to it but that they were far away from home and thrown together in very terrible circumstances. Why, Baby, do you know they were working right over there behind the front lines night and day, cutting off arms and legs and heads and everything else? And you just don't know what you'd do in a situation like that."

Another time, when one of the cousins lost her husband (who had been some sort of off-brand Baptist or whatever), Auntee brought back the following report from the funeral: "Well, after she moved to Memphis, Irene always did have the most peculiar-looking friends. I don't reckon they ever *stole* anything, but it certainly wasn't because they didn't look as if they could or would. But anyhow, when we got down there for the funeral, do you know that Irene had a woman to preach his funeral? Named 'Sister' something or other. Anyhow, I looked over

at Irene's niece, Mary Elizabeth, who's right civilized, and raised my
eyebrows; but she just nodded and went right on. So I gathered there
wasn't anything earthshaking about such doings among that set of folks.
And, Baby, do you know one thing? Sister Do-funny or whoever she
was made a real good talk too. On the text 'Thou preparest a table before me in the presence of mine enemies,' which I did think rather
strange in view of the fact that Irene was always the world's worst cook
and lazy into the bargain. But then, you know, there's just no account-
ing for tastes."

Another time, when one of her sourpuss friends (that same Miss
Susie Larrimore probably) remonstrated with her for not attending
church more regularly, she snapped out, "Well, I just don't want to
be struck by lightning! Because the last time I set foot up there in the
Methodist Church (where I was born and raised) I looked around at who
was there, and I never saw such a bunch of sots and backbiters and
whoremongers in my life. And that's the God's truth. But do you know
one thing? God Almighty's not going to stand for all that carrying on
forever, and someday He's going to take a hand up there, and I don't
particularly care to be there when it happens! I know I'm a sinner too,
just like everybody else; but I'm not a fool. And I resent all that crowd
sitting up there on Sunday looking as pious and sanctified as a herd of
white-faced cattle. I don't know what the Lord thinks about it all, but
they sure haven't fooled *me!*" Then there was the Sunday when one of
her contemporaries asked the *whole Sunday school class* what they would
think if she carried her senile older sister to a matinee at the picture
show *on Sunday* and some of the class members expressed reservations.
When Auntee got home, she exploded, "Thunderation! The poor de-
luded old thing don't know who or where she is or one day from another; but if it will help her sister, who's been nursing her night and
day and who's really the one to be considered now, I say go ahead on
and *go.* The Lord has certainly got more things on His mind than to
worry about some old women desecrating the Sabbath. But then most
people don't really like to credit the Lord with having more sense than
they do."

No prude, no hypocrite, Auntee always faced the truth, told the
truth, and finally, I think, *did* the truth—but always with joy, almost
zeal, you might say. (When I was growing up there was a section in the
Methodist hymnal that fascinated me: "Activity and Zeal." What it all
meant was beyond me, but the hymns therein were some of my favor-

ites: bold and militant, even sanguinary, but full of fervor and a joyful noise.) Life might not have seemed to deal Auntee a very good hand, but what cards she had, she played whole-heartedly and well. She had nursed and buried an old husband and then nursed and buried an old sister. But neither of them was able to bury her. She had no children of her own, so she became an aunt to all other people's children. In more ways than one, she was a life-giver, not a death-dealer; in more ways than one, she never stayed home and held her hands. And always there was joy, even when she began her pronouncements with "Now, Baby, do you know one thing?" The world was good; the world was bad, usually a mixture of the two. The wonder of it all never ceased to amaze her and ultimately to give her joy—that she had been privileged to be part of such a spectacle, such a drama.

Once when we were driving home from a day in Memphis, she looked out at the lush West Tennessee countryside in the summer twilight and observed, "How beautiful it all is, and it's only *lent* to us for such a little while! How can people go through life just making money, 'getting ahead,' as they call it, accumulating *stuff* really, and just working and sleeping and eating and not having any *joy?* I never have understood that." Some years later and after I had moved away, she went to bed one night and just never woke up. But I understood that she had told the next-door neighbor the night before that she had had a sudden yearning for some catfish that afternoon and had just gone downtown and bought some to fry for her supper. And she had said, "I know it seems like a fool thing to do, but I wanted the fish and I had the money. And if I can't please myself in my old age, I might just as well not have lived at all. And do you know one thing?" And I could imagine her adding "Baby" if she had been talking to me. "If I die before morning, you can just tell everybody that here's one old woman who died with a belly full of catfish. And died happy too!"

I Never Have Been
a Well Woman

You know, I never in the world thought I'd live to be this old—a hundred! And that's exactly what I told that young man that came round to interview me, as they call it, for the television the other day. As I told him, I really never have been a well woman. Oh, nothing ever really bad wrong that I couldn't get over, but—especially since I've gotten so old—just aches and pains and that old arthritis and what that new young doctor called an allergy when he examined me about ten years ago. In my time, there weren't any such things as *allergies;* you just had a breaking out and called it nettle rash and went right on. And to tell you the truth, I don't know that they can do much more than that now.

Of course, I never married; so I never had any children of my own (just taught other people's)—even if I'd wanted any, which I'm not too sure I would, considering what the world seems to be coming to these days. On the other hand, folks have been saying that about the younger generation from time immemorial, I suppose; and the world keeps right on going. So I don't suppose now will make any difference. Anyhow, I don't know that people really improve or not as they get older; mostly, I think they just get more the way they already were. So you can look at it either way.

But anyhow, after I fell and broke my hip about five years ago, my nieces and nephews got together and decided this nursing home would be better for me. (All of them think I'm going to leave them something when I die, but I may live it all up myself first!) So I gave up my house and moved in and here I am, and I reckon here I'll be till they carry me out feet first. I'm more or less used to it now, which I suppose is a good thing if you look at it one way but a bad thing if you look at it another. Maybe I'm really getting "institutionalized," like you hear about in those "public-health scandals" they're always revealing in whatever you read or listen to now. On the other hand, I'm certainly not going to lie here in this bed or roll around in that good-for-nothing wheelchair and give up the ghost either. You have to stay up and get around and be up and about and be *interested* in folks and in the world if you want to live a long time. And God knows, I have; and I guess I still do. Why, I fight old age every day of my life!

That young man the other day wanted me to say what all I had *learned* in my "first century," as he put it. And goodness knows, I wasn't sure of anything I *had* learned, which sounded, I suppose, as though my whole life had been nothing but a water haul. But when you come right down to it, I don't suppose many of us can ever say just exactly what it is we have learned. Like I said, I don't think people improve with age—not like a wine. Of course, the silly ones just get sillier and the fools just get more foolish: time don't do a thing for them, I can tell you. Like that silly Mildred Perkins down the hall from me—won't even look at the dance numbers when they show them on the television—thinks they're godless or something. But what else can you expect, with her such a *big* Baptist and with maybe grandparents that weren't but just a jump away from being Holy Rollers or Pentecostal Nazarene or God knows what? Anyhow, she sits beside me at nights when we watch; and every time somebody prances out in an abbreviated costume and begins any kind of gyration, Mildred automatically ducks her head and won't look up until it's over, except occasionally to ask me, "What are they doing now, Myrtle?" And I tell her, for God's sake, use the eyes she was born with and look for herself. We're all more than twenty-one out here. But I don't think Mildred has ever gotten away from Mamma's apron strings, and she's only a couple of years younger than I am right this minute. If I weren't right here beside her, I suspect she'd put the clock back more years than that, but she can't fool me. I've known her ever since she grew up right next to us out in the country (we didn't move into town until long after I was grown) and ran after my brother Ben until he positively had to get himself married to somebody—anybody—else, just to get away from her.

He married Ona Mae Stanley from over on the other side of the county, who didn't have the sense God gave a billy goat, but she made him a good wife all the same—raised some fine children, too: that's the nieces and nephews I was telling you about. And Ben and Ona Mae are both gone now, so it's just me and the nieces and nephews; but I see as little of them as possible because there's no point in having them come out here and get all upset because I'm ailing: at a hundred years old, what else do you expect? All things considered, I think I'm doing pretty well.

And that's what I told that young man when he interviewed me the other day. Wanted to know what were the main changes I had seen in my lifetime and what all. And I said, well, folks out in the country had electricity and indoor plumbing now and people didn't die of typhoid and pneumonia anymore; and, of course, there's always the automobile, which to my way of thinking is an infernal machine in almost every sense. But as to whether there were better or happier people these days as a result, the quality of their lives improved, I really wouldn't know. And I think he was sort of surprised. Probably thought—most folks do—that just because things were different—changed—they were bound to be better. But I've lived too long to believe in any of that. Like I said, people—*folks*—don't change; and you're a fool if you believe they do.

Of course, there's not as much sheer drudgery as there used to be. I don't think people are as much worked to death, literally, as they used to be—on the farms and, I suppose, in the factories. But then, so what? So they don't have to earn their bread by the sweat of their brow as much as they used to, so they do have more free time; what do they know to do with it all? That's always been the question as far as I could see. And more and more folks, it seems to me, are afraid of good, honest work. And the way the government's going, you might think Washington was conniving at that too. Like one of the Negro maids out here told me the other day: her sister didn't have to work, she said, because she was "drawing," which meant she was on welfare or social security or God knows what other form of "relief." But nowadays it's not just restricted to *them;* white folks are just as lazy and ornery, as far as I'm concerned. And Jews are just as bad as Gentiles and Catholics like Protestants. I am certainly *not* prejudiced. I just believe in Original Sin, which covers a lot of things I can't understand any other way. Just like it used to say in the Episcopal Prayer Book (but that's one more thing they've gone and changed): "We have left undone those things we ought to have done and we have done those things we ought not to have done and *there is no health in us.*" And the longer I live, the more I want to shout "amen" to that.

You know, I was a school teacher for nearly fifty years—yes, a real old-maid school teacher, just like you hear and read about. And if

I learned anything in all that time (I just taught the first grade, but it's all the same: nobody, young or old, much wants to learn *anything*), it was that human beings have an amazing capacity to resist enlightenment. And considering the homes that many of my pupils came out of, I thought it might be a merciful dispensation if they didn't learn too much because then they'd wake up and see what a really terrible mess their lives were in (father a drunk and mother a slut and God knows what for brothers and sisters), and then they really would be miserable! Quite often, you know, ignorance really *is* bliss. When I was younger, I would have thought that shocking for anyone to admit, especially a school teacher. But I guess that's one of the things that you notice as you get older: fewer and fewer things have the power to shock you. After a while, you just feel like relaxing and saying, "Well, yes, I have seen the nature of the beast; so tell me something else I didn't know."

Does this mean that age hardens you? I hope not, really; but you just don't make a big hurrah about a lot of things anymore: eventually, you just feel there won't be any more surprises. But that's a dangerous way to look at it, too: the Old Adam is still up to his old tricks, and there still ain't nothing like *folks* anywhere. So that's why I don't get much excited one way or the other about who's president (and this one sent me a birthday telegram—did I tell you?) or congressman or what not: they're all pretty much cut out of the same bolt of cloth—and the people who vote for them are no better. I tell you, it's a pretty widespread ailment—Original Sin. But we Americans particularly, I think, put our trust in princes and in machines more than we ought. We go wild over personalities and pretty faces and whatever other gadgets get thrown at us all the time on the "media," as they call it—whoever makes the most noise is what it amounts to, really. And to tell the truth, it's all just like we were deciding on which new car to buy—a *product*. Or so it seems to me. And most of it leaves me quite cold, I can tell you. If I've got *convictions* about anything, I don't change them to suit the season, like they were clothes or something. They're *there* and they *stick,* if there's anything to you at all.

And that's what I guess I've learned in my life, if I have indeed learned anything. And that was what I tried to tell that young man when he asked me all those questions in that interview the other day. God knows what he must have thought of it all—and of me. But one thing he did say, before he left, was that I ought to be declared some sort of national monument. And I haven't yet decided whether that was a compliment or not. But I'm going to take it as such anyhow; I'm sure he meant well.

Well, I'm sorry you have to go now; but be sure you watch the six o'clock news tonight: that's when my interview is supposed to be shown. That young man promised.

Up on the Corner,
on the Dogleg

———————————— • ● • ————————————

Jackson Street, the street we lived on, made a sort of dogleg before it got to our house, coming out from the square, and for almost a block ran sideways to itself before it righted its course, if I make myself clear. They never bothered to change its name either: it was still Jackson Street, no matter which way it ran. And it never occurred to me that that was in any way peculiar till we had a cousin come out from Memphis to visit one time, and she said it just didn't make sense and showed a lack of urban planning or something of the sort. But my mother just said everybody in Woodville knew what it was and where it was going, and that was good enough for *them.* (The cousin was not a close one anyway. And my mother didn't see any use in taking her *seriously,* especially when she had come from out at Fisher's Crossing in the first place, where hardly anybody had ever heard of a stoplight, much less urban planning. And anyway, she was my *father's* cousin.)

But I always thought it was interesting, in any case—that Jackson Street could still be itself even when it ran sideways. And I even wondered whether that sort of arrangement maybe did something to the people that lived on the dogleg and certainly the ones that lived up on the corner from us. Did it mean that they were just a little out of step with everybody else or that they sort of enjoyed being contrariwise to the prevailing opinions of the day and the ordinary ways of doing things, like material cut on the bias? Of course, they were still themselves, no matter what—just like Jackson Street, no matter which way it ran. Certainly, our town, Woodville, was peculiar in its layout— mostly existing on the ridges that lay between the ravines (people said it was a city set on a hill), and all radiating out from the square like spokes in a wheel with few conventional blocks to be seen, no "grid" at all. And you had to go back to the square—the hub—and start over to go almost anywhere, certainly to go from one side of town to another. But the dogleg on Jackson seemed rather extreme, even for Woodville.

But it might have been just the folks that lived up on the corner from us, as Jackson Street straightened itself out to run parallel to its first section leaving the square, that made me wonder about it all in the first place. Not that they were *peculiar* or all that different from anybody else: I've always said that if you knew Woodville, Tennessee, you could go round the world with few surprises. But maybe they were just more obvious. Of course, you could argue that a small town like that had more than its fair share of anomalies: some people would have you believe that right now, especially if the towns are down south. But again, I think not: everybody is just closer to everybody else and there are fewer secrets, fewer places to hide—that's all. In any case, I thought the people up on the corner, for good or for ill, might just possibly be more *Woodville* than anybody else I could think of. And I always more or less made a sort of private study of them, watched them, thought about them, to see whether they added up to anything special.

But what could be all that unusual about them? They weren't hiding any bodies in the basement or imprisoning lunatic members of the family in upstairs bedrooms or defiling the purity of family life by illicit affairs with their colored servants—or, for that matter, with each other. Nothing lurid at all—certainly nothing for the national "media," as it's come to be called, to get up a sweat about. But what they all were, first and foremost and very emphatically, was themselves— what my father would have called their own boss and manager. And they didn't mind being different, but they didn't make any big deal out of it either. That's just the way they were, and I suppose they thought everybody else in the world was the same—or ought to be. (Again, who cared which way Jackson Street ran?) Maybe I never would have thought there was anything unique about them either unless I had grown up and gone away to earn my living in Memphis and then could look back on Woodville as where I was *from*. But this is all forty years ago now, and maybe Woodville has "progressed" and gotten to be like every other place you can think of. I'm almost afraid to go back there now, for fear of finding out that it has.

I do know that some years ago the Board of Mayor and Aldermen hired a big-city firm of "consultants" (all the way from St. Louis, I think) to come in and take a look around and recommend whatever they thought fit to improve Woodville's "image" and its economy, or something of the sort; and one of the first things they lit on was the dogleg on Jackson, which they labeled a very back number indeed and a holdover from simpler times. They very strongly urged its elimination—or rather just its renaming, the sideways part, that is. But the people up on the corner weren't having any of that, and they all showed up in a group before the board to protest. Some of them were old and feeble too; some had hardly been downtown or even out of the house in a good while. But they thought it necessary to take a stand on such an important matter. And the board listened too—and granted their request to leave Jackson Street alone.

I was living in Memphis by then, but I saw the whole thing prominently written up in the *Commercial Appeal* and read it all with considerable interest—and amusement. And I thought, well, Woodville never changes, and there's no other place like it, and hurrah for all those stout-hearted old folks that wanted to live and die on Jackson Street, dogleg or no! We need more people like that in the modern world, I thought, and score another one for the American Resistance Movement! But I wondered whether it was just change of any sort they feared, or did it go deeper than that? And why would they really want to hold on to such a confusing anachronism or whatever you wanted to call it? Come now, tell the truth. Wouldn't it really make things simpler for all concerned if the Jackson Street dogleg got itself straightened out and into the modern world? The people up on the corner would still be themselves, still be the same. But then of course, I gathered, *they* didn't see it that way.

So I began to think about them, individually and collectively, and to wonder whether they were all that different or were they just trying to cash in on whatever nuisance value they had and get themselves a lot of notoriety thereby? (My mother never distinguished between *celebrity* and *notoriety,* and she may have been ahead of her time because there really doesn't seem to be any difference now.) God knows, there seems to be plenty of that sort of thing in the world today, with demonstrations and martyrdoms for all to see, on very short notice, on worldwide TV and everything else. (Of course people like me always wondered whether there would be so many martyrs if the witness-bearers weren't so sure of an audience.) Whatever the case, these people—

up on the corner, on the dogleg—were not your everyday, garden-variety sort of folks; that much was certain.

Just to start off, the two old bachelor brothers Fitzpatrick—Dr. Will and Mr. Jim, one a doctor and the other a lawyer—who lived in the big brown house were not without some interest. I don't know why neither of them had ever married: some people just thought they never had gotten around to thinking about it, they had been so busy getting started in their respective careers and then making money when they did get established. And maybe there was no passion for that in them anyway; but there certainly was for other things—hunting, for instance. Wherever either of them went, he was usually accompanied by one or more dogs, and of course the house literally swarmed with them. I don't recall hearing that Dr. Will took them into a sickroom (and this was back in the days of house calls, remember); but wherever he went, day or night, one of the dogs was sure to ride along, in the backseat of his little car. (For some reason, doctors then seemed mostly to drive coupes, just as they always seemed to have their home and office phones on the same two-party line—so you could find the doctor instantly, I suppose—and the same way all their offices were down on the square up over one of the drugstores.) Mr. Jim was the same as Dr. Will. He never took a dog into the courtroom as far as I know, but there was always one sleeping in the doorway that you had to step over when you went into his office, which was up over the bank.

Dr. Will had a rough tongue, especially for people that wouldn't follow his advice; but he was considered to be very good always with children and old people—people who mostly couldn't or wouldn't talk back to him. And when he gave doctor's orders, they were just that. Once he laid my father out when he stopped taking some medicine Dr. Will had prescribed as soon as he began feeling better: "I said for you to take the whole bottle of medicine, and I meant the whole bottle too." And my father then meekly obeyed. When Dr. Will was finally able to persuade Cousin Serena Cobb, whom he had been treating for a chronic urinary infection for years, to let him take out her tonsils because he feared they were badly diseased, he took one look, after he had gotten her all laid out on the table in his office and deadened with some sort of local anesthetic (we didn't have a hospital in Woodville back then), and exploded: "Good God, woman, I've been working on the wrong end of you all this time! Your kidneys aren't even in the running: these tonsils are as big as a bear!" This sort of thing didn't endear him to some of his patients; but then my mother, who was always the most sensible of women, said you didn't go to him to be flattered: you went to be cured and whatever it took to do that was certainly all right with her. She had long ago lost any illusions she had ever had about the way things *looked*.

Dr. Will didn't miss much. When he was a very young doctor just out of medical school, he had been taking some special courses up in New York one summer; and he took in all the sights too, including the trial of Harry K. Thaw, who had killed Stanford White in a much-publicized "society murder" but was duly exonerated because he was supposed to have had a "brainstorm" at the time. There was naturally some skeptical opinion about that. Because of Thaw's wealth and position, it was suggested that the brainstorm theory was nothing but a kind of rich man's alibi. But not to Dr. Will: he said you could just take one look at that fellow and tell he was crazy. And anybody that would shoot his wife's lover in such a public place as the rooftop restaurant of Madison Square Garden had to be either crazy or stupid. And he didn't think Thaw was stupid, though he ought to have known better than to marry a chorus girl in the first place.

Mr. Jim didn't seem to be so colorful, but I do remember that during World War II he tried to run his old car on a mixture he concocted out of coal oil and cleaning fluid. That was his answer to gasoline rationing. So whenever you saw him coming, he was attended by a good deal of smoke and a considerable smell as the old Chevy lurched down the street. But it kept running all through the war, and that was what he wanted. Their married sister, Miss Olivia, who lived in Memphis, used to worry about them a lot: who would look after them in their old age, and were they eating properly, and why hadn't they ever married? But they seemed to do a good job of looking after each other, and you never would have known they felt the lack of family life. I remember my mother said that, if you ever called up there late at night for Dr. Will, Mr. Jim would always answer the phone; and you never knew whether Dr. Will was there either till Mr. Jim found out who you were. For that matter, the community itself did a pretty good job of looking after them. When Dr. Will had his first heart attack (the first time, I remember, I ever heard the word *coronary*), the town stationed a policeman on down Jackson Street, right in front of our house, to reroute traffic around by the primary school so the noise wouldn't bother Dr. Will when he was so sick. (He was sick at home because they hadn't been able to move him to the hospital in Memphis.) And I remember my mother kept the policeman supplied with all the coffee he wanted while he was on duty: she said she couldn't do anything for Dr. Will himself, but she could do that.

Old Mr. Conner, who lived across the street from Dr. Will and Mr. Jim, was another matter. He and his family had moved into town from out in the country years ago: he was supposed to have made a good deal of money somewhere along the line and sold his farm and was all ready to retire. But my mother said she never would believe he had done all that well just in farming—and certainly not on the kind of land he owned; and, to cap the climax, he was supposed to be some sort of jack-leg preacher on the side, and that didn't help. Why, he might have spoken in tongues, for all she knew. When she talked like that, my father would always profess himself embarrassed: he never thought she respected the ministry as much as she should. But she just said, never mind, he would see; and he did. Because "Brother" Conner, as he had first insisted on calling him, seemed to be up to all sorts of tricks in the way of mortgages and lawsuits; and it looked as though anybody that had any sense ought to think twice before getting involved with him in a business transaction. They even told it on him that he once moved into a house he had bought and nailed down the rugs before they could be removed and thus was able to argue that the rugs had gone with the trade. But what really opened my father's eyes, apparently, was hearing the old boy preach, which he did once at a funeral of a tiny baby that was held somewhere out at a country church. "Brother" Conner held forth for nearly two hours on the subject of infant baptism! And my father was scandalized and never referred to him as "Brother" Conner again: usually it was just "that old devil" from that time on.

Since I've been grown and no longer live there, Mr. Conner's granddaughter has told me (and we grew up together) that he still continued to perform funerals into his very old age. Once she drove him out to a church somewhere in the tall and uncut; and just before they arrived, he told her he had forgotten whose funeral it was to be. She naturally asked him how he could officiate under such circumstances, but he merely replied that he would know whose funeral it was when he got there and saw the family. And anyway, he added, you always said the same thing. I was sorry then that my parents weren't still around to hear that one. I don't think either of them would have been surprised.

Mr. Conner was sometimes a trial to his neighbors, especially after his wife died—a silent little old woman that I never heard say a word. Old Mrs. Higgins, who lived on one side of the Conners, said she was sorry the old boy was so lonesome now but she couldn't take him on with all the rest she had to worry about: running a boardinghouse along with, in summer, fighting the weeds in the yard with only a bunch of no-good Negroes to help her and, in winter, keeping the pipes from freezing underneath that great big house that had no underpinning at all. Her hands were full, and she let him know that right away when she told him her hens wouldn't lay on coffee grounds. She said he was just that lonesome: he would come traipsing over to give her chickens his "table scraps," just so he could pass the time of day with her. But she said she didn't need anything *he* had to give her. Whether she was conscious of the innuendo I don't know: she certainly wouldn't have been embarrassed if she had been. My mother certainly wouldn't have been either. My father, though, like many men of his generation, was more prudish (and less realistic) than many of his female contemporaries. He was definitely outraged when another old man of his acquaintance once confided to him that a man his age didn't need sexual intercourse but about once a year and then went on to add, "But my wife—she don't mind."

On the other side of the Conners lived the Malones, with "more beautiful women in one house than you ever saw in your life," people used to say (they had five lovely daughters and their mother had been a beauty too). But everybody said it was just as well Mrs. Malone *had* been beautiful because she certainly couldn't have counted on her brains. One time, I know, after she got up in years, she broke her hip; and my mother went to see her when she got home from the hospital. She told my mother that the doctors had all assured her that, no indeed, that leg wasn't going to be one bit shorter than the other one after it got well: if anything, it was going to be a little bit longer!

Next to the Malones—and just before you came to our house— was old Mrs. Scott—"Miss Alma," as most of her friends called her. I've tried writing about her elswhere, but I doubt that I'll ever be believed. Still, it won't hurt to add a little more here. Having outlived her husband by a good many years and raised assorted children and grandchildren, Miss Alma was naturally the one you *turned to* when you were in a tight place. One time, I remember, my mother was horrified to find that the country ham she had planned to serve the Tuesday Bridge

Club was much too salty, and the "girls" were due in only an hour's time. But Miss Alma didn't turn a hair: she told her just to put it on again in cold water and bring it to a boil. And that was that. She was that way about everything else: when she had grandchildren running in and out of the kitchen all day long, she said she just turned the handles of whatever she had cooking on top of the stove to the inside so the children couldn't knock it off and went on her way rejoicing. By mistake, someone called Miss Alma on the telephone once, under the impression that she was the Mrs. Scott whose husband had a little machine shop, and asked whether he was still sharpening lawn mowers. To which Miss Alma quickly replied that he *could be:* he'd been dead five years and she didn't know what he was doing now! Oh, I could tell you a lot more, but Miss Alma needs a whole story to herself. *Down to earth* is putting it mildly.

The upshot of all this is that the folks up on the corner, on the Jackson Street dogleg, weren't any different mostly from anybody else. That's something I know now—as I look back on them after all these years. They were just highly visible, that's all. Their situation was somewhat different from that of the rest of us—out of kilter, as my mother used to say. And so you just noticed them more. But they did like who they were and where they were, and they knew where they were going too. And it didn't matter really which way Jackson Street ran. I'm sure there were probably a lot more people around town just like them too, but I don't think there are so many people like them in the world today. We don't seem to have as much room, as much time to spare for people a little out of kilter or cut on the bias, people who live on doglegs. And I think that's too bad. But the times have changed, the world has changed, and I'm sure Woodville has changed too. (I hear they've even got a shopping mall there now.) But then you can look at it another way. My mother always said that, give or take so much, people were always pretty much the same wherever you found them, and the human animal didn't really seem to vary much from time to time and place to place. Whatever the case, she said, you just couldn't ever really beat *folks*.

Miss Effie,
the Peabody, and Father Time

———————— • ● • ————————

"**W**hy, when she first came here as a young married woman, she was as wild as a buck!" That was what my father said to me about Miss Effie Herrin, who was the grandmother of my closest friend, John Howard Herrin, back when we were growing up in Woodville in the 1930s. John Howard had all his grandparents still alive then, as did Mary Sue Green, who was a good buddy of ours; and I was jealous because all I had to show for any of it was just one ancient grandfather whom we all called Pa. And he was cranky as the Devil and ate peas with his knife, and all his children (my father included) were still afraid of him, lo, these many years later. Every time they all talked about Pa as the sole survivor of the Good Old Days—my father and his brothers, that is— I would think, well, History was OK, but you didn't want to let It get you down or hold you back either, especially when History had a mind you couldn't change with a sledgehammer and didn't want to bathe any oftener than It could help.

On the other hand, there was Miss Effie Herrin, who looked and (I thought) acted just like a grandmother ought to. She had put on some weight as she got older, they said; but she had a warm smile and a twinkle in her eye and was always very comfortable to be around. And she obviously adored John Howard, who of course returned the compliment. Her hair was snow white, and she wore it in a very dignified "up-do" like the ladies—or the older ones, at any rate—were all messing around with in those days: swept up on top of her head, which my mother said gave older women especially a distinguished look. The only thing was, she said, it was hard to arrange yourself: you might just have to break down and go to the beauty parlor. And she didn't think much of that: you ought to be neat and clean always, she said; but as for trying to look any prettier than the Lord had made you, well, she had better things to do with her time. It was mostly just women who didn't really have enough to do around the house—the ones that were too lazy to really *keep* house, the ones who *wouldn't* cook (always the worst thing she could say about another woman)—who resorted to beauty parlors and such like. Her own hair was naturally curly; and every time somebody would ask her who gave her that lovely permanent and when, she would observe, "God Almighty gave me this permanent the day I was born." And that would settle that. But then she took a dim view of anything that tended toward the voluptuous, to say nothing of the sybaritic. The idea of even a tame little bubble bath was abhorrent to her. "Now as far as I'm concerned, a bath is strictly a business proposition, and I just get in and get out and don't waste any more time in the tub than I possibly can," she would say, "and besides, with skin like mine, you don't need any more soap and water than you can help anyhow."

Her skin was not her "long suit," as she would have told you herself. Once when she was afflicted with two different kinds of "breaking out" at once, our family doctor sent her to Memphis, to see the great Dr. McCall, who was the *leadingest skinologist* in those parts back then and, according to my mother, the ugliest white man she'd ever seen in her life. However, she wasn't going to him for his *looks* but because he knew skin backwards and forwards, she said: first things first. And after he completed his diagnosis, he told her that however many times a week she bathed was just that many times too many and she could just keep clean with cleansing cream for a while until her trouble cleared up; besides, God Almighty hadn't given her very pretty skin to start with. When one of her friends asked if that hadn't made her mad, she said no indeed, she knew it was the truth and she hadn't needed *him* to tell her that. There was nobody like my mother for facing facts.

But to get back to Miss Effie Herrin. I can't remember now what provoked my father's remark about her "wildness," probably some observation of mine that she always looked stylish and well dressed, even if she was John Howard's grandmother. Maybe I even said her outlook on life was still young or something of the sort. In any case, he was very quick to put both me and Miss Effie in our places. And when I ventured to demur, saying something to the effect that I could hardly believe in her past "wildness," she was such a sweet and loving grandmother, he snorted and said, "Why, son, Father Time has caught up with her!" Then he clammed up right away: he wasn't about to get into any kind of discussion with me about sex or anything connected therewith. God knows, neither of my parents ever told me even the rudiments of the "facts of life." And what I finally learned, not always strictly accurate, I should say, I learned from my contemporaries. Of course, the secrecy in which much of the information (or misinformation) was communicated, the whispers and the bated breath only emphasized the shame and the distaste. Why, Mary Sue had even told John Howard and me (you always have to have at least one good girlfriend who is not a romantic attachment to *tell* you things) that her mother hadn't told her a thing about what to expect when she got to be a teenager, and the only reason she hadn't been scared out of her wits when she began having her periods was that some of her older girlfriends told her what it was all about.

So my father didn't say any more than that: I was just supposed to *know* something about Miss Effie's lurid past in spite of her domesticated present—at any rate, know enough. My mother did observe, when I asked her, that it was common knowledge that Miss Effie and two other young matrons (they were young *then*) of very correct background had once been asked to leave the Peabody Hotel in Memphis. And that did open up exciting prospects for speculation, but I couldn't imagine *what*. The Peabody was unquestionably the great hotel in everybody's life in those days—everybody in the Mid-South, as they used to call it. And most of us thought if we'd been very good, we should get to go there when we died! My mother had even told me, when I was very little, that since my name was Drake, the celebrated ducks in the lobby fountain were some of my kinfolks! As for anyone's misbehaving amid all that elegance, it was inconceivable to me. Why, all the bridal luncheons, all the debutante parties in that part of the world were held in the Peabody's Skyway, up on the roof; and you weren't legally married if you didn't spend at least your wedding night there. So what could Miss Effie and her friends have *done?*

Auntee, who believed in the Old Adam more strongly than even my mother did and was always the one I could *ask* things, said, "Oh, Baby, you know it must all have had something to do with *men*." But that was all she would say, not from any reticence or squeamishness, I felt, but just because she wasn't really very much interested. Neither the Peabody nor Miss Effie's alleged misbehavior was any news to her. There wasn't really anything glamorous about either one, certainly not anything worth making a production out of. And as for getting all dressed up and going down to have lunch in the Skyway or the Venetian Dining Room on some festive occasion or even listening to the music of Jan Garber ("the Idol of the Airlanes") or Clyde McCoy, who had composed "Sugar Blues" and played the trumpet part himself when they broadcast from "the breeze-swept Plantation Roof," well, she couldn't be bothered. She could eat better in her own house anyway, she said, and she certainly didn't need some black former field hand right out of the Mississippi Bottom to explain a French menu to her. Miss Effie herself had originally come from over in Jackson County, where there were Campbellites and Republicans just as thick as ticks on a hound dog, she went on to say. So what else could you expect? And pretty was as pretty did, for both Miss Effie and the Peabody. If truth were told, they were all of them probably just as loose as a bucket of juice! And then she cleared her throat and pulled her corset down, to indicate there was no more to be said on *that* subject.

So I grew up and passed on into adolescence, never *knowing* about Miss Effie and always *wondering* about the Peabody. It looked, to say the least, as though you couldn't count on appearances: more often than not they would deceive you. And yet, of course, you wanted things to look nice, to look good. Even in my speculations about Miss Effie, she never took on any other guise than the sedate, eminently respectable white-haired grandmother of John Howard Herrin, even if she did have a twinkle in her eye. I simply couldn't imagine her acting otherwise. Even when, prompted by my father's assertion that Father Time had caught up with her, I began to conjure up visions of that encounter, Miss Effie always looked and acted as she should. In the back of my mind, every time I thought about her, I could see her, clad in a long white night-gown (with bare shoulders, though), her hair neatly swept up on top of her head; and she was running long and well across the green lawn in front of some stately home. Father Time, dressed for some reason as a clown (Death as the ultimate joker?), was pursuing her closely but not with a scythe; instead, he was fiercely gaining on her with a lawn mower! Now what Dr. Freud might have made out of all this I can't imagine, but I think I now read it as some sort of fable about life and death. Life *would* go on, even in the immediate proximity of the end, with death gaining on it every moment. And death *was* funny, to think he could compromise you in any way, cramp your style. Who did he think he was anyhow, to come cut you down in your prime, as you'd always been told he might—before you'd had time to do all you wanted? Better to

think of him as somebody straight out of a Marx Brothers movie, a joker
like Harpo, chasing the girl in the grass skirt with a lawn mower,
something fairly lunatic and making no more sense: that would put him
in his place. And in my fantasy he didn't faze Miss Effie either. She ran
smoothly and serenely on before him, not batting an eye or in any way
compromising her dignity. You had to admire her imperturbability:
she had *style!*

Oh, it was titillating to think that that dignified old lady might
have kicked up her heels in the old days; and you could rejoice to think
she hadn't yet been made to feel her age, to grow old, to lose her
"rhythm," as a friend of ours lamented about her only daughter (whom
they all called Sister) when she changed music teachers: Mrs. Johnston
had taken every bit of the rhythm out of Sister, she said. Miss Effie was
like a very stately old gal I encountered many years later in a very proper
hotel lobby in Texas—the St. Anthony in San Antonio, to be exact. I
was sitting there, comfortably ensconced in a deep sofa, reading a detective story, conscious that there was a sound of revelry by night coming
from the ballroom that opened off the lobby—a wedding reception,
probably. And here came an old lady slowly wending her way down the
length of that long, elegant lobby, where a string quartet played every
day during the luncheon hour. She looked like a queen dowager at a
state reception—and was dressed very much like one too, in evening
gown and jewels. I looked up, impressed by the spectacle, to follow her
progress. But when our eyes met, she simply nodded and said, "There're
lots of drunk little girls back there." And that was all. At first it seemed
almost indecent, to have heard such a thing from her lips. Then it
seemed funny, to think of the incongruity. Finally, it seemed rather
sweet, to understand that age need never stop you from living, from
participating in life. Something like this was what I felt in the years
ahead, whenever I thought of Miss Effie. Well, good for you, old girl,
I thought; they haven't gotten you yet, they haven't taken the rhythm
out of *you!* And you keep right on outrunning that clown-driven lawn
mower, as long as you can. And long may you wave!

Something of the same thing I also felt about the Peabody all those
later years, as the times changed and the world that the Peabody had
served changed too. I saw it begin to go downhill, going through several different ownerships and managements. (As my mother and her
generation would have said, of a restaurant, a department store, or anything else, "It changed hands and went down." But then, as one friend

pointed out, did you ever hear of anything that changed hands and went up?) And I saw the downtown district of Memphis declining, almost by the day, the familiar stores fled to the suburbs, the movie theaters now dark and deserted. Hardly anybody would be left there before long but bankers and lawyers, one of my cousins remarked. And finally, I read in the Woodville paper (I was long gone from those parts but, of course, continued to take the weekly newspaper) of Miss Effie's death. I had heard, too, that the Peabody had been closed by order of the bankruptcy court. Now it just sat there, in the middle of downtown Memphis, all locked up.

But do you know this all has a happy ending all these many years later? Because I've only recently returned from a visit back home, to Woodville; and while I was there, somebody asked me to lunch in the newly reopened Peabody. And I found it marvelously restored to its former elegance in decor though not up to par yet in the catering. And the whole lobby, which had been modeled on the courtyard of a Venetian palazzo, I believe, has now been turned into a gigantic bar, to the scandal of the abstemious. You can sit anywhere in the place and order a drink! Mercy! But the ducks are still there in the fountain, and now the management makes a big thing of bringing them down from the roof (where they sleep) every morning and returning them there every night—a real ceremony. And I suppose before very long, they'll start having bridal luncheons in the Skyway again. Already they're having Sunday brunch there—unheard of in the old days—complete with champagne too! And so I was cheered up, to think that grand hostelry was back in business again—and winning new fans among the next generations.

Nonetheless, the best news of all was something I learned on the same visit. Calling on an old friend, who had known who was who and what was what back in the old days before I came along (she was a generation older than I), I idly remarked that I had just been to see the resurrected Peabody and loved it, that it had always been *the* great hotel in my life, and it was still so beautiful, perhaps even the unseemly might be glamorized if connected with its name. But all my life, I added, I had wanted to know just what Miss Effie and her friends had actually *done* to cause their ejection all those years ago. To which my friend said, "Good Lord, I can tell you all about that. Nothing to it, really. Old Effie and her buddies were going off to Memphis on Saturday and meeting the traveling men at the Peabody, having a few wild parties, and

only getting back home just in time to sing in the choir on Sunday
morning!" And we both exploded into laughter. So that was all it
amounted to—what an anticlimax! No grand passions, no torrid ro-
mances, no gilded halls of sin, really, but just the good healthy vul-
garity of the jokes that used to be told in the smoking car about traveling
salesmen and farmers' daughters. All very tame and somehow very engaging, I thought. But at the same time it all gave me a good feeling,
about both Miss Effie and the hotel. The Peabody had managed to escape death and destruction; it had held the wrecker's ball at bay, to be
restored to life and looks. And in a way, I thought, Miss Effie had survived too, as comfortable as ever, the twinkle in her eye still intact. In
the back of my mind I could hear that lawn mower still whirring away,
but somehow I could also see her, in the long white nightgown and
swept-up coiffure, sailing serenely on ahead.

II

ANN LOUISE: THE MAKING OF A SURVIVOR

The First Year

———————— • ● • ————————

Nineteen hundred thirty-nine. That was the year Ann Louise Parker finished the third grade and entered the fourth. And it was the first year she ever remembered being conscious of as a year. At times during the summer, in the middle of whatever she was doing, she would suddenly stop and say to herself, "This is 1939; it never has been before and never will be again." And then she would practically have goose bumps from thinking about it—that it was unique—the way she also had from thinking about eternity when the preacher talked about it in church. But in that case she would practically get dizzy from thinking about something that went on and on, for ever and ever, world without end, amen. . . . When Brother Howell would say, "This present time isn't a drop in the bucket compared to eternity," Ann Louise would see a great water faucet dripping into an enormous bucket drop after drop, but somehow never filling it up, despite the fact that you knew it had to. It was right scary.

Why was 1939 the first time this had happened? There had certainly been other memorable years in her life. 1936, when she started to school, for example; and her teacher was Miss Rosa Moss, who had taught her mother and father and practically everybody in Woodville. And there was 1937, when the Mississippi River flooded almost worse than it ever had before. That was certainly an important year, but she supposed now she didn't know it at the time. And it was *time* that was the clue here, she reckoned; she was becoming conscious of *time,* that it was passing, that it was even running out—that some day that water bucket might really fill up. And she herself would pass from the scene. She couldn't have put it into those words then herself, but it was all hovering there unstated, in the back of her mind.

She supposed part of what was different was what was happening in Europe, with another war about to break out there any minute. War, of course, was something she'd known about all her life: *the* war, in which her grandfather (whom she remembered quite well) had fought for the Confederacy, and since which time things in the South had never been quite the same, everybody said. Then there was the Spanish-American War when everybody nearly, except Teddy Roosevelt and his Rough Riders, had gone to Cuba and Puerto Rico and died of yellow fever. (Ann Louise herself had had malaria, and *that* was bad enough.) And, most recently, there had been the World War, where a lot of our boys had died in the trenches over in Europe, and a lot of the home folks had died right here of the flu. (Ann Louise's mother told her people had died so fast in Woodville, they had run out of coffins to bury them in and had to make them!) That was all *history*, in the schoolbooks certainly, but also in the memories of people she knew or had known herself. (Her grandfather had actually been at Appomattox and seen General Lee on Traveler! Think of it!) And now with a new war about to get started, Ann Louise felt that history was about to happen to her; she would be a part of history herself. And that was an exciting prospect. She would be in a war—or at least on the sidelines of one.

Sure, she had had history at school; and she also had had it at the picture show in what they called costume dramas, in glorious Technicolor, with Errol Flynn as Robin Hood and Don Ameche as Alexander Graham Bell and swords flashing and hoopskirts flying all over everything. But there were other forms of history too. There was always, once a week at the picture show, another installment of *Paramount News*, just as there was *Life* magazine, which came, as a rule, on Thursday or Friday, and was almost as great to look forward to as the weekend. Already Ann Louise had seen enough Germans running all over Europe pushing people out of their homes and turning them into *refugees* to last her the rest of her life: they were just like the Mississippi River, she had decided, that overflowed its banks every year or two and washed people's houses and land away and turned them into *refugees* that had to be *evacuated*. And that was the first time she remembered ever hearing those two words, in the 1937 flood. She privately thought it might be a good thing if they built a fence or a levee around the Germans, too, to hold them in, the way they did the river; but she never had settled on who this "they" was going to be.

Vaguely, in the back of her mind, there were memories of the Japanese a couple of years ago doing something like this to the Chinese, running them out of their homes, turning them into *refugees*. (She never could remember whose eyes slanted up and whose slanted down: one country did one way and one the other, she thought.) And she remembered seeing a headline about the Spanish Civil War in the *Commercial Appeal,* which they read every morning, and realizing, for the first time, that civil war wasn't just something that happened between North and South. She remembered also one hot summertime a couple of years ago, with her mother stretched out on the daybed in her parents' room, and reading her a scene from *Gone With the Wind,* which had just come out and everybody was reading and talking about. (One of Ann Louise's aunts had a chance to borrow the book—it cost $3.00, which was a whole lot to pay for a novel, people said—for just three days. So she just told her husband he could take over the housework—he was a farmer and already had his cotton crop laid by—and she went to bed and hardly got up for three days until she finished it at two o'clock in the morning.) Anyhow, the scene her mother read her was the one when the Yankees were coming, probably to steal and burn, and Scarlett got the whole family, white and black, to leave (*evacuate?*) and go hide in the swamp. And as she prepared to leave herself, it seemed to her that all the family heirlooms—the furniture and such like—were saying, "Goodbye, goodbye, Scarlett O'Hara." And she knew she might be seeing Tara for the last time. She knew she might be on the verge of becoming a *refugee.*

Well, Scarlett was right in the middle of history; there was no doubt about that. And Ann Louise wondered whether she knew it or not; did anybody ever know it at the time? Had her grandfather, the Confederate veteran, known it? Had he pinched himself right then and there so he would always remember Appomattox and General Lee? Maybe, on the other hand, they all just thought, "Well, this is life and that's the way it is" and let it go at that. *History* was what you called it after it was all over. That is, unless you had somebody practically standing at your elbow telling you that it *was* history, right here, right now. Maybe that was the function of newspapers and radios, maybe even the picture show, to tell you what was history—or going to be. Ann Louise knew that they were making a movie of *Gone With the Wind* out in Hollywood right that minute, and she was dying to see it. But of course that was different: it was a "story" and only *based* on history. In that sense, it wasn't the real thing.

But what was happening right now in Europe was real, and what had been happening right here at home was too—the Depression, which she knew meant lots of people being out of work and being poor and not having enough to eat. But things didn't seem to be better or worse than usual in Woodville: nobody had ever had much there, her father said. And, he added, you could always sell your cotton for *something;* and her mother said, yes, and eat lots of sweet potato pie, which Ann Louise loved anyhow. And so nobody was starving around there; breadlines and soup kitchens were just something you heard about. But her father said he thanked God every day he lived for President Roosevelt: whatever you thought about him and the New Deal and all those alphabetical agencies, he had saved the country from revolution, without a doubt. And he just couldn't wait to vote for him for a third term.

So Ann Louise knew she was on the verge of something, that the times were *momentous*—not like the Baptist preacher, Brother Scoggins, had said at chapel that time when he talked to the whole school about the end of the world and got them all scared to death, looking for the signs and portents that would signal Judgment Day. They weren't *that* momentous, she felt. But they *were* dramatic and bold and something was happening—or about to happen. You felt that history was on the way to happening. The question was where it would strike first.

And, of course, where it struck first was where Ann Louise had least expected it. Her best friend, Martha Alice Craig, came down with acute appendicitis and had to be rushed to the hospital in Memphis in the middle of the night and practically operated on before they could get her out of the ambulance: it was just that close, that much of an emergency, they said. Ann Louise was naturally jealous because Martha Alice was getting so much attention now and later on she would have all that to look back on and talk about *for the rest of her life.* And she had come through it all and lived to tell it. (Was that what history was— what you had come through and lived to tell? But then suppose you didn't come through and just got turned into a dead body and a tombstone? That was history too, wasn't it?) But, in this instance, Martha Alice was a survivor, who would get to tell her tale at the drop of a hat (even drop it herself, Ann Louise suspected) for ever and ever. And she had a *scar* to prove it too, which of course she insisted on showing Ann Louise when she took her some flowers after she got back home from the hospital. The scar *proved* everything she had been through: it was a *record* of what had happened. It was history.

Ann Louise didn't think of it all that way at first. It was just something that had happened—something dramatic all right—to Martha Alice, which caused her to get lots of attention too—what Ann Louise's mother called *notoriety,* which could just as easily have referred to a lurid divorce trial, like the one she had heard about right there in Woodville, involving Leroy Duke and Ida Nell Griggs, where people went and took their lunches so they wouldn't have to give up their seats. (Of course, if Martha Alice had died, she would have gotten even more "notoriety." Every time there was a sudden or a dramatic death around town, Ann Louise's mother would nod and look very wise and observe, "That'll be a *big* funeral." And if it was somebody rich, she would add, "I expect they'll preach him right on into Heaven.") But the more Ann Louise thought about it, and especially with all the airs that Martha Alice was beginning to give herself (like she had just come back from a harrowing adventure as a missionary in the Amazon jungles), the more she realized that history happened off the front page, maybe even could happen without any particular drama: the drama was what you saw afterwards, maybe even helped to create yourself, as she suspected Martha Alice was doing. Ann Louise had sense enough—and she thought she was honest enough—to admit to herself that she wouldn't have a bit minded some of the attention Martha Alice was getting right then; but she certainly wasn't going to go out and break a leg to come by it. On the other hand, maybe that could be history too—nothing happening, nothing glamorous, at any rate.

So when school opened in September and the Germans goose-stepped into Poland and the war really did begin, Ann Louise was more or less ready for it—and maybe clearer-eyed about what was really happening. Because now they were in Miss Kate Harrington's fourth grade, and Miss Kate bore down heavily on geography. (Miss Kate didn't go in for window dressing; she stuck to fundamentals, Ann Louise's mother said.) So they started off the first day talking about the war and following it on the map. And then the *Life* magazines began to come, with all the war pictures; so there it all was—real as anything in this world. And, of course, there was *Paramount News* too. Yet there was also Martha Alice, back to normal again, still with her scar, but with her operation receding further every day into the past: it was now just something she had *had*. Was that also what history meant—no big headlines necessarily, no big deal at all, but just something you *had* and not necessarily glamorous or dramatic either?

What would all those big-hatted, blue-haired ladies in the D.A.R. say to that, she wondered. (They had just refused to let Marian

Anderson sing in their auditorium in Washington because she was a Negro, and Mrs. Roosevelt had resigned in protest.) But anyhow, who wanted to hear it all? She remembered the night the evangelist who was holding their revival had asked for people to come up and kneel at the altar rail who wanted to testify to God's providence in their lives. And old Mrs. Taylor got to going so strong that the evangelist—he was a brought-on fellow from somewhere up in Kentucky—finally had to go over and nudge her with the toe of his shoe and say, "That's enough, sister, that's enough." *Everybody* had history; you needn't get on a high horse about it.

Was that the real truth even about her grandfather, the Confederate veteran? He had fought for the Confederacy all right, but he was also lazy and didn't bathe very often. (She had heard her father—when he didn't know she could hear him—say that if it hadn't been for his mother, the whole family would have starved to death.) Was history then pretty much like your skin—you had it and couldn't get rid of it and couldn't change it and you'd be a fool to try? In other words, was it that history simply *was* and you had it whether you liked it or not? Was it like those old jokes they always pulled on little kids: "You have *ancestors!*" or "You *hesitated* on the sidewalk!" or "You *slumber* in your sleep!" You couldn't get away from it, but it was no big deal. Would all years, to some extent, now be like 1939? It was just her realization that it *was* 1939 that made it different, that made it, in some ways, her first real year. Ann Louise now saw all the years of her life opening out before her: history literally loomed ahead. But now, she thought, she knew what she was getting into.

The Operetta

Ann Louise Parker would have rather been shot dead than be in the operetta, that summer she was ten years old. But she and all her friends had to take part in it because, her mother said, it was all for the P.T.A., which was trying to raise money to buy a new baby grand piano for the high school auditorium. And the Lord knew they needed one, she would always add, with that old upright they had to use for all the recitals and commencements and everything else sounding like a washboard or a dishpan, to say the least. But Ann Louise thought it was asking a lot of them all—when they might just as well have stayed home and been cool on the front porch, playing Authors or Rook or maybe even Monopoly—to trudge down to the high school every morning in the hot weather and sit there in that oven of an auditorium waiting their turn to go on in the rehearsals.

The operetta, which was called *The Stolen Flower Queen,* was being directed by one of Ann Louise's mother's friends named Eva White. And she was so small (and awfully proud of her tiny hands and feet, which showed she was a *lady,* Ann Louise's mother said) that most everybody called her Little Eva. But, of course, not Ann Louise and the other children: that would have been disrespectful. Mrs. White had taught *expression* (what everybody said used to be called *elocution*) before she moved to Woodville with her husband (who sold insurance and was named Orval) and her son and daughter. And everybody said she could really manage children, though you wouldn't have known it to look at her, Ann Louise always thought: ladylike hands and feet, a faint, faraway look, and the breathless air of always being late or running behind time. But it was just another case of the iron hand in the velvet glove, Ann Louise's mother said; and the thing was, Little Eva had enormous staying power. Everybody in town said yes indeed, and she was a brave woman to be putting on the operetta.

But Ann Louise thought it was all the silliest thing she had ever heard of—all about the Flower Queen, who had been abducted or kidnapped or something by the Weed King and was being held for ransom till her friends among the flowers and fairies or whatever could get her set free. And practically every child and teenager in town had been hauled in to play the part of a flower or a fairy or something else equally ridiculous. Over the whole thing there was flitting about the Fairy Queen, who was nobody but old Isabel Edwards, a high school girl all dressed up in white and leftover Christmas tinsel, with an oar from a rowboat down at the lake to paddle through the air with when she wasn't supposed to be flying, looking helpless and confused and trying to get her good friend, the Flower Queen (Janelle Holmes, who had taken dance lessons for years and wanted to go off to New York and study the ballet), out of the Weed King's clutches.

Ann Louise had made up her mind right away that she wasn't having any of all that foolishness. And it was all so namby-pamby anyway, with everybody being sweet and wholesome all over the place. She had much rather have been in one of the "living pictures" from the Bible they always put on at the Methodist Church Christmas pageant: there wasn't anybody there always running around being sweet. What's more, she had thought for quite some time that she could make a good shepherd or Wise Man if she put her mind to it—or maybe even King Herod. (Being an angel or even the Madonna wasn't any kind of challenge.) Now she was definitely on the side of the Weed King, who was played by Bobby Jack Morton, a senior in high school who smoked cigars and drove a pickup truck to the rehearsals. Indeed, he had dark brown eyes and a deep bass voice; and you could see the hair on his chest coiling out of his shirt collar right that minute. He was as cute as a bug; and Ann Louise had already made up her mind he could abduct or kidnap her anytime he wanted to.

But anyhow there she was, along with her best friend, Martha Alice Craig, both of them all signed up to be rosebuds or something idiotic like that and having to go out to Miss Rose Tatum's to have their costumes fitted every few days—all cheap material cut and sewed to make them look like whatever they were supposed to represent, with their heads as the flowers' "faces" exploding from a bunch of petals and leaves and naturally looking like perfect fools. On the other hand, Ann Louise had decided, it could be worse: they might have been fairies, like the smaller girls, and have to stand around with those damned wings

on their backs and wands in their hands and unable to sit down or lean
up against the wall or do much of anything else. (The wings were the
main drawback to being an angel in the Christmas pageant, she had
always heard.) The littlest girls of all—first-graders—were snowflakes
and mostly just got to wander around and look aimless, which wasn't
any trouble for them at all. And the older girls got to be chrysanthemums, which did have possibilities, Ann Louise decided, because they
got made up to look like Japanese women—with yellow skin and slant
eyes and their hair all slicked up on their heads—and carried parasols.
And that at least looked dramatic or maybe even like a *femme fatale* when
Bette Davis or Greta Garbo played her in the picture show—what Ann
Louise used to call a *sireen* until her mother corrected her. At any rate,
it was interesting and not like some damned rosebud, which really
couldn't *do* anything. Ann Louise had decided long ago that it would
never be her lot in life to sit around looking pretty; and she wasn't sure
if she was talented either, which people always said was a help if you
weren't pretty. But when all else failed, she thought, you could always
be *dramatic*. You could always *perform*.

The boys at least got to do something. The ones her own age were
mostly elves or gnomes or something like that, all sewed into violent
green costumes that reminded you of children's pajamas, with the head
pieces and the footgear all attached to the body of the garment, and
peaked caps and turned-up toes too. And what was worse, they wore
padding, to make them look chubby and cute or something of the sort—
maybe like overgrown teddy bears. Their job was more or less just to
dance attendance on the Weed King and look mischievous. But at any
rate, it all gave them character and showed they could do something
besides wander around and look cuddly. The smaller boys got to be
bumblebees, and that was even better. They got to dart around all over
the place, seeming to terrify all the flowers and make them all tremble
with fear. But then after all that carrying on, they always made friends.
And Ann Louise wasn't sure she really understood that. Why should
they, flowers and bees, go through a whole big song and dance like that
and then kind of just kiss and make up? It didn't make sense. But Mrs.
White just said airily it was all part of "the romance of nature" and
they would all understand when they got older. But Ann Louise didn't
know what there was to understand: if Bobby Jack Morton wanted to
menace her right that minute, that was perfectly all right with her. She
certainly wouldn't scream or run away. And she didn't see that she

needed to be any older to appreciate that.

But anyhow here they all were, with the next few weeks of their summer vacation already tied up with the rehearsals and costume fittings. And Ann Louise was already sick to death of the whole thing. She couldn't have cared less about getting the high school a baby grand piano. The agonies she had been undergoing when she played in Miss Caroline Miller's piano recitals she didn't think would be appreciably diminished, whatever breed of instrument they played on. At least now they were spared Miss Caroline during the operetta because she had gone on an excursion to the World's Fair in New York (and doubtless would be asked to "tell her trip" at every women's book-club meeting in town when she got back); and the pianist for this whole shooting match was Miss Berniece Robbins, who played the organ at the Methodist church and had lots of beaux, one of whom always sent her an orchid every Easter. And she was pretty to look at but inclined to be excitable in a crisis, like the time she started in on the wedding march before they had brought in the mothers at Emma Lou Johnson's wedding and had had to back up and start over, while they practically *trotted* old Mrs. Johnson down the aisle. Well, for good or for ill, that was one thing about Miss Caroline: she *wasn't* flighty. And it was things like that you appreciated more as you got older, Ann Louise's mother always said— folks being in the right place at the right time and doing what they said they were going to do. And then when time came to cut the head off, why then, cut the head off! Or at least that was the way she put it. But Ann Louise's father said that was all very well, he still thought Miss Caroline had missed her calling: she should have been the kaiser of Germany.

So the days went on and the rehearsals progressed and the costumes got fitted, and things began to "tighten up" for the big night. There were some hitches, of course, like when Isabel, the Fairy Queen, got mad because she didn't get to sing as many solos as she had expected and she decided to go on strike or something. What she did, of course, was go home and go out in the back lot and get up on top of the barn and refuse to come down till Mrs. White herself came and asked her to, even promised her another solo. And in a way, it all sounded rather grand and theatrical, Ann Louise thought—like Sarah Bernhardt laying down the law to a producer or Katharine Hepburn walking off a movie set because it was all a matter of *principle.* But Ann Louise's mother said all that so-called principle wasn't a thing in this world but pouting and it all came from having a bad temper and being spoiled rotten. And if she had been Mrs. White or Isabel's mamma, she would have worn her out.

All the paraphernalia like the lighting and the scenery were supervised by Mr. Morrison, the football coach, who everybody said was a real whiz at that sort of thing, even with limited resources. There wasn't anything he couldn't do with some canvas and a spotlight and a couple of extension cords, they said. And then he could always press the football team into service, even in the summertime. So he had lots of hands and backs and shoulders at his command. Of course, it all seemed like a pretty limited thing to Ann Louise after she had been to Memphis and seen *The Wizard of Oz* at Loew's State; but she had to concede that, for a small town, it was pretty good. And she didn't think you had to low-rate romance just because it might be home grown. Anytime you said "once upon a time" or even "let's play like," Ann Louise was ready to roll; and she didn't much care how it was done or what it led to. So she more or less had to go along with the operetta and Little Eva and Miss Berniece, to say nothing of all the other children-performers. Isabel Edwards wasn't Judy Garland, and Janelle Holmes wasn't Ginger Rogers. And Ann Louise had sense enough to know she herself wasn't any Shirley Temple either. But you couldn't finally vote against romance.

The only thing was—just what did you mean by romance? Was it all just a pack of lies that, for the moment, turned everything into Technicolor you knew couldn't last and then always let you down with a thud; or did the lies or the magic or whatever you wanted to call it spill back over into real life and change the way you looked at everything the rest of your days? What did it really mean, anyhow, to live happily ever after? Ann Louise well remembered that *The Wizard of Oz* had begun and ended in black and white (or was it what they called sepia?); and the Technicolor was only for Oz itself. But nothing would ever be the same for Dorothy after she came back home to Kansas. And Ann Louise thought that might be important. All these questions were more or less bubbling around in her mind now as the rehearsals went on, but there was nobody to talk to about them. Certainly not her mother or, God help her, Little Eva. Even Martha Alice, though she would doubtless be sympathetic, probably wouldn't understand.

So the big night finally came—late June and hot as all get-out. And there the children all were, back behind the stage, practically sealed into their costumes and sweating away for dear life. Of course, they were already beginning to be uncomfortable if they had forgotten what Mrs.

White had told them about *avoiding liquids*. Isabel and Janelle were humming away over their solos, afraid they might forget; and Bobby Jack Morton was swaggering around in his wild array as the Weed King and flirting with all the older girls. Somewhere along the line, the plot was going to call for his submission to the Flower Queen and asking her forgiveness for trying to carry her off and vowing to be her servant from then on, forever and ever, amen: weeds must always give way to flowers was the idea. And that always upset Ann Louise, who had been on his side all along and didn't see how anybody in this world could agree to take a backseat to Janelle Holmes in anything going. Ann Louise thought Janelle had the ugliest legs she had ever seen, and anyway she didn't think Bobby Jack Morton ought ever to be tamed by anybody, and any sensible girl ought to know better than even to try. That's what Olivia DeHavilland would have done, she knew. Now even the elves and fairies were running through their numbers, rehearsing their dance steps and choruses. And Johnny White, Little Eva's son, was bragging that since his mamma was putting it all on, he was getting to lead the elf procession onstage while Miss Berniece thumped out "March of the Wee Folk" on the old upright. He said he was the *lead elf*.

But there was only one thing, really, that was worrying Ann Louise. And that was the duet she and Martha Alice had to sing just before the big number at the very end—what Mrs. White called the *grand finale*. It was all about love and forgiveness and all the flowers and fairies and tiny creatures great and small and everything else in their little nests agreeing. Every time she sang it, it made Ann Louise want to throw up. There wasn't a word about marigolds, which smelled bad, or wild flowers that were beautiful, or even poisonous spiders and snakes or anything else of the sort. And, of course, no mention of weeds at all. It was all just too deodorized for her—like Walt Disney's animals: Ann Louise was sure they were all house-broken. Certainly, there wasn't anything on hand to compare with Margaret Hamilton as the Wicked Witch of the West, to scare the pants off you, and nothing to tie all the romance in with where you were right then, whether out on the plains of Kansas or down in Woodville, Tennessee. It was all, finally, a cheat. You could go only just so far to Never Never Land; Ann Louise had sense enough to know that. She hadn't seen that many picture shows.

And so that idiotic duet she and Martha Alice shared always gave her the willies. And she was torn between bursting into laughter or else putting "something real ugly" into the lyrics—she wasn't sure just what but some word or words she would have gotten her mouth washed out with soap for using at home. Of course, she had told Martha Alice all about it, and that had set her off as well. When they got like that, they were a dangerous combination—like the time at the Baptist revival (under a tent, down on the square) when Ann Louise had egged Martha Alice on to go up and "rededicate her heart to God" when the evangelist asked for mourners to come forward at the end of the sermon. The next day Martha Alice woke up to find that, without knowing it, she had joined the Baptist Church thereby; and her mother had to call up the Baptist preacher and tell him everybody in town knew that they had always been Methodists and Martha Alice really didn't mean it. Another time Martha Alice had sent mean old Mrs. Kimball, their third-grade teacher, a very rude comic valentine and signed Ann Louise's name to it. Their parents were always threatening to keep them from playing together if they didn't quit misbehaving like that.

Now Ann Louise had been studying up ever since the rehearsals for the operetta began on what all she and Martha Alice could do to show how they felt about the whole thing that wouldn't get them into terrible hot water at home. It had to be something *ambiguous,* she decided—a word she was just beginning to learn, something that could be taken in more than one way, that would leave people just *wondering,* though it would probably give them all a sneaking idea of the way she and Martha Alice felt. But right off, neither she nor Martha Alice could think of anything it might be. They couldn't very well belch in the middle of their number; everybody would think it was just an accident and nobody would really know what they were doing. And other, even ruder noises were out for that, if for no other, reason. And if they forgot their lines, who would know what it all meant anyhow? But then what about this? Instead of singing something about welcome sweet spring-time, hurrah for the stolen flower queen stolen no more, why not do a quick-change act, a substitution or something—pretend they'd forgotten their words and were singing something else in desperation? And then it could be something like "A sunbeam, a sunbeam, Jesus wants me for a sunbeam." And everybody would have to say it was sweet whether they wanted to or not. But that wouldn't show what they really *thought* about it all.

That was as far as they had gotten in their scheming right up until the moment before they went on—right before the grand finale. And then, almost in the twinkling of an eye, almost like a revelation, it came to Ann Louise what they had to sing, what would be absolutely perfect for the time and the place and the way she felt: "Ding! Dong! The witch is dead!" And that was just what they did now—over Miss Berniece's confused fingering at the piano, even ignoring Little Eva's frantic gestures from the wings. (Once, during rehearsals, Mrs. White and Miss Berniece had been almost vying with each other to see who could get the most up in the air over the confusing stage directions for one number. And Miss Berniece, jumping all over the piano bench with nervousness, whispered, loud and clear, "Mrs. White, Mrs. White, where do you want the little fairies to go?" But Mrs. White rose to the occasion with all deliberate speed and, in her most carrying elocution voice, replied serenely, "I don't want them to go anywhere." And of course Ann Louise and Martha Alice had had the giggles. Nevertheless, it had seemed to settle that. It was all because Mrs. White was a *professional,* Ann Louise's mother said, and not just a pretty girl who played for church.)

But in due course now Miss Berniece improvised until she could come right in on the "witch" as though that was what had been intended all along, with Ann Louise and Martha Alice looking their most innocent and imperturbable. Out in the auditorium one or two college students home for the summer, who had been forced to come catch their little brothers' and sisters' acts, started to snicker but quit when they realized they weren't getting any support. And Ann Louise could see her mother, right there in the front row, looking extremely uncomfortable at first, then gazing about her with a satisfied air, as though she had known all along about this pleasant surprise. (Her father, of course, didn't change his expression one way or the other. He looked just as he had all evening—as if he wished he was anywhere else in the world but where he was.) How Little Eva and Miss Berniece were taking it she didn't really know or care. But at least now, she thought, she had been *dramatic,* she had *performed.* She figured it would be some time before they heard anymore about stolen flower queens and such like around town. And that really cheered her up. Maybe it would even put the quietus on the very idea of an operetta for a while, though she feared that might be too much to hope for. Whatever the case, Ann Louise knew that she herself would probably always be on the side of the weeds.

The Veteran

———— • ● • ————

Miss Fanny Hamilton was an old lady who lived down the street from
Ann Louise Parker back when she was growing up in Woodville during
the 1940s. And Ann Louise thought she must be at least a thousand
years old because there was very little in this world that she seemed to
have missed out on. Indeed, in some ways she seemed History person-
ified. Her father had been an officer in the Confederate cavalry under
General Forrest and had taken part in the famous lightning raid on
Memphis, when the general rode his men right up into the lobby of the
Gayoso hotel, the same place where, many years later, Ann Louise's own
parents spent their honeymoon. For all Ann Louise *knew* (she was born
within the year after her parents were married and had counted the
months on her fingers), she might even have been conceived right there;
in fact, she rather hoped so. After all, it was General Forrest who said
to "git thar fustest with the mostest"; and that had always seemed to
her like a sensible, no-nonsense rule to conduct your life by. Of course,
the general had been a slavetrader before the war. And maybe he had
been the imperial wizard of the Ku Klux Klan afterwards too. (Nobody
had ever proved it one way or the other.) But the main thing was, he
didn't just fool around but went on and did something. And that was
what Ann Louise always admired. She even liked it when the Bible said,
"Let your word be yea, yea or nay, nay."

Her father's father, whom she could remember very well, had
been a Confederate veteran (the last one in the county), with a big wal-
rus mustache and a peremptory manner, a Virginian who had come out
to Tennessee after the war. And *he* had been at Appomattox and seen
General Lee riding on Traveler. Not even Miss Fanny could top that.
But Ann Louise's grandfather ate peas with his knife and hadn't been
overly fond of bathing, and she wondered whether all that went with
age or was it maybe the Confederacy? Did real history *smell?* The only

history Miss Fanny cared to talk about was thoroughly deodorized—all
full of Jeb Stuart's plumes and the purity of Southern womanhood and
such like. ("I remember quite well the first time I ever saw a woman
riding astride, and I thought it perfectly scandalous too!")

Anyhow, when Ann Louise would drop by to see her—in the
winter sitting in the back bedroom with a fire going in the grate and
all the ancestral portraits looking down from the walls or else out on
the front porch sheltered by the big wisteria vine in the summer—it
took very little to get Miss Fanny started on the old tales and the old
times. And Ann Louise would be partly fascinated and partly put off
because of the stranglehold Miss Fanny seemed to have on history and
modern times too. There never, of course, had been a father like her
own—handsome, brave, and true. Also, there never had been any cause
like the Confederacy and nothing had ever been "normal" since it failed.
Ann Louise would get right tired of all this from time to time, for all
that she found the old lady, who must have been in her nineties, mostly
fascinating. Ann Louise privately thought she herself would have dearly
loved sitting on the front porch (or was it the verandah or the piazza?)
in a hoopskirt while both the Tarleton twins flirted with her like they
did with Scarlett at the opening of *Gone With the Wind*. And as for slaves,
well, there were definitely times when Ann Louise just knew she was
born to be waited on. (Her mother had observed the same thing about
her, but not by way of a compliment.) On the other hand, all those ancestral portraits and that historical stuff could get you down. Can you
live up to us, can you be worthy of us? they all seemed to say. And between her schoolwork and her piano lessons (under the iron hand of Miss
Caroline Miller, who could have shown General Forrest a thing or two,
whether as a slavetrader or cavalry leader), Ann Louise just didn't believe she could take on anything else. Sometimes, after a session with
Miss Fanny, she would stomp back home and declare that she had had
enough history for a spell and it would do Miss Fanny a world of good
if she could just forget about the Confederacy for a while and go to the
picture show and see *real* romance, with Clark Gable or Errol Flynn or
Tyrone Power making passionate love to the most beautiful women in
the world. Honestly, she said, Miss Fanny seemed to think all you
needed to get through life was a Bible and a copy of *Gone With the Wind*.
And who did she think she was anyway—just a dried-up old woman
living in a tumbledown old house and poor as Job's turkey too? Why,
at her time of life, she was lucky, Ann Louise told her parents, to be

still stirring the waters around there; really, she ought to be sitting by the fire reading her Bible!

At this point Ann Louise's mother would always break in and say that that would do, it was what Miss Fanny *stood for* that mattered; but her father would usually mumble something to the effect that he didn't think much of all that broken-down aristocracy either. As far as he was concerned, it didn't even have nuisance value: it was just a decoration, and *that* had never put food on the table yet. But anyhow, what *did* Miss Fanny stand for, Ann Louise always wanted to know. Well, said her mother, the old days and ways, the old traditions, back when life was less hectic and hurried and people had time—took time—to be more gracious. (Yeah, back when they all had lots of Negroes to wait on them, Ann Louise always thought.) And, her mother went on, it mattered then *who* you were and *who* your folks had been and *what* they had done, what all was *behind* you, you might say. (Um-huh, Ann Louise said to herself, how much money they had had.) But she never bothered to argue with her mother about any of it: it would probably be just one more thing that there were two mutually exclusive views on—the grownup's and the child's. And anyway, she didn't really want to quit going to see Miss Fanny, who continued to entertain her as well as infuriate her from time to time. It was just like going to the picture show, only this all had really happened—or at least most of it had, Ann Louise thought. She was sure Miss Fanny wasn't beyond touching it up just a bit too, just to make the story better. She had already heard enough good tale-tellers to know that was part of the game.

The first thing, of course, was *Family*. And Ann Louise always thought in capitals whenever Miss Fanny used the word. Because that had obviously been the main thing in her life: "Papa" riding with General Forrest, and "Mamma" presiding over the old plantation home (burned, of course, by the Yankees), and all her brothers and sisters well married and intermarried and having children and grandchildren—yea, unto the third and fourth generations. Ann Louise had often wondered why Miss Fanny herself had never married. Because she was the youngest, were her parents reluctant to give her up? Was she herself reluctant to go? Had her suitors all been killed in the war? Or was it that there just wasn't anybody good enough for her? (Maybe there just wasn't *anybody*, period, Ann Louise sometimes thought. Had Miss Fanny always been an unsought maiden lady, an old maid?) But anyhow, there she still was, living on in the old house her parents had built when they moved into town from the country all those many years ago. And she was still her own mistress and running her own show, still paddling her own canoe. Whatever you felt about her, you had to hand it to her for that. She was bossing the job herself; there wasn't anybody telling *her* what to do.

Sometimes she had great-nieces and nephews staying with her that Ann Louise could play with; but mostly Ann Louise liked it best when they could visit alone. When she had first started going to see Miss Fanny, at about age five or six, she was halfway afraid of the old lady, whose high-handed ways were rather off-putting. But she suspected even then that though Miss Fanny might seem formidable, even intimidating to the outsider, nevertheless she might be lonely and glad to see some company. Her manner and her memory were sometimes almost too grand, however. Once she observed: "I had rather be dead than to live without servants. Why, Papa kept two Negroes doing nothing but just polishing silver the year round!" (But yeah, look at how many she had now, Ann Louise thought, only just old Mammy Sue, who had been born into slavery on the Hamilton place and practically grown up with Miss Fanny.) And where was all that silver anyway? Did the Yankees get it or did they have to sell it to pay off the mortgage and save the old homestead? The same was true of the furniture. Miss Fanny would observe that after the war times were so hard, nobody had anything left much except a lot of land and some nice furniture. Ann Louise would then quietly look around the house and wonder where all the Hamiltons' furniture had gone in that case: had they had to sell that off too? It was all very provoking, with Miss Fanny populating the bare rooms with all those vanished glories and faded splendors. To hear her tell it, even her hardships had been special: "People talk about this Depression, but they should have lived through Reconstruction!" Why didn't she live in the real world, Ann Louise thought, and face up to it that nobody much cared anymore who you were or what your folks had done or what they'd had—or lost?

But somehow Ann Louise couldn't quit going to see Miss Fanny, if for nothing else than her entertainment value, which, as Ann Louise grew older, she thought bordered more and more on the absurd, even the outrageous. And she began to savor, even treasure, what she called the *Miss Fanny-isms*—the views on modern men and manners as reflected in some of her memorable sayings. ("I never did understand why women were so anxious to vote: I never wanted to vote in my life. Anyway women are much smarter than men and always have known how to get what they want—vote or no vote. Sometimes I feel downright sorry for men.") For Miss Fanny, the world had mostly stopped in 1865 or else just lasted on in a sort of twilight until the World War, which, she always said, was the very last of the old order anywhere. (Yeah, Ann Louise thought, all those old kaisers and czars had lost their thrones and sometimes even their heads; in any case, they didn't have anybody to order around anymore. They didn't have anybody to wait on them.) And Miss Fanny said she had seen all these changes reflected on a small scale right there in Woodville too, which was certainly more "democratic" (and she pronounced the word as though it had the most sinister implications) than it used to be, with people "going places" and "doing things" they certainly couldn't have before. (Before what, Ann Louise always wondered—Appomattox or the Armistice or the W.P.A.?)

Of course, Ann Louise noted that Miss Fanny didn't quit going places herself just because the world had changed. She was right there every Sunday morning, in her spats and carrying her father's goldheaded umbrella, in her pew at the Methodist church. She once grandly observed to some younger person who had been off on a trip to New York and Boston and made bold to compliment the church music in those cities, "We have a good choir too." Because, for good or for ill, Miss Fanny never went back on her own. Of course, the U.D.C. couldn't have functioned without her, since she was one of the last of the "real daughters." Even her house, which had obviously seen better days, she and Mammy Sue kept swept and garnished as for a royal visit; and it was painted afresh every couple of years— "the whitest white house in town," as she remarked to an old acquaintance. And there she would sit entertaining Ann Louise with tales of the days before, asking questions about Ann Louise's own world as though it were another planet and not yielding a jot or a tittle to the world around her, scarcely even for the claims of humanity itself. Ann Louise had suspected for some time that Miss Fanny wasn't about to subscribe to the notion that all men were *brothers*. She did, however, always contribute to the Red Cross, she told Ann Louise, because that was the closest thing we had to the Savior's own ministry and, after all, the whole thing had been founded right here by Miss Clara Barton during "*the* war." And of course Ann Louise had long since learned which one that was; there was no mistaking that.

And that was the way it stayed, all the time Ann Louise was passing out of childhood into her teens, even approaching what Miss Fanny called young ladyhood. Sometimes she would forget about Miss Fanny for weeks at the time, she had so many new things to think of, at school and in the world. Why should she bother with that tiresome old woman who mostly just lived in the past and hadn't really approved of anybody since 1865? (Ironically, Miss Fanny herself couldn't have been much more than a teenager then, Ann Louise reflected. How could she possibly have known what she really thought about anything?) A lot of younger people in town had never even heard of her; and if they had, they probably thought she was dead long ago. But then something would come over Ann Louise and she would recollect Miss Fanny, who, whether you liked it or not, had *lived* and could tell you about it too. That somehow ought to be worth something, Ann Louise thought, even if it mostly pointed the way to what not to do in the modern world. There Miss Fanny sat, usually dressed in black or gray, with a lace jabot and a cameo brooch at her throat and smelling of lavender sachet; and she wasn't about to get up and go anywhere else. She was just a fact, in Woodville and the world. And you couldn't ignore her.

But it was right then that the modern world began to close in with a vengeance on all of them. The Japanese bombed Pearl Harbor; and the country landed in the middle of a new war, which most people had seen coming for some time. ("We were going to have to get into it sooner or later. Now let's go on and get it over with.") Ann Louise wondered what Miss Fanny thought of all that. Would it be too remote from her own world; would she regard any new war as but an upstart affair after the real thing of 1861-1865? Would she even condescend to take notice of it? Ann Louise had her answer soon enough the next time she went to see Miss Fanny. (And Ann Louise had discovered by now that, for some reason, she couldn't leave Miss Fanny alone.) No sooner had she entered the house and taken a seat than Miss Fanny exploded. And as she talked, her fury grew. "So now we've got another war on, but that's nothing new. All wars are really the same, you know. It's just one set of folks trying to take other folks' homes and their goods and chattels—their whole way of life—away from them. And folks are always right to defend that. Indeed, what else do any of us have to live and die for?" And Ann Louise didn't know what else to say but, "Yessum, I guess so."

Then the old lady went on, "It was so in 1861 and 1914, and it's the same today. And the Germans and the Japs are no better than the damned Yankees—*foreigners* all of them and always wanting to push other people around. Always have been that way too, all of them. And I hope they get roundly served for their trouble—and that I'm spared long enough to see it happen. I've already been spared to see—and live through—a great deal; and I can certainly manage this." And here she drew herself up as straight as if she'd just swallowed a ramrod and looked Ann Louise right in the eye and gave a grim chuckle and continued, "Indeed, I intend to *survive* it. And I'd like to send a message to that effect to those rascals across the ocean and let them know here's one old woman they can't push around." And then she stopped to catch her breath and think for a minute but continued more calmly, "I've lived a pretty quiet life lately, maybe thinking too much about my age and my various aches and pains, hardly getting out of the house, really, except to go to church. But the time has come for me to think of higher claims, considering who I am and the way I was raised. Now what sort of war work do you think I'm best suited for?"

Ann Louise's head was reeling by now, and she couldn't have spoken to save her life. But Miss Fanny continued, "I don't quite see myself, at my age, wearing trousers and working in what they call a munitions factory; and I don't suppose I could be a 'hostess,' doing the jitterbug at one of those Stage Door Canteens they keep talking about. But I'll bet I know what I *could* do. I could go talk to the wounded boys in the hospital and listen to them tell about their experiences and then tell them one or two of my own. And then I'd remind them that one set of villains is about the same as another, when it comes to things like this. I've survived mine; and, God willing, they can survive theirs. We're all *veterans* here, one way or another, you know." And then she paused and almost glared at Ann Louise, as though daring her to contradict her. "Now what do you think of that, young lady?"

But Ann Louise, who had almost stopped breathing by now, broke out in a big grin and said, "Miss Fanny, I think you're dead right." And with that she just jumped up and went over and hugged the old lady around the neck—and kissed her on the cheek too.

I Am Counting with You
All the Way

———————— • ● • ————————

"Now, remember, I am counting with you all the way!" That was what Miss Caroline Miller used to say to all her piano students just before she propelled them, already pop-eyed with terror, onto the stage at her annual recital. And that naturally scared some of them worse than ever, to think that Miss Caroline, who had for the past year practically supervised their every waking hour, would follow them in spirit right onto the stage, out there before all those people. That was almost too much.

Because Miss Caroline's recitals were like military campaigns, perhaps even battles; and you started getting ready for them weeks, almost months ahead of time. Of course, you had to get eight hours sleep a night. And you couldn't go to the picture show, and you couldn't drink coffee or tea; indeed, you couldn't even read "stimulating" literature. (Some people definitely reacted differently to this regimen. One older woman in town said she remembered perfectly well having had nervous prostration just from resting for one of Miss Caroline's recitals years ago.) Now Ann Louise Parker, who was twelve, had been reading *Gone With the Wind* on the side after getting all her homework done every night. But when she happened to mention it to Miss Caroline at the end of her lesson one day, Miss Caroline hit the ceiling and told her that was not the sort of book for a young girl to be reading, and there were a lot of things in it she simply wasn't "mature" enough to know about. Ann Louise didn't tell her, of course, but she already knew where babies came from, so that was no big deal when Scarlett had to deliver Melanie's baby. And as for that night of passionate love between Scarlett and Rhett (after he had carried her up the stairs), well, Ann Louise had already seen enough picture shows to know what that was all about. She thought it was all rather dull too. The best part was all the things about battles and soldiers and the damned Yankees, which was what her father always called them; but she knew Miss Caroline would object to such name-calling. Because Ann Louise could remember her grandfather (her father's father), the Confederate veteran. And she liked to think he could have given those blue-bellied Yankees (she had heard somebody else call them that, and *belly* was a bad word too) a run for their money.

That was the story of her life, Ann Louise had once decided—having to take things off people, whether it was at home or at school. And as if that weren't enough, she now had Miss Caroline too. Everybody—at least all the girls—in town had to take music lessons from her sooner or later even if they weren't talented because, their mammas all said, it would all give them an *appreciation* of music, just like dancing lessons were supposed to make you *graceful* even if you weren't any good. But fortunately, Ann Louise had escaped *that* because the old Jeff Davis Hotel, where Miss Leila Maud Fields, the dancing teacher, gave lessons in what she called the ballroom (Ann Louise's mother said it was really a "sample" room for traveling salesmen to show their wares in) had burned down about that time. And that suited her just fine because she thought if there was anything in this world that looked silly, not to mention tacky, it was a teenage girl in real short shorts—with skinned knees from falling off her bicycle—trying to tap dance. Waltzing or the fox-trot (maybe if you were Ginger Rogers in the arms of Fred Astaire) might be OK for a while, but tap dancing was something she just wasn't prepared to think about, not even if you were Eleanor Powell or Ann Miller. (Every now and then some movie magazine would tell you that one of them could do 100 taps a minute—or however many it was. So what, thought Ann Louise: what did that prove? It all sounded to her like a steam drill.)

Of course Miss Caroline's piano recitals were *productions,* and you wore a costume too, so to speak—the frilliest organdy or chiffon dress your mother could get you into. And it was usually made by Miss Rose Tatum, who was so gifted that all the high school girls, getting dresses for the beauty revue or the senior prom, would just gesture and say, "Miss Rose, I just want a real full skirt and then a little thing here and one here"; and it would come out looking just like that—perfectly beautiful and light and airy, like whipped cream or even a cloud. And everybody said Miss Rose had a natural talent, just like playing by ear. So the recital dresses all looked light and summery (it was always late May) and of course ladylike because that was Miss Caroline's big thing—to turn her students (they were all girls) into ladies. On the whole, that was the farthest thing in the world from Ann Louise's mind right then: she had much rather have been Scarlett shooting the Yankee on the staircase.

And so there had more or less been a running battle all along between Ann Louise and Miss Caroline. Yet Miss Caroline held all the cards; Ann Louise knew that—even when she told her mother that Miss Caroline ought to shave; she had a thin little gray mustache on her upper lip. And Ann Louise's mother told her it wasn't ladylike to make such *personal* remarks, but Ann Louise could see that her mother was tickled but wouldn't admit it. And she knew, then, for the first time, something about the *double standard.*

So Tuesdays and Fridays, the days she took her music lesson, were always dangerous times because of what Miss Caroline might say or do and how she might react. One time, Ann Louise's best friend, Martha Alice Craig, who took her lesson right before hers, hadn't learned her new piece all from memory like she was supposed to; and Miss Caroline had really blessed her out, whereupon both Martha Alice and Ann Louise had then gotten scared and run home. But her mother hadn't done a thing in the world but make Ann Louise go right back up to Miss Caroline's and apologize to her. And then Miss Caroline had embraced her and Ann Louise had had to "hug her old neck and get scratched by her old mustache," as she put it later on.

Then on top of all that, there was Miss Caroline's music club, the Junior Beethoven Club, which they all had to belong to and go to once a month. And it was all nothing but another place for you to play your new piece at, only this time you had to play before all Miss Caroline's other students, some even in high school; and sometimes you had to "give an article" out of the *Junior Music Magazine* about the childhood of some great composer or the history of whatever was the Hymn of the Month. The pictures there all made you wonder about your future if you "went on with your music," like people always said you ought to do if you were talented. Because they were all either of foreigners with long beards (composers or performers, the magazine said) or else old women (music-club leaders) with the biggest bosoms and bottoms you ever saw in your life. And at the music-club meetings you had to be on your best behavior both during the "business session," which was always conducted by "parliamentary law," and also during the program and even in the social hour, when they served refreshments, which was the only part of the meeting Ann Louise could really enjoy. She was always scared to death if it was her turn to play or even "give an article" on the program, and the refreshments were something to look forward to. But even then Miss Caroline kept tabs on you—whether you ate too much when they passed the finger sandwiches and peanut butter cookies or made too much noise drinking your Coca-Cola. And God help you if you belched. The worst part was trying to balance the "tempting party plate," as it was always recorded in the minutes, complete with a cup of hot chocolate, on your lap, which Miss Caroline said all ladies had to learn to do. And Ann Louise wondered how on earth boys and men managed, with no skirts to make a real lap out of.

It was all a preparation for the recital, of course, the biggest event of the year for both Miss Caroline and her students. And she had them all "going into training," as Ann Louise's father always put it (after he had raised his left eyebrow), from about the first of March on. It was just like credit opening for the new cotton crop, her father said, only taking music from Miss Caroline was much more hazardous. (Ann Louise's mother always pursed her lips and frowned at him then, but she never *said* anything.) And it was from then on that you couldn't do all those things that might undermine your health or unsettle your nerves. Ann Louise used to wonder whether Miss Caroline had any time left over from bossing her piano students for anything else, and sometimes she supposed not. She had been married to a man Ann Louise always privately thought of as "Mr. Caroline" Miller, but he had been dead for years. Miss Caroline's only child, a daughter named Melissa May, was married and lived in Memphis, but she never came home, and somebody said she never even went near the piano anymore. So the field was more or less left clear for Miss Caroline and her students; and Ann Louise's father had in fact once said (and he didn't even raise his left eyebrow that time) that Miss Caroline could easily have been the kaiser of Germany and he just wished to God they had her up there in Washington.

One part of the recital that Ann Louise always hated, almost as much as playing her piece, was the "program note" she had to recite to the audience (hands clasped together in front of her just like she was going to sing) before sitting down at the piano. And it always began with "I shall play *Such-and-such* by *So-and-so*," almost like a proclamation or even a threat. And then you went on, in great detail, to describe what everybody would hear in the piece: "the tiny feet of deer splashing in a mountain stream" or "fairies gliding through the forest glade," and once, from one of the high school girls, "Slavonic fire and passion." Ann Louise would have given anything in the world to play a piece like that; but when she asked Miss Caroline why not, Miss Caroline just looked very wise and said she was much too young now and would understand when she got older. Anyway, here she had this lovely piece called "Scarf Dance" and maybe next year she would be up to "Rustle of Spring." What more could any little girl want?

So here she was now, twelve years old, and stuck with that eternal "Scarf Dance," which was written by a Frenchwoman named Cecile Chaminade, which sounded like the name of a fancy dessert. And Ann Louise thought, yes, that was just about her style. But at any rate, she had been spared another minuet, like the one she had played the year before. So maybe now she could just really imagine herself twirling in the arms of Fred Astaire, though for some reason she suspected that a scarf dance was more of a solo performance. She also remembered once having seen Groucho Marx do some sort of dance with a scarf when he was alternately courting and insulting Margaret Dumont. And that also cheered her up, but she thought she had better not mention it to Miss Caroline.

So there they were now—all Miss Caroline's students, the ten girls she always "took" and no more because, she said, she wanted to give them her undivided attention. And there they sat behind the stage in the high school auditorium, their feet up on chairs in front of them so as to relax and, incidentally, keep the long skirts of their evening dresses from getting soiled or torn. Each one sat there, feet up, hands in lap, eyes straight ahead, thinking of her piece, all of them, despite the resting and the dieting, scared to death but nevertheless strangely calm. Ann Louise was as bad as all the rest, all the way from the smallest first-grader, who would play "Magic Music," up to old "Slavonic fire and passion" herself. And Ann Louise couldn't remember a single bar of that damned "Scarf Dance." Once she even tried playing the opening line on her lap; but Miss Caroline (herself all decked out in her ironclad corset and that everlasting black lace "dinner gown" she wore every year) spotted that and shook her head and whispered sternly, "You don't have a thing to worry about: you know your piece, and I know you're ready to perform. I wouldn't let you if you weren't." And she wondered how Miss Caroline could be so sure. Why, Ann Louise might just have the hysterics like Ida Lupino in *The Light That Failed,* or she might go blind at any minute like Bette Davis in *Dark Victory.* How did Miss Caroline *know* she wouldn't?

And then there was only one piece (Martha Alice playing Paderewski's "Minuet in G") left before Ann Louise had to go and duel with "Scarf Dance": out there mostly before parents and friends, who *had* to come, and the stage all made up (by the mammas) to look like an elegant drawing room, with presents and gift baskets of flowers banked at either end of the footlights, and the baby grand piano the P.T.A. had given the high school specially tuned for the occasion. And it was all as artificial as a wedding or a funeral, Ann Louise thought, with the congregation saying, right on cue, that the bride was beautiful or the corpse looked natural. For two cents, Ann Louise would have jumped up and run out the back door. But Martha Alice was into the home stretch, the last repeat of the Paderewski piece now; and Ann Louise made up her mind to die with her boots on, like Errol Flynn as General Custer. And she thought about Rhett Butler saying, "Frankly, my dear, I don't give a damn." That was the way she would act now and *to Hell with it!* And tomorrow *was* another day. So here now came Martha Alice, still alive and blooming with relief, and the dutiful applause still sounding out front. And Ann Louise stood up and went over to the wings, where Miss Caroline was waiting for her. (Miss Caroline hardly ever sat down during the performance; she was roaming all over the backstage area, checking on the girls, keeping her eye out for any signs of fainting or failing, which certainly would not be allowed.)

Miss Caroline came and stood right behind Ann Louise and put her hands on her shoulders and said, "You've worked hard, and you know your piece, and you have nothing to fear. And remember, I am counting with you all the way." And with a little shove, she pushed Ann Louise out on stage. There was the piano, and there was the audience. And yes, there was Miss Caroline behind the stage. No surprises. She launched into her "I shall play . . ." speech without a bobble. And then she spread her long skirt, as Miss Caroline had taught her, and sat down before the keyboard. Yes, she had done it all before, and she was perfectly calm now. She knew Miss Caroline was behind the stage, counting with her all the way; and they were held together by something that went beyond either one of them alone, beyond the audience, even beyond the recital itself. And Ann Louise realized now that it was this really that she had been preparing for all year long— just as surely as "Scarf Dance" was fixed forever in her memory and now, at her command, came cascading out of the baby grand, into the darkened auditorium, full of life, full of joy, and right on cue.

Remember the Errol-mo!

————————— • ● • —————————

"Remember the Errol-mo!" That was what Ann Louise Parker and her best friend, Martha Alice Craig, kept shouting at each other all that summer after they were in the seventh grade. Then they would explode into laughter because it was a private joke between them and all had to do with sex and where babies came from and everything else connected with "all that," as they called it. You could hardly get away from it anywhere right then either because that was the year when there was a rash of paternity suits brought against movie stars like Charlie Chaplin and Errol Flynn, and the Memphis papers didn't leave very much of it to anybody's imagination. There was even a breach-of-promise suit right there in Woodville, brought by a woman, who said she was a nurse, against one of the local doctors; and it received generous press coverage too. The woman even testified that she had gone off to a medical meeting in Chicago with the doctor and, on the train coming back, left the day coach, where she had been riding, and moved back into the Pullman with him *because she thought she deserved it.* And so that became another rallying cry between Ann Louise and Martha Alice: "Out of the day coach and into the Pullman!"

Anyhow, Ann Louise's mother said she didn't know what the world was coming to and it was a good thing her own mother wasn't still alive. What would she have thought if, right there staring her in the face at the breakfast table, was a front-page story in the *Commercial Appeal* detailing the number of times and the places, even, where and when all the "intimacies" had gone on? She said she was surprised they didn't have *pictures!* And why didn't they publish more "elevating" items anyway? Everybody knew things like that went on in the world, but why *dwell* on them?

But Ann Louise's father just told her not to be an ostrich and she might as well join the twentieth century, which was going on its merry way with or without her. There was no use worrying what her mother would have thought because she would have had to make the best of it all, just like everybody else. And it might all have done her a power of good, to open the doors and windows and let in a little air: he well remembered, he said, that she never even acknowledged the existence of sex, and babies were never spoken of till they were born. Naturally then it was all very "sweet." Women didn't have *legs* either: their shoes were just sewed to the bottom of their skirts! But then Ann Louise's mother said that was quite enough: he had made his views known. And besides, her mother had too admitted that there was such a thing as sex in the world: why, before she had married, her mother had told her, whatever she did, never to economize on her nightgowns. But then she remembered Ann Louise's presence and hushed.

It had all started that last year, back in the seventh grade, when their teacher was Miss Elizabeth Johnson, who was young and pretty and had lots of beaux. Ann Louise was still taking music lessons from Miss Caroline Miller, who was well past middle age and had a thin gray mustache; and that year her recital piece was "To a Water Lily." Anyhow, Miss Elizabeth was the first young teacher Ann Louise and her friends had ever had. Before that they were all old maids like Miss Clara Davis, who pulled her girdle down in a very businesslike way whenever she had anything important to say, or else old women like Miss Caroline, who had either outlived or otherwise disposed of their husbands and now had the decks cleared for action on their own terms. And they all of them *meant business* too; in fact, Ann Louise sometimes thought they ought to have "no foolishness" carved on their tombstones when they died—if they ever did.

Sometime after Christmas that year, back in January, when everything was dull and depressing and there wasn't much to think about except your first-semester grades, one of Miss Elizabeth's friends—a young woman only married the year before—came by the classroom one day to see her. And it was obvious that she was going to have a baby almost any minute: Ann Louise even thought she might not be able to get back home before the stork arrived. You could tell all that even underneath what Ann Louise had heard her mother call a "maternity dress." Not that she had ever opened her mouth to Ann Louise about any of "all that" except for the barest minimum of information about what she could expect when she "became a woman." What Ann Louise knew about "all that" she had picked up mostly from the movies and *Life* magazine and her friends, most of whom didn't know much more than she did. There *was* a column called "Tell me, Doctor" in the *Ladies' Home Journal* every month, which was all about women going to the doctor with the most hair-raising things in the world wrong with them; but Ann Louise was usually too scared to read it.

It was all of it a dark and mysterious subject to most of them: they hardly even mentioned it to each other, let alone any of the boys. It just sat there like an open secret that everybody skirted gingerly and everybody knew about and knew everybody else knew about too but didn't mention. Nobody could bring himself to let on to it in public. But Miss Elizabeth's friend broke the ice for them. Because when Miss Elizabeth stepped out into the hall to speak to her, the whole class went up in a great giggle; and nobody even had to explain why. There was all that rampant pregnancy, to say nothing of the antecedent sexuality, whose fruits were all too obvious. Not even an ostrich could have done much in the way of ignoring it. It was all simply right there in your face, as Ann Louise remarked to Martha Alice later on; it *was* a fact of life.

It was from then on that the whole crowd began to make references to sex, even sometimes tell a mildly dirty joke, which they didn't always understand, even the boys. And they all began to relax, as though to say, we don't really know what this is all about, but it's apparently part of the whole package deal and somehow has to be dealt with and dealt with now. (Ann Louise even heard her father tell her mother one night after she told them she had just been invited to her first dance that he *thought* it was about time for the sap to begin to rise. But she couldn't hear what her mother said to that, and she wasn't even sure she understood.) At any rate, some of the things that had always puzzled Ann Louise began to come into focus, like the plots of several novels and operas—even ones she had had to listen to on the radio on Saturday afternoons to report on at Miss Caroline Miller's music club, when she had much rather have been at the picture show watching Hopalong Cassidy or Johnny Mack Brown. But she still didn't see why there had to be such a hullabaloo raised about Little Emily and Hester Prynne and Marguerite. Okay, so you got caught with a baby: you should have been more careful. That was what Ann Louise thought. On the other hand, she couldn't see any particular charm in marriage: people just wanted to settle down and get turned into old, middle-aged people like her parents quicker than a wink. *She* wasn't going to have any of that: *she* was going to go to New York and get a job as private secretary to somebody like Cary Grant or Tyrone Power and have her own penthouse apartment like Betty Grable. *She* was going to have fun.

Her views on the matter had become solidified when World War II broke out and young men were going into the service all over the place and there was a whole slew of elopements and "secret" marriages, usually performed down in Mississippi or over in Arkansas because Tennessee had stricter marriage laws then. For one thing, you had to wait three days to hear from the "blood test," which always puzzled her. But when she asked her mother about that, she just said it was something Ann Louise, *with her background,* would never have to worry about, thank God, and that was all she needed to know right then. And the elopements and "secret" marriages, Ann Louise noticed, were almost always followed by a baby—and sometimes within a very few months. Of course, she had heard some of the older girls say the records down in Mississippi or over in Arkansas could sometimes be rearranged (for a consideration) to show that the marriage had taken place *a full nine months* before any baby appeared on the scene. And Ann Louise didn't doubt that either, from such a jumped-up, jackleg way of doing things. If you were just determined to get married, she thought, you ought to do it with banners and bugles—a big church ceremony and veils and trains and the whole shooting match. In other words, *drama.* Ann Louise was always great on drama.

That was part of the excitement of sex, she thought: it had ceremonies, as in mating dances and practices, and it had romance and glamor, at least in the movies and in novels. Of course, there was the other side—where people got caught off base and had babies they didn't mean to and where "ladies" got turned into "fallen women." And, of course, there was always white slavery right around the bend. Again, she had learned "all that" in her reading and at the picture show. (Her parents didn't seem to worry what she read or what she saw. And Ann Louise used to wonder at that—how trusting they were—when she got older. Then again, maybe it was part of the ostrich act: things were all right as long as you didn't acknowledge openly you knew what was going on.) And so it was all dramatic, whether glamorized or sordid. But there was another side to sex too, and that was what Ann Louise and her friends were only beginning to realize that summer after they had been in the seventh grade.

And Errol Flynn did it all. Ann Louise had always been wildly in love with him ever since she had seen him in the *The Sea Hawk,* which was always described as a *swashbuckling* adventure story. Ann Louise never knew what that meant except that when you ran around having sword fights and jumping off the decks of ships, all for the honor of Queen Elizabeth (who was played by Flora Robson), or else to win favor in the eyes of your lady love (Brenda Marshall, who was married to William Holden in private life), and all of it somehow mixed up with the wicked Spanish Inquisition and the Armada, *swashbuckling* just sounded right: a combination of sword play and gallantry whether on ship or on shore. It was unforgettable the time Errol Flynn played General Custer and *died with his boots on* (which was the name of the picture) and Olivia De Havilland, who played Mrs. Custer, slid to the floor in the most graceful faint Ann Louise had ever seen when she got the tragic news. But, of course, they didn't show you any *scalping:* it was all horses and bugles and dashing plumes.

So anyhow Errol Flynn was now being sued by some "starlet" or other for being the father of her unborn child, which she said she was determined to have and no bones about it. (No back-street "illegal operations" for *her,* she said. Ann Louise wasn't even sure what that meant, just like in *Blossoms in the Dust* when Greer Garson, who was a *moral crusader,* shouted down into the Texas legislature, from up in the gallery: "Bad girls don't *have* babies!" It was all very confusing.) Anyhow, Ann Louise didn't know just how the girl had any legal hold on Errol Flynn: after all, she had presumably known what sort of risk she was running when she had "granted him the last favor," like it said in some of the older novels. And the more fool she. So Ann Louise didn't see what she had to complain of, but then she had always heard that California was a peculiar state. And she didn't doubt they might even have a special department out there just to deal with the private lives of movie stars. Because the movie magazines were always telling you what the Hays Office or the Production Code wouldn't let you do in the movies, like have twin beds closer together than two feet or whatever and then, if a man and woman were on a bed together, they had to keep at least three feet on the floor! And she well remembered when David O. Selznick had had to get special permission just to let Clark Gable as Rhett tell Scarlett, "Frankly, my dear, I don't give a damn!"

So her attitude now toward Errol Flynn wasn't one of disillusion or disappointment, really: it sort of went with his daring roles on screen to be something of an adventurer elsewhere. Ann Louise really didn't care how much *notoriety* he got. But she didn't think much of the girl who was trying to get all his money just because *she* hadn't had the guts—or the sense—to say no. And besides, from all the testimony, which she couldn't wait to read in the paper every day, Ann Louise didn't see how anybody could know who the baby's father really was. Just like in the novels, the "starlet" had apparently "distributed her favors freely."

And so when the court returned a verdict of "not guilty," Ann Louise was tickled to death because it now meant that Errol Flynn could keep on swashbuckling and romance wasn't dead either. (Apparently his name was almost a byword for that in Hollywood. Some comedian even made a joke over the radio once about a great lover who was so quick on the trigger he was "in like Flynn"; and he got cut off the air too! Or that's what Martha Alice told her.) Anyhow, Ann Louise was delighted Errol Flynn didn't have to go to jail or even pay a lot of money in damages; and she couldn't wait now for him to make a movie with Bette Davis (another Warner Brothers star, so there wouldn't be any problem about "loan-outs") that was wild and passionate and naturally fatal. And then they could both just act all over the screen. Of course, Bette Davis played mainly two roles: she was either doomed or damned, sometimes both. And in her secret heart, that's what Ann Louise really wanted to be, even more than being Betty Grable with her own penthouse apartment. But anyhow, she thought Bette Davis would really be worthy of him—that is, of course, if she couldn't be there herself.

So it was all a great victory for romance—*and* sex—as far as Ann Louise was concerned. And somehow it was all a great victory for *fun* too—maybe even something that went beyond fun. From the way he acted both in the courtroom and outside, you could tell Errol Flynn didn't make any big deal about sex: it wasn't dirty and it was all perfectly natural. And it could be very enjoyable too, but you shouldn't kid yourself about it either. It was all something like the frame of mind she thought Rhett Butler must have been in when he refused to marry the girl he was supposed to have compromised: he said they hadn't "done" anything and the girl was a fool. That was the first thing Scarlett ever heard about him, Ann Louise remembered; and he had gone up in her estimation right then. Surely there was no need for that "starlet" to get up on a high horse now about it all: she had known what she was getting into. When she said as much to Martha Alice, Martha Alice said maybe she ought to be more sympathetic to the woman: wasn't that what the *double standard* was all about? But Ann Louise said she had heard one of her mother's old-maid cousins say time and time again that, where men were concerned, women were such fools.

So long live Errol Flynn, as far as Ann Louise was concerned. That was when she and Martha Alice went on to invent their new slogan: "Remember the Errol-mo!" This, of course, was based on what they had read in school about Davy Crockett and the Alamo. It wasn't the same thing, but somehow Ann Louise felt like Davy Crockett wouldn't have taken anything off a "starlet" any more than he did the Mexicans, and he had died with his boots on too. She thought it would be a very fine thing if there were more men around like him. She already felt that way about Errol Flynn.

Football Queen

Ann Louise Parker, who was fifteen and a sophomore in high school, would have given anything in the world to be elected Football Queen. But in order to do that you had to collect the most money of all the candidates—a penny a vote. And the money all went for a good cause—to buy new equipment for the team, which they never would have gotten otherwise, there was so little money for athletics in the official budget then. Anyhow, that was certainly all right with her: what she mainly wanted was simply to be crowned at halftime during the annual Thanksgiving Day game with Woodville's arch-rival, Jimson, which had the only other high school in the county, and then have the privilege of sitting on the bench with the team all during the next season. There was only one drawback. The Woodville and Jimson Queens always had to exchange bouquets halfway across the field on the fifty-yard line as part of the halftime ceremony, and Ann Louise would have to give up her purple and white chrysanthemums (the Woodville colors) for the tacky old ordinary yellow of Jimson's. But she reckoned she could rise to the occasion if she had to.

Anyhow, this was all better, to her way of thinking, than being chosen Miss Woodville in the annual beauty revue and getting to represent the town at the annual Strawberry Festival over in Crockett City. All you got out of that was mostly your picture in the Memphis *Commercial Appeal* and a chance to ride a float in a number of parades. And none of that could compare with sitting on the bench with the football team. Besides, Ann Louise could always face facts: she knew her looks were not her strong point (her nose was no good, for one thing) and she was never going to be a beauty queen. If she was anything at all, she had always told herself, she was a realist.

She never was really sure just how she had gotten into the race for Football Queen anyhow. Each of the four high-school classes had to choose a candidate, and somehow she had gotten elected for the sophomores. She was already a cheerleader, and maybe that had put ideas in somebody's head—that she could advance to the greater dignity of Football Queen. Because everybody said she had great spirit and lots of pep, whatever that was. And yes, she did enjoy getting to wear the purple and white cheerleader's uniform—purple and white sweater and a purple skirt with a white underside that you could see when she did cartwheels. And God knows, you got to be as conspicuous as all get-out, which was what Ann Louise's mother said she was afraid she mainly wanted anyway.

In general, her mother took a dim view of all such affairs: they were all too "stimulating," she said, even "demoralizing," and took your mind off your studies. But then as long as Ann Louise could show her she had a very respectable report card, especially in English, Latin, and algebra—what her mother called the "fundamentals," her mother would pretty much go along with whatever she wanted to do in the extracurricular line. And Ann Louise thought perhaps that, all things considered, her mother might be getting more broad-minded as the years went along. (She could wear long hose on Sundays now and even a little lipstick to school—but not too much.) Then, too, now that Ann Louise had quit taking piano lessons (she had decided not to "go on with her music," as they said), she had more free time; and perhaps her mother thought it was just as well to have something else acceptable to fill it up with.

Anyhow, she had always suspected that her best friend, Martha Alice Craig, had somehow engineered her being chosen the sophomores' candidate for Football Queen (she wasn't sure just how) because then *she* could get to manage Ann Louise's campaign. And if there was anything in the world Martha Alice loved, Ann Louise knew quite well, it was getting to *manage* something—whether it was an election campaign or a Girl Scout drive to collect kitchen grease to help the war effort (World War II had just ended) or even to sew pink and blue flannel squares together to make blankets for the Red Cross to send the Londoners who had been bombed out of their homes during the Blitz.

Ann Louise had always wondered about all that—how all that left-over grease from bacon and chicken frying was going to avenge Pearl Harbor and what the English would think of those thin, flimsy blankets. And she sometimes had fantasies of greasing all the tiny little Japanese so they couldn't get into their suicide dive-bombers; and she would dream about the freezing London homeless huddled under the pink and blue blankets in the London underground, which was what they always called the subway on the radio and in the newsreels. But then you just never knew what might happen from even the smallest things, for good or for ill: there had been the little boy with his finger in the dike and the kingdom that was lost for the want of a nail. And whatever you were doing in the world, you had always better watch your step because, like they were always telling you back during the war, *careless talk costs lives.* So every little bit helped, as her mother had always said when she wanted Ann Louise to dry the dishes after supper and, as she always went on to add, every step Ann Louise took saved *her* just that much.

But however Martha Alice had managed it—or not managed it— Ann Louise *was* the sophomore candidate; and, on the whole, she didn't think much of the competition. The freshmen had chosen Sandra Sue Davis, a tiny little thing that everybody always called "adorable," though Ann Louise had never decided on what grounds other than the fact that she *was* small and had eyes that tended to violet and a little tee-wee voice that mewed like a kitten. And the juniors had picked Bonnie Jean Dougherty, who had the ugliest legs Ann Louise had ever seen, and you certainly got to see them often enough because she was a drum majorette with the band and the highest stepper Woodville had ever seen. The seniors, however, who never had been able to elect a Football Queen (after all, when would she reign, she'd be gone the next year?), put their shoulders to the wheel and got behind Juanita Stanley; and Ann Louise had sense enough to know that here finally was some real competition. Because Juanita was really pretty, with naturally curly hair; also, she had dimples and a great smile and used them both quite often. People *liked* Juanita too, even if she had been going steady with the man who drove the Wonder Bread truck and was going to marry him as soon as she graduated. But then Ann Louise never had seen any future in that: why would anybody want to get married and settle down and turn into an old woman any sooner than she had to? So what if you couldn't afford to go off to college? You could always go to Memphis and get a job and maybe even have your own apartment. And the possibilities that might come out of that were practically limitless, Ann Louise thought.

But then why would anybody want to go steady anyway? In 1945, the more boys you could keep dangling at one time, the higher your stock rose. Ann Louise would never forget that only last Easter, Marcelene Vaden—who everybody always said was faster than greased lightning, but you never could prove it—had gotten six corsages from six different boys and somehow managed to wear them all in the course of the day: one for Sunday school, another for church, and so on throughout the day, ending up with the Training Union and evening service that night. But her mother told somebody later she couldn't have made it without the kindness of her neighbors: she sent her rolls and dessert for dinner over to the Wheelers next door, to keep in their refrigerator because there was nothing but all those corsages in their own.

Ann Louise wasn't sure she wanted to be all that spectacular herself; but then she had always had a hankering to be like Scarlett O'Hara and have the smallest waist in five counties—seventeen inches—and be *courted* and *sought after*. If truth were told, she supposed she really would like to have lived back in those days—at least for a little while—and been a *belle* and have lots of *beaux*. But then she knew she would have gotten tired of all those hoopskirts. And maybe she was more cut out for the Reconstruction period anyway: she knew it never was going to be her fate in life just to sit around and look pretty, but she had gumption and believed she could have run a sawmill right well, like Scarlett after the war. Whatever the case, Juanita and her Wonder Bread man were the farthest things in the world from her mind: *she* was going to *go places and do things and have fun*. And only last year, when she was a freshman, she had been voted into the Subdebs and got to go to their Christmas formal with Billy Higgins from down the street, who was already a junior; and she had dated him and a couple of other boys on the weekends since then, even gone to a dance over in Crockett City, which was twenty miles away, as a guest of her cousin, Paul Andrews. She didn't think there was any limit to what she might do before long— maybe even the Cotton Carnival in Memphis!

Being Football Queen would certainly be a step up—there was no doubt about that—and it wasn't something that was too narrow or limited either. If you were a beauty queen (which, let's face it, she hadn't been born for), well, there really wasn't much you could do—just ride floats and smile and wave at people, maybe for the rest of your life. Because Ann Louise had already noticed that being a beauty queen seemed to do something to people: older girls and women who had been one always seemed to be posing for the camera or else expecting to be photographed everywhere they went. But it was really all downhill from then on. After all, what could they do for an encore? But then, on the other hand, you could be real studious and make the highest grades in your class and win a scholarship to college and go on and be a Phi Beta Kappa (like Mrs. Coleman, their algebra teacher, who wore her hair like Popeye's girlfriend, Olive Oyl). But then that all seemed to put a crimp in your social life, and you ended up wearing glasses before your time and not having many friends or dating much because everybody thought you were a brain. Football Queen seemed like a sensible middle course then: it showed you were *popular* (a word that Ann Louise had come to respect a great deal) but had your feet on the ground. And your head wasn't too much up in the air either. And you had plenty of sense and weren't just boy crazy, with nothing else on your mind. For that matter, Ann Louise had always made the honor roll; and, on the whole, she thought her mother had probably always been right about *putting first things first.* But then, of course, you didn't want to overdo it either: you might end up looking like Mrs. Coleman.

So anyhow, they had three weeks to mount and carry out their campaign, as Martha Alice put it; and she told Ann Louise she was determined to do something different, something that would attract attention, and not just go around with a tin can soliciting money—and votes—like it was just one more fund-raising thing for the war effort. Everybody was sick of that, and you could really get them to sit up and take notice only if you came up with something new and different; you had to do some *merchandising.* And so what she hit on was the *Sophomore Scandals,* to take place the last week of the campaign on one morning during the activity period in the school auditorium.

Everybody else had been doing what seemed rather piddling things: the freshmen, with little tiny Sandra Sue as their mascot, held a bake sale, which Ann Louise thought might just as well have been a return to the days of Girl Scout cookies. The juniors—with Bonnie Jean leading the way, of course—staged a band concert, though there was nowhere for Bonnie Jean to strut her stuff as a majorette. But she did get to sing (not her strongest point, Ann Louise thought) what turned out to be a medley of war songs, all dressed up in an Uncle Sam costume but without the beard. By then everybody was sick to death of the war, and that was the last sort of thing they wanted to hear. "Remember Pearl Harbor" and "The White Cliffs of Dover" were already back numbers. The seniors really didn't do anything much, just had lots of posters put up all over the place, with Juanita's picture on them, looking sweet and pretty and saying, "Let's make it a first: elect a senior

Football Queen." But they really didn't say much about Juanita: her photograph and her name were just more or less left to speak for themselves, which all seemed pretty desperate to Ann Louise. Still, what *could* you say about somebody like Juanita? There wasn't anything about her that was dramatic or glamorous or even scandalous. She was just *nice,* and she was going to marry the Wonder Bread man, and there was no *news* about any of it.

Anyhow, Ann Louise knew that if you were going to get anywhere in this world, you had to *hustle* and get your product out before the public. And she thought that applied to Football Queens as well as soap powder or anything else. Certainly Martha Alice, whose father had the Ford agency, was of the same opinion. She told Ann Louise her father had been nearly crazy these last few years, during the war, with no new cars to sell: all he had to offer was service, which put food on the table all right but wasn't exactly the most exciting or interesting thing in the world. But now he would soon be having those big, beautiful machines in his showroom again, and there was already a long list of customers with cash money ready to buy the first cars that rolled off the assembly line. (Mr. Craig kept the list in his safe, and nobody ever quite knew what the order of the names was either. That was his trump card, Martha Alice explained.) And so Martha Alice thought up the idea of the *Sophomore Scandals,* which would be a sort of variety show or maybe like old-time vaudeville was supposed to be, with everybody in the class doing whatever act he would be best at, and the whole thing capped off with a striptease number performed by *masked dancers!*

Sometimes Ann Louise just had to wonder where Martha Alice got all her ideas. Even if her father was a car salesman (and if she'd heard right, could really sell you the Brooklyn Bridge or anything else he wanted to), that was pretty advanced for Woodville High School in 1945. But, of course, it wasn't as if they were really going to *do* anything. The strippers would just start out fully clothed—in their most fetching party dresses or formals but swapped around so people wouldn't know exactly who was who—and, after shedding whatever was in between, end up with bathing suits on. That seemed pretty tame. And all the while one of the other girls in the class would be playing slow, slinky music on the baby grand piano the P.T.A. had given the school some years before. Ann Louise, who wasn't performing herself, could have done that part easily; but she thought that since she was the heroine or the honoree or whatever of the occasion, it would be more suitable if she stayed back behind the scenes and just mainly gave moral support. But she had something of a giggle when she stopped to think of what Miss Caroline Miller, her former music teacher, would have said if she ever heard of such a thing. Miss Caroline should have been a German general, Ann Louise had decided long ago, with maybe a dash of Emily Post thrown in. She had ruled the lives of her piano students— all of them girls whom she was determined to turn into *ladies,* if not pianists—down to the last participle. And what she would have thought of "her girls" (Martha Alice had taken lessons from her too) being involved in such an event just didn't bear close examination.

Ann Louise didn't say anything much about all this at home. In fact, she hadn't said much of anything about her campaign for Football Queen. She knew enough to know that her mother wouldn't be too keen on the idea, despite the fact that she always wanted Ann Louise to be "popular"; on the other hand, her mother didn't take much stock in the royalty or the beauty business either. She said she could think of a lot more things for Ann Louise to be in the world besides a beauty queen, which Ann Louise thought was just as well considering what *she* had to work with. Her father usually just kept all such woman-foolishness at arm's length and had as little to do with it as possible (as a rule, he disappeared behind his newspaper); the happiest day of his life, Ann Louise had decided, was when she stopped taking piano lessons and he knew he never would have to go to another one of Miss Caroline's recitals again. But in any case, she thought it would be just as well to keep them in the dark about the striptease.

So the day for the big performance came; and every sophomore that could sing or tap-dance or do a waltz (like one brother and sister duo) or recite (like some of the ones who took "expression") or just play the piano (but preferably nothing "classical") was right there, ready to give it his or her all. And Ann Louise was all over the place back behind the stage, giving aid and comfort to the ones who had suddenly come down with stage fright. Martha Alice, who had billed herself as "producer and director" in all the advertisements, was looking very important and commanding, as she ran around seeing that everybody was in the right place for every number. And then she gave the signal to start, and the curtain went up, and the show was on. It all went well too. Everybody in the audience (which was a large one) knew all the performers, of course, and urged them on, even shouting to them by name from time to time. It was all about as undignified and unlike one of

Miss Caroline's recitals as anything on earth could possibly be. But then Ann Louise decided that was all right too: this was certainly no time for Emily Post. In any case, it all now seemed to be going well; and though most of the performers were all the rankest of amateurs, there was nobody you really had to feel *sorry* for.

Eventually the grand finale—the masked striptease—was ready to begin; and Ann Louise suddenly wondered whether it was all going to go off all right. Had they gone too far for Woodville; were they too "advanced" and ahead of their time; what would everybody say? She really hadn't ever thought that far ahead before. Mainly, she had just thought the whole thing *sounded* deliciously wicked; but that was about all—nothing really *risqué,* of course, and mostly just the power of suggestion anyway. But now all of a sudden she began to wonder what the harvest would be. And pretty soon she wasn't in any doubt. The boys in the audience began to whistle and holler (things like "keep it clean"); then they stomped their feet and made some even ruder noises. But it wasn't like they were *offended,* more just like they were making fun of it all. Looking out from the wings, Ann Louise could see many of the girls in the audience beginning to leave: Sandra Sue and Bonnie Jean and their supporters, she noticed. But she didn't think for a minute they were *outraged;* they were just showing off. She noticed that Juanita had stayed put and wondered what the Wonder Bread man would think. Finally, after the girls had got down to their bathing suits, which after all was as far as they were going to *go,* there were very few people left in the auditorium but mostly just some rabble-rousing boys, none of whom Ann Louise would have dated on a bet. And here came the principal, Mr. Venable, to say to Ann Louise and Martha Alice that he thought the performance had gone on quite long enough and they could bring down the curtain now. (No other teachers were present, and Ann Louise was certainly glad of that.) Mr. Venable assured them that he would say no more about the matter, yet he looked amused. And Ann Louise wasn't sure but what he was trying not to laugh when he said he would always wonder just *who* the "masked ladies" were but wouldn't inquire further.

Well, it was just the worst time ever in her whole entire life, Ann Louise decided right then and there. And she would gladly have crawled off somewhere by herself and died or else thrown up or had the hysterics or *something;* but she was too well schooled in "appearing before the public," as Miss Caroline had called it in her recital days, to act like

that. That was one thing Ann Louise had learned from her for sure—
self-control and maybe something else Miss Caroline always vaguely referred to as "presence." And it really paid off now. She just told all the
performers she really loved what they had done for her and would always appreciate it, but this was the end of her election campaign and
now they would all just wait for the results, to come in two days' time.
She and Martha Alice didn't dare look at each other now; they might
have laughed or cried or done both. But what they wouldn't have done
was get mad at each other. They were much too close and had been
through far too many things together for that. She could imagine what
she might have to endure when she got home later on: her mother would
probably have a fit when she heard about it, but she didn't think her
father would much mind. After all, what she had done showed her *ini-
tiative* and her *resourcefulness;* and her father was always on the side of
things like that. (He wasn't a banker for nothing, Ann Louise had decided long ago.) And if she wasn't quite in harmony with the public
taste right then, well, she had shown that she had get-up-and-go and
maybe was ahead of her time.

It was nevertheless a very bad time for her right now, and so all
she could think of to do was go to the rest room: at least there she could
sit down in one of the stalls and be alone for a minute or two. She really
didn't *need* to go at all. But she went on anyway; and when she closed
the door, she saw some new writing on the back of it she hadn't seen
there before. It was all in big, bold, block letters too: LIFE IS A BITCH,
it said, AND THEN YOU DIE. And it sounded almost like an Old
Testament prophecy or else one of those roadside signs that urged you
to prepare to meet your God, just before you went round a hairpin curve
up in the Smoky Mountains. In any case, it looked—and sounded—as
if it had been put there by somebody who knew what he (or, in this
case, presumably she) was talking about and who *meant business.*

Ann Louise sat there for a good while thinking about it; and the
more she thought about it, the better she liked the idea. It was all perfectly true, too: that's just the way it was—life, the world, folks, whatever you wanted to call it. And whatever you did, it was going to be
too little or too late or too early or ahead of its time or out of its time
or something else. Who knew what the arrangements might be like on
the other side—or who was going to be there anyhow? So who finally
could give a damn anyway? And the more she thought about it, the
better she liked the idea of that sentence being chosen for the rest-room

door. What better or more suitable place could there have been for it? Maybe the anonymous author and/or perpetrator was the wisest of philosophers. At any rate, it pleased her right then to think so. And she began to laugh.

From that very moment her spirits slowly began to rise and continued steadily to do so, until two days later; and then they positively soared when the election results were announced and it was found that, for the first time in history, the seniors had elected a Football Queen. Now Juanita Stanley would get to be crowned at the Thanksgiving game; and the next year, if she chose and the Wonder Bread man didn't mind, she would get to sit on the bench with the team at all the games.

Fairy Tale

———————— • ● • ————————

Ann Louise Parker stood there, in the vestibule at the back of the Methodist church, waiting for the wedding march (or the "Bridal Chorus" from *Lohengrin,* as they called it) to begin. And she thought it was all just like one of Miss Caroline Miller's piano recitals back when she was growing up. Of course, this time she would have her father's arm to lean on, and he would be giving her what they always called moral support. But it was still the same sort of thing—a *production* that was done more for the benefit of the audience than for the participants themselves. As for herself, she never had thought she'd want a big wedding, parading around all over the church in a veil and train, just for everybody to look at and say "how sweet!" and wonder how much it all cost. On the other hand, Ann Louise knew her mother would have died if she hadn't agreed to be married in the church: that way she could show everybody what her life's work was all about, and it would be the culmination of all her dreams—to have a daughter, whom she had literally *produced,* the central figure in one of the oldest of all dramas. (And, of course, her mother was producing that too.) So Ann Louise had thought, well, all right; and she reckoned she could stand it. Also, she never had really thought much of home weddings, where you were all just standing there with all that emotion right in everybody's face and everybody could just reach out and put his hands on you and hug and kiss you and cry over you, and it all made you choke and want to throw up right then and there just from thinking about it.

It wasn't that Ann Louise wasn't romantic or vain either for that matter: she didn't at all mind being the main character in the play, but was this the right play? Everybody in Woodville would be there, and they all knew about her already and vice versa; and she didn't see that that would be anything to write home about for her or them or anybody else. It wasn't as if she were Scarlett O'Hara marrying by candlelight in the front parlor at Tara or even Dorothy skipping down the Yellow Brick Road to meet the Wizard of Oz. It would all be just home folks, and there really wouldn't be anything sensational about any of it. After all, she was too old for that kind of thing anyhow: she had already been out of college for a couple of years and taught school in Nashville. And she didn't imagine anybody wanted to think of her as a heroine or a debutante or anything else like that. Of course the groom, Johnny Emerson, was a "brought-on fellow" from St. Louis; and that might carry a certain amount of interest. But then everybody in Woodville had already gotten to know something of him after he started coming down to see Ann Louise when they were both at Vanderbilt. So again, that was no big deal.

Johnny had had to have a lot of things explained to him at first— what it meant to live in a small town and why you always automatically looked around the room before you opened your mouth when you were going to tell a tale, because you had to be sure you weren't talking about anybody's kinfolks, and how you always had to consider what everybody else would think of what you did or didn't do. (He used to tell Ann Louise that she spent most of her time worrying about what "they say" and "everybody thinks.") But gradually, he got so he felt at home there and even came to entertain the possibility of living there after he and Ann Louise were married. He said St. Louis, for all that it was next door to the South, was getting too "modern" for him and before long it wouldn't be anything but one big shopping mall after another and you wouldn't be able to see any real dirt anywhere for all the concrete and asphalt. He never had thought he would live to say such a thing because, after all, he was a city boy born and bred. But he didn't relish the idea of spending the rest of his life in what he called the Great American Plug-in Civilization, where you just automatically moved every few years from one suburb to another, with the same stores in the same sort of shopping centers. And everybody you knew worked for one big corporation or another, and it was really all the same to them where they worked or lived, and you couldn't imagine any of them outside their jobs. Whatever Woodville would have to offer, he said, it wouldn't be that. Anyhow, Memphis would be close enough if you just had to have a whiff of the big city from time to time.

And it all worked out after Johnny decided he wanted to go into school administration or something like that. (He would have liked to coach football; but he said he already knew something of the precarious lives of such men, especially in small towns, and he wasn't sure he had the nerves—or the guts—for the job.) Anyhow, that was when he and Ann Louise got engaged—when they both stayed on in Nashville after graduation to work on their teacher certification. Ann Louise well knew his folks up in St. Louis weren't altogether happy about what he had decided to do and the sort of place they were going to live. But his folks seemed to have sense enough to let him alone while he was deciding and afterwards too. Any maybe in time Johnny would get acclimated to Woodville, where they both already had jobs in the school system for next year; but she didn't think there would ever be any danger of Johnny turning into a Good Old Boy and driving a pickup truck.

That was the game plan, anyhow. And now here she was, all dressed up in satin and lace from the Bridal Salon at Goldsmith's in Memphis—veil, train, and all the rest—all ready to play Cinderella or Queen for a Day and give the paying customers their money's worth. She was being supported by Martha Alice Craig, her closest friend and fellow conspirator from childhood, who was naturally her maid of honor now. There were also a couple of girls she had gone to college with as bridesmaids—one from Memphis and one from Nashville—just to let Woodville know she had more strings to her bow than just the home talent; and, of course, there were even a couple of Johnny's friends from St. Louis to act as ushers, to say nothing of his parents (his father was best man) and his married sister and her husband. So at least she was getting part of the glamor of marrying "off"—but not too far off. After all, they would live in Woodville and stay right there in the Methodist church; it wasn't as though Johnny was a foreigner or a Roman Catholic or anything else that might cause trouble. (She didn't think she ever could have made up her mind to be *immersed* if he had been a Baptist.) And she supposed everybody would think it was all very "suitable" and everybody was happy. Indeed, it all seemed to be going right by the script. So far, so good.

Ann Louise had been thinking all this in the twinkling of a eye, while they were all getting lined up there in the vestibule, with Miss Sophie Caldwell, the florist, fluttering over the whole wedding party like a mother hen with her chicks. She told them all how to act and what to do and, of course, got everything completely turned around from the rehearsal the night before until Ann Louise wondered how anybody in the world would know where he was supposed to stand or what on earth he was supposed to do. But Miss Sophie, she had always thought, was one of those people for whom speech was not a gift but an affliction and sometimes didn't really know herself what she was saying. Everybody in town knew her and how to take her; and anyhow, she did know what flowers were all about and so you just more or less put up with her. (Maybe that's what small towns were all about finally: you learned how to put up with people.) And now the organist, Imogene Morris, was well into the last piece before the processional: the hymn "O Perfect Love." Imogene had always played the recital pieces Ann Louise envied, back when they both took from Miss Caroline Miller—mazurkas and polonaises and such like, teeming with what Miss Caroline described as "Slavonic fire and passion" in the program notes she always wrote for them to memorize and recite before they played their pieces. So Ann Louise never doubted she could handle something as tame as "O Perfect Love" now. (Miss Maud Simpson, Ann Louise's mother's closest friend, *had* to be asked to sing; and she had already rendered "Because" and "I Love You Truly." So now, thank God, *that* was over. And fortunately, Ann Louise had managed to spike a suggestion that Miss Maud might sing "The Lord's Prayer" while she and Johnny knelt at the end of the ceremony.)

Now it was time for the mothers to go in, Johnny's mother first, then Ann Louise's; and everybody would know the show was really on the road. It was June (what else?) and, at five in the afternoon, hot as a firecracker: few churches were air-conditioned in 1955 and the window fans just stirred the heat around without cooling it. And so some of the white gladioli behind the altar were drooping, and many of the candles had begun listing either to port or starboard. The ushers were sweltering in their navy blue suits; and more than one fan—palm leaf, Japanese, or funeral home—was going full tilt out in the congregation. In any case, it was time to begin, time for the curtain to go up. And now Mrs. Emerson was taken in, to sit in the left-hand front pew; and then Ann Louise's mother, who would sit on the other side, across the aisle. And everybody would look at her and her dress ("toast chiffon," Goldsmith's had called it) and automatically forgive her for *everything* because of what she was going through now. And she would cry a little— but not too much; that was on the program too. They were really down to the wire now: old Imogene struck *five* on the chimes and then followed with the chords that were the fanfare for the "Bridal Chorus."

And then came the moment that Ann Louise had always heard about but wondered whether it would really happen to her. What was it—stage fright or something more than that? She suddenly thought, I'm getting married, right this minute and right here in front of all these people who have known me all my life; and they think they know me and I think I know them. And there up by the altar will be somebody I've known for a couple of years and think I want to share my life with. But do I really know him too? Suppose it doesn't work out. What will I do and what will people say? And here is my father right beside me, who I've always thought wasn't too important in my life. But maybe he was disappointed because I wasn't a boy and so just let my mother run the show where I was concerned. Still, a moment ago he had tears in his eyes when he hugged me and said, "Baby, Daddy will always love you." And now she almost gulped. It was almost like one of those nightmares where you all of a sudden realize you're out in public, in church or up on the stage or somewhere formal and dignified like that, and you're absolutely stark naked. Or what was worse, like one of the nightmares you used to have about Miss Caroline's recitals, where you forgot your piece and wanted to cut and run.

And that's what Ann Louise would have liked to do now—after all the hullabaloo, all the showers, the parties, the presents, and the whole shebang. She wondered what Miss Caroline (if she were alive) would say. Nobody ever dared to panic at one of her recitals: that would not have been *professional*. Ann Louise wondered, did she really *want* to get married anyhow? Would any of it be even remotely like the fairy tale you were brought up on? And was Johnny her Prince Charming now or ever? Or was he just a fine boy she thought she knew and somebody who really could, because he loved her, come and live in Woodville the rest of his life? Could you ever really be certain? And what would you do anyhow if the movies (or the picture show, as they used to call it) really started coming true? Did people really ever live happily ever after, and would you like that anyhow? Besides, *what would you do for an encore?* (She had long ago decided that that might be the ultimate question in life.) It might all be something of a bore or a letdown—like the day after Christmas. She and Martha Alice used to sit up nights, back when they were in high school, just wondering about things like that. Even after they thought they knew all about sex and "all that sort of thing" (mostly from the *Ladies' Home Journal* and their "hygiene" classes, and very little from their mothers), they used to talk about what might come after all that sort of thing. And who ever knew for sure, and anyhow what could you do about it? Was it simply a risk you had to take—on faith, in the dark—and just hope to God it would work out all right? Whatever the case, it looked as though somewhere along the line you simply had to take the bit between your teeth and go on and do *something;* you couldn't just stay out of water till you learned to swim. You had to trust somebody or something.

Now the bridesmaids had started down the aisle; and here came Martha Alice as maid of honor to take her place right before Ann Louise and her father. She and Martha Alice had always planned it like that: they would be each other's maid of honor or matron of honor, depending on whoever married first. As it was, Ann Louise was only going to have a brief headstart on Martha Alice, who was going to marry Don Phillips from Woodville as soon as he finished medical school in Memphis at Christmastime. So she knew her days of seniority in the married state were numbered, but then she and Martha Alice had always gone neck and neck in whatever they did.

Suddenly, Martha Alice turned around now and poked Ann Louise in the ribs and hissed, "Remember, I am counting with you all the way," which was what Miss Caroline had always said to her students just before they started out onto the stage at her recitals. And somehow that always galvanized them into action, terrified as they were. Such was the case with Ann Louise now, as they both started giggling right there on the brink of matrimony, right there on the very verge of life. And so now she squared her shoulders and looked straight ahead—on past all the congregation, who were mostly, after all, just folks she had known all her life, and on past Martha Alice, with whom she had been through so much, now halfway down the aisle, and on up to the altar, where Johnny already stood waiting for her and grinning from ear to ear. She thought, well, he's no Prince Charming and a far cry from Rhett Butler; but then I'm no Cinderella or Scarlett O'Hara either. I'm going to survive this and live to tell the tale, too. (She nearly laughed out loud when she realized she was sounding almost like Scarlett when she vowed she would never be hungry again!) It's probably not going to be any fairy tale either, and we may not live happily ever after. But we're going to do the very best we can and maybe even have some fun along the way, which is all you can ever ask of anybody. And who knows but what telling the tale afterwards may not be the best part of all anyhow?

And with that, Ann Louise squeezed her father's arm and whispered, "All right, Daddy, let's go."

1975 Has Come and Gone

—————————— • ● • ——————————

"The year 1975 has come and gone, and we're still not wearing hoop-skirts!" was what Ann Louise Parker—who had married Johnny Emerson—hollered to her old friend, Martha Alice Craig—whom she hadn't seen for a long time and whose husband, Don Phillips, was a big cardiologist in Memphis—when they happened to be seated near each other at a Kenny Rogers concert. Martha Alice had promptly snorted with pleasure, but there was no time to pursue the matter right then because the music—or rather, the sound—was getting under way. And afterwards the two couples had time for only the briefest of greetings, since the crowd was so large and the next day was Monday. Larry Gatlin and his brothers actually introduced the program, which was just great as far as Ann Louise was concerned, though, if she'd been consulted, she would have had the program the other way round, with Kenny Rogers doing the introducing and the Gatlins the main attraction. But she wasn't going to worry about that, only about getting prematurely deaf from the sheer noise of all the music, which most people seemed to be used to: she reckoned they'd been to so many such affairs they'd lost a lot of their hearing. In any case, while it was all so loud that Ann Louise couldn't have understood the lyrics if she hadn't already known the songs, most people just sat there taking it all in, as happy and unconcerned as if they had good sense.

What the "1975" and "hoopskirts" was about, as Ann Louise explained to her husband when they were driving home, was all to do with when she and Martha Alice were growing up in Woodville and playing with their *Gone With the Wind* paper dolls, shortly after the movie had just come out and everybody was going to Memphis on Saturdays and taking their children to see it. Martha Alice had seen fit to hold forth then on fashion and style: how things came and went and were the height of fashion today but out of date tomorrow; and she had proclaimed that it was all perfectly clear to her that hoopskirts, which they both just adored, would certainly be back in by 1975. She would brook no argument, either, not that Ann Louise was disposed to give her much of one. For one thing, as Ann Louise afterwards told Johnny, who hadn't grown up in Woodville—where they still lived and he was the high school principal—when you disagreed strongly with Martha Alice in those days, she might bite you. And she could still see those teeth marks on her hand yet, too. She said she wasn't sure that biting you ever convinced anybody that you were wrong and Martha Alice was right. But anyhow it somehow proved something and, if you'd ever been bitten by Martha Alice, you'd be more or less inclined just to let matters stand as they were. Martha Alice was always more or less *positive* about everything, and hoopskirts were no exception. It all came from her mother being a Russell, Ann Louise said: too much temper all the way round. And their men all drank too.

But they were the dearest of friends growing up and always would be. It was just too bad that Martha Alice lived in Memphis now and she still lived in Woodville, which was fifty miles away; it all might as well have been on the moon for all they got to see each other anymore. They had grown up just down the street from each other and were the same age, and every afternoon of the world their colored nurses would take them up to play on the steps of the Methodist church, where all the other children in town who had nurses would be also. The nurses could all have a good visit and talk about their boyfriends while all the children told secrets and giggled and played hide and seek, in and out of the flying buttresses, as their mammas and daddies called those supports on the sides of the building.

Later they started to school together, in the class of Miss Rosa Moss, who had taught the first grade in Woodville so long that she had had three generations in some families. They went on to take piano lessons from Miss Caroline Miller, who had a thin gray mustache and who Ann Louise's father said could have been the kaiser of Germany. (Miss Rosa Moss said she'd never seen a child yet she couldn't control, but in her case it was all done mostly with love and affection, unlike Miss Caroline and the Reign of Terror.) In fact, the first evening dresses she and Martha Alice had ever had were made for them to be in Miss Caroline's recitals, which were somewhat like stage productions on the one hand and military drills on the other—as Ann Louise had tried many times explaining to Johnny, who hadn't grown up in a small town and didn't understand things like that.

He thought it all mildly amusing but more from the standpoint of a missionary learning tribal rites in darkest Africa, Ann Louise suspected. She was always having to remind him that, however funny you might think it was now, it had all been perfectly serious back then—and maybe to some people it still was today.

Like cheerleaders and drum majorettes in high school, she used to tell him. Nothing in your life could ever be quite so grand as being one of those (she'd been a cheerleader but missed out on the other). But all the little Bertha Jeans and Betty Sues had had their day right then and there and never would get over it. Think of them in later life, she reminded Johnny: they all got married right after high school, mostly to boys named Junior and Bubba, who drove trucks and drank Pabst Blue Ribbon. And almost immediately they all had four children with dishwater blond hair and snotty noses. They themselves weighed two hundred pounds in five years' time. Furthermore, Ann Louise said, their idea of being dressed up was to have their hair all teased and colored up like a new kind of cotton candy to wear with yet one more polyester pantsuit with jacket and trousers in complementary designs and preferably in what you might call *wedding reception green.* This got its name from a Baptist wedding where you had the reception in the church basement and so you couldn't have anything to drink but Kool-Aid punch that usually had lime sherbet melting in the middle of it. It had all been downhill after their high-kicking days, she told him. And as for the subsequent lives of beauty queens, Ann Louise said they simply didn't bear contemplation. As one of her great-aunts used to remark contemptuously of such like: "Pretty, pretty . . ." But pretty was as pretty did; and none of it would get you anywhere at all, she implied. Yet to Ann Louise and Martha Alice in high school, it had all been deadly serious, even heart-breaking. (Martha Alice lost out because her mouth was too big, they said; but maybe somebody also remembered her sharp teeth.) Ann Louise supposed they could have tap-danced, which even then she knew was the tackiest thing of all; but their mammas had thought they'd be better off with Miss Caroline and the Girl Scouts: that was quite discipline enough.

And it was about that time, anyway, that they began to go to dances and discover boys—just as they entered high school; and that Christmas Mary Lou Sanford—who always did everything before everybody else and her mother before her too—as Ann Louise had overheard her mother tell her father one night, invited the whole class to their first real dance. And the girls all wore their mothers' fur coats and their last year's recital dresses and felt terribly grown up. But Billy Joe Martin (whom Ann Louise had had a crush on all fall, but he wouldn't look at her except to scowl when she trapped him in Latin class and got a headmark before he did) danced cheek to cheek with Martha Alice before he even danced the first dance with her. (Somebody had turned all the lights down low in the Sanfords' basement recreation room.) Ann Louise's evening was spoiled. There was one bright moment, however, when Harry Johnston got carried away and got up on the Ping-Pong table and invited everybody to a dance at his house on New Year's Eve; and his mother, who Ann Louise always thought looked like an anteater because her lips were almost always pursed in continual disapproval of *something,* didn't know a bit more about it than a spook. And she had to make the best of it, and the dance took place too. But Ann Louise would always remember that Harry's mother, after having been dragooned into letting Harry give a dance that way, sat there all evening right back in the hall, apparently absorbed in her book-club book and rocking away by the Heatrola, never once looking up into the living room but with her ears bristling like antennae for the first sounds of rape or riot. That night Billy Joe Martin did dance cheek to cheek with her while the record player played "Moonlight Becomes You," but by then Ann Louise had decided his cowlick wasn't going to be nearly as cute in a couple of years as it was right then and Martha Alice could have him.

And so they proceeded, more or less neck and neck—she and Martha Alice—neither of them ever really *leading* the other but both mostly holding their own, which was probably why they stayed good friends. Martha Alice had stopped biting by now; but she had other ways of making her displeasure known—raising her eyebrows and shrugging her shoulders about anything she felt superior to, making sounds of nausea when it was anything she violently disapproved of. (Ann Louise had to content herself mostly with her ability to belch on cue; but she had discovered there was a limited audience for that sort of thing, to say nothing of what her mother would say if she caught her at it.) Martha Alice was still inclined, though, to get on a high horse from time to time and lay down the law like she had done that time about them wearing hoopskirts by 1975. There was just no question, she once told Ann Louise, but that it was really better the North had won the Civil War; and that way they would always be one country. And Mrs. Roo-

sevelt certainly did look a lot better since she was in that car wreck and
got her buck teeth knocked out and replaced with some false ones. Ann
Louise, who remembered her Confederate-veteran grandfather (of whom
she was always afraid) only too well, said, well, maybe it was but she
sure hoped hoopskirts were coming back in 1975 anyway. And whoever
said Mrs. Roosevelt was supposed to make her living by her looks anyhow? When you heard the president give one of his "Fireside Chats"
on the radio, you just knew that there was somebody up there in Washington who was going to *take care of you* and you didn't have a thing to
worry about. Besides, they couldn't help the way their children had
turned out.

Martha Alice *was* probably the only one of Miss Caroline's piano
students in captivity who ever ventured to stand up to her. And she did
it in style. When Miss Caroline blessed her out for not having memo-
rized all of her recital piece, which that year was going to be Brahms's
"Hungarian Dance No. 5," Martha Alice just jumped up and called
her an old Gestapo agent and snatched up her music and ran out the
door and never had gone back either. It made you right weak to think
about it; but, Ann Louise decided, you had to admire it. The only thing
Ann Louise had ever done even remotely comparable to that was when
she was ten and she had stuck an old-fashioned hat pin she had found
in her mother's dresser drawer in Miss Evelyn Hartman's behind at Vacation Bible School. Miss Evelyn had been wearing them all out with
stories about all the poor people starving to death in India and China;
but since she herself weighed close to three hundred pounds, Ann Louise
decided that none of it would ever come nigh her, and anyway, what
were they all supposed to do about it—stop eating? So she stuck the hat
pin in Miss Evelyn; and Miss Evelyn promptly turned on her, with tears
in her eyes, and said, by way of rebuke, "It just hurts me to think that
you don't have any more Christian love in your heart than to do me that
way." And Ann Louise smirked and said, "It hurt something else too,
didn't it, Miss Evelyn?" But Miss Evelyn just looked at her sadly and
shook her head and didn't say anything else; but that night Ann Louise
got a first-class spanking at home as a result.

So she and Martha Alice were never rivals but perhaps copartners
in crime, colleagues, you might say—as she had tried to explain to
Johnny. When they were sophomores in high school, Martha Alice had
even produced the *Sophomore Scandals,* complete with a masked striptease (just half a dozen girls stripping down to their bathing suits while

Doris Arwood played "Malaguena" on the baby grand piano back behind the stage), in an abortive attempt to help Ann Louise get elected
Football Queen. And when they were juniors, they had sneaked off all
by themselves one Saturday, when their mothers thought they were at
a big music-club district meeting in Memphis, and had lunch at the
Peabody Hotel up in the Skyway. Later they cried all the way through
a rerun of *Wuthering Heights,* which they had missed the first time around
and was then playing at the Malco where, between showings of the
movie, Milton Slosser groaned up out of the dark mounted on a snow-
white Wurlitzer, and they would all gallop off into community singing. She didn't know whether Martha Alice had ever tried explaining
it all to Don, the cardiologist. But then he came from Woodville too,
so perhaps he would naturally understand. And it didn't matter, really,
that they hardly ever saw each other. Martha Alice had always worked
part-time after her children had got big, and Ann Louise always seemed
to be involved in so many local good works (to say nothing of substitute
teaching) that she seldom got to Memphis. But what they had been
through together, what they had both lived to tell was, after all those
years, still a bond as strong as death. One time, as she had tried telling
Johnny about it some years after they were married, she had exclaimed,
"Why, sometimes, when I'm doing the dishes at night—or the laun-
dry, after you and the children have gone to bed, I could just cry about
the things Martha Alice and I did when we were growing up, the things
we *shared.* I don't think you ever get over that."

     She never was sure Johnny understood; and, she supposed, it was
maybe because he had grown up in the suburbs of St. Louis, where
everybody's father mostly worked for a big corporation and automatically got transferred every few years to another suburb just like the first,
whether it was in Detroit or Cleveland or somewhere else. And no, she
didn't have to *see* Martha Alice now to keep their "relationship" going
because it all went far beyond seeing. Further, it wasn't a "relationship" either: they had simply grown up together. They didn't even have
to *talk* periodically either; they simply had each other on the mind and
knew what the other must be up to—almost like telepathy. That was
even the way it had been when they had gone off to college and Ann
Louise had pledged Theta at Vanderbilt and Martha Alice had gone Chi
O at Ole Miss—both the same but different, if you knew the two
schools. And Ann Louise had met Johnny, who was also in school there;
but even then Martha Alice had always known she would come back

home and marry Don, who was already in medical school in Memphis. In those days, when they were going together and Ann Louise would try to explain to Johnny about her closest friend, he would say, "Well, then, you're sort of like sisters." But she would reply, "Yes and no. We grew up together in a small town, just down the street from each other. And we had everything in common—likes and dislikes, not just families, the way it can be with sisters, who may not really *like* each other. And all around us, twenty-four hours a day, was Woodville and everybody in it. We knew everybody there and everybody knew us and our families back to the Year One. And you didn't have to *explain* anything to anybody because all of you there had it all in common. You never get away from it either. I've already found that out. When Martha Alice and I are together right now, we don't even have to talk if we don't want to: we seem to follow each other's thoughts anyhow. The main thing is, no matter where each of us is in the world, she knows the other one is somewhere else in the world too. She just *is,* and that's enough."

So by the time it got to be after 1975 and Ann Louise and Martha Alice, who hadn't seen each other for some time, were both old enough to start having grandchildren, Johnny should probably have understood something of their long association, their rooted connection, which all came out, all over again, in Ann Louise's greeting to her old friend at the Kenny Rogers concert. Maybe he never would understand it altogether because he hadn't grown up in Woodville; maybe, as one of his friends there used to tease him, you not only had to be born there, you had to have been conceived there as well! But he knew enough by now to understand that they were, in this barest of gestures, somehow touching base with each other, saying little but implying the whole world: "1975 has come and gone. . . ."